Ask a Shadow to Dance

Ask a Shadow to Dance

Linda George

Five Star • Waterville, Maine

First Edition
First Printing: December 2005

Published in 2005 in conjunction with Tekno Books.

Set in 11 pt. Plantin by Minnie B. Raven.

Printed in the United States on permanent paper.

Library of Congress Cataloging-in-Publication Data

George, Linda.
    Ask a shadow to dance / by Linda George.—1st ed.
    p. cm.
    ISBN 1-59414-367-6 (hc : alk. paper)
    1. River boats—Fiction.   2. Time travel—Fiction.
3. Memphis (Tenn.)—Fiction.   I. Title.
PS3607.E664A93 2005
    813'.54—dc22   2005027045

For Chuck, with all my love.

Acknowledgments

In 1993, I came across a news article about a riverboat that left Memphis, then disappeared without a trace. A lover of time-travel, I immediately wondered what it would be like to see my own name on the list of passengers who disappeared—along with the name of someone I loved.

A month later, I flew to Memphis to research this novel, and returned in the spring to finish that research. I found the people of Memphis friendly and willing to help in any way to make this story as accurate as possible—on the trolleys, in Sleep Out Louie's, in the museums, and especially at the Memphis Queen Riverboats. Captain Dale Lozier and her excellent crew answered dozens of questions for me and helped me learn about navigating the Mississippi and how things run on a riverboat. Any deviations from what they told me were made in favor of the story, and not because I wasn't listening.

Many thanks to everyone at the Memphis Queen Riverboat Line who contributed valuable information and tidbits, and also to those at the Peabody Hotel who were pleased to have another author feature the grand old lady in a novel. The ducks were less enthusiastic and said, "Quack."

Thanks, also, to Phyllis Peterson at the Mallory-Neeley House for the wonderful photographs of the furnishings, and for allowing me to wander around and get to know this incredible house and use it as the model for the Morgan home in this book.

And, thanks to the kind man on the trolley who saw me writing in a notebook, asked if I was a student, then, hearing I was writing about Memphis, asked, "How can I help?" Everyone in Memphis was just as eager to help, and the details in this book are my thanks to them.

Thanks, also, to my family and friends who supported me through the writing of this book and for encouraging me to wait for exactly the right time to publish it. I love and appreciate all of you.

Chapter One

Saturday, November 14, 2009

There. In the shadows.

She stood just out of the soft glow of the tiny white lights laced among the rose filigree cornices throughout the room. David Stewart took a step closer. No one. Had he only imagined the black dress and dark hair, draped with a veil?

"Uncle David, I'm going to get some punch."

He nodded to his niece, Marilu, then glanced around the room. The second deck of the *Memphis Queen III* had been transformed into the perfect setting for the gala ball. Parents, sponsors and young people clustered near the refreshment tables, near the orchestra and at private tables all around the narrow dance floor. The ladies dressed in keeping with the Victorian theme made it easy to imagine being in the late 1800s. Their elaborate ball gowns swept the floor and gave them the illusion of gliding rather than dancing.

Once again. In the shadows.

He could see her better now. She stood near the far exit, alone, dressed completely in black, from the tip of her chin to her toes. The black veil had slipped to her shoulders. Lights reflecting in her hair revealed auburn highlights, running to spun copper. He hadn't imagined her after all. She seemed confused, retreating farther into the shadows, then completely out of sight.

David skirted the room, hurrying to where she'd disappeared. She must have gone outside onto the landing. He pulled the door open and stepped into the cool, moist breeze, rich with the clean mud smell of the river. The constant vibration of diesel engines turning the huge red paddlewheel at the stern made it easy to get lost in the rhythmic tuck-a-tuck-a-tuck of the paddles dipping into the Mississippi, propelling the boat north along the Tennessee side of the river. A thick cloud-cover reflecting the lights of downtown Memphis and, on the opposite bank, the distant lights of West Memphis, gave the river an eerie glow. The north wind swept briskly over the bow.

A narrow metal staircase led onto the third level. He hurried up the steps. Open bow to stern, with the pilot-house above the center section, the deck was rimmed by a metal railing. No one else braved the wind. He wandered toward the stern, feeling the engine vibration more and more as he neared the giant wheel. The splashing of the paddlewheel complemented the November evening.

Heading back toward the bow, David pulled at his tight, fancy collar, feeling slightly disoriented. A chill played along his spine.

She stood silhouetted at the far end of the deck, where no one had been standing before. He took a step closer. She gazed at the river with a wistful smile. The full moon cast a magical glow on everything, kissing the river with silver, bathing her face and shoulders in tremulous beauty.

"Excuse me, Miss . . ."

She whirled around, her eyes wide. Haloed by moonlight, errant strands of auburn hair danced about her face. The veil draped over her shoulders, fluttering in the breeze.

"I'm sorry, I didn't mean to startle you. But, inside, you seemed . . . lost . . . or upset. May I help?"

She relaxed somewhat, touching her fingertips to her

slender throat. Her breasts rose and fell with quickened breaths.

"I . . . we haven't been formally introduced, Sir."

"I'm David Stewart, a doctor here in Memphis. And you are—"

"Lisette . . . Morgan. I, too, am from Memphis. Have you been there long?"

"All my life." As they spoke, his heart pounded. Her voice was elegantly southern. Her skin, gossamer and translucent, appeared so delicate a mere touch might bruise her. He guessed her age at late-twenties, yet something about her suggested maturity beyond so few years.

"You're staring, Sir."

"Sorry. I'm wishing we'd met before."

She pointed toward the bridge. "I'm wondering about those lights."

He went to the rail and stood beside her. The pulse throbbed in his throat. "You mean the lights on the bridge?"

"Yes. It looks likes a fancy necklace across the river. When did they build the bridge?"

"Years ago. It's called the Hernando de Soto Bridge, named for the explorer." She must have been away from Memphis for quite some time, not to know about the bridge.

Without warning, the lights blinked out.

"What happened? They were lovely."

He searched the river. "Do you see that light, against the Arkansas bank?"

She followed where he pointed and nodded.

"That's a barge tow. The bridge lights cause a glare on the water, so southbound boats can turn them off until the barge is past the bridge. Then, the lights come back on.

They can do it electronically, two and a half miles upriver, where Wolf River enters the Mississippi, or where that boat is now, by shining a spotlight at a sensor on the bridge."

" 'Electronically.' What an intriguing word. You seem to know a lot about these things."

"I love the river."

"So do I. I envy it."

"How?"

"It travels where it wishes, hundreds of miles, wandering, seeing new places, different people. I wish I could go with it."

"Where would you like to go?"

Her eyes gleamed with excitement. "Anywhere—other than New Orleans. I'd really love to see San Francisco. Afterward, I would close my eyes, turn in a full circle with my arms outstretched and go wherever I might be pointing when I opened my eyes again. I'd love to see the whole world." She looked away, embarrassed. "You probably think me silly."

"Not at all. I love to travel."

She focused on him with renewed enthusiasm. "Where have you been?"

"All over the United States and Canada. Not much abroad, but I've always wanted to go." She clearly envied him. "Do you work somewhere?"

Her expression hardened, eyes blazing with anger. "Certainly not."

He rushed to apologize. "I didn't mean to offend you." He would have to be more careful. The fact she was attending a dance on a riverboat, dressed completely in black as though in mourning, and insulted by the suggestion that she might actually work, meant something. Although, he could not decide exactly what.

She backed away. "I have to go now." Pulling the veil around her head, she clutched it beneath her chin.

"No, don't!"

"I beg your pardon?"

"I mean, you can't leave so soon. We've just met. How will I see you again? May I call you?"

She considered a moment. "You may call on me if you wish. I'll be living with my father now and Aunt Portia. My father is Jacob Morgan of Morgan Enterprises. I'm sure you've heard of him."

David knew no one by that name and had never heard of Morgan Enterprises. Saying so might offend her. He'd have to guide the conversation and gain more information about Jacob Morgan. Maybe get her telephone number and address.

Lisette went down the stairs. David followed a step behind. Her perfume was intriguing, a fragrance he didn't recognize, something entirely natural and completely feminine. "May I ask the name of the perfume you're wearing?"

She hesitated, then smiled. "Lemon verbena. Do you like it?"

"Very much." He'd find it, buy a gallon and have it sent to the Morgan home. "Would you like to dance?"

"It wouldn't be proper. Perhaps another time."

When she reached the landing, she hesitated. He touched her arm briefly before reaching to open the door. For an instant, she trembled. If only they could talk longer, get to know each other better . . .

He opened the door, waited for her to step inside, then followed, pushed aside the fronds of a fern sitting beside the door and closed it securely. Judging from the brown tips on the fronds, not everyone had been as careful to avoid crushing them. When he turned around . . . she was gone. "Lisette!"

Marilu approached from the refreshment table, holding a cup of red punch. Everyone milled around, between dances. There was no sign of Lisette anywhere.

"Uncle David! I've been looking everywhere for you."

"Did you see the woman who came in just ahead of me? Black dress. Long hair and a black veil." He scanned the room again but there was still no sign of her.

"Black? How dismal. It looked like you came in alone." Marilu straightened her pink-as-a-cloud ruffles. Her blond curls cascaded past her shoulders like silk.

"Do you think anyone is ever going to ask me to dance?"

"How could any young man resist you?" He took her hand and squeezed her fingers. If he were also fifteen, he would monopolize every dance.

"You look so handsome tonight in your tux." Her grin was impish. "You said you were thinking of cutting your hair and shaving your beard. I'm glad you didn't. You look more old-fashioned with longer hair. Perfect for this dance."

"I'm glad you approve." She was teasing, he knew. She'd always liked his hair collar-length and his beard neatly trimmed. She thought it made him look distinguished. He sometimes cut his hair and got rid of the beard during the summer. His older brother Joe—Marilu's father—thought it made him look younger. At thirty-five, he was just beginning to give that consideration some thought. Fran had preferred him without the beard. Every time he thought about shaving it, he saw Fran's face in the mirror, heard her laughter. In time, maybe he'd be able to shave it. But not yet.

A five-piece orchestra on the port side of the room played modern easy-rock selections as well as classic favorites. The room had been decorated to resemble its late nineteenth century counterpart, even though the ballrooms of the truly palatial riverboats would have been much larger, with chandeliers and grand staircases. Servers in black tuxedos threaded their way through the dancers with trays of canapés and sparkling white grape juice in champagne glasses. Pink and white flowers, floating in crystal bowls of tinted water, scented the room as the water swayed gently with the movement of the boat.

David had been glad to escort Marilu when Joe couldn't attend the important function. A photographer elbowed his way past, around the perimeter of the dance floor, snapping pictures of dancing couples for the *Commercial Appeal.* If Marilu didn't dance soon, she might be overlooked and miss the opportunity to have her picture in the newspaper tomorrow. David couldn't let that happen.

"May I have this dance?" Her fingers, long and graceful, nails polished to the same hue as her dress, felt cool in his hand. Debutantes once wore gloves, but that custom seemed to have been abandoned. Fran had worn gloves even though the fashion had passed. She liked the gentility of quieter, more peaceful times.

A tap on his shoulder interrupted the waltz.

"May I cut in?"

The young man was dressed in tuxedo pants with a white dinner jacket. A pink rose decorated the lapel. His dark hair shone with careful grooming. His eyes never left Marilu's face.

Watching them waltz away, David envied them. They were young and full of hope and expectation.

He'd been full of hope at fifteen, too. His dream to become a doctor had been realized when he graduated from the University of Tennessee with honors. Then he met Fran during his first year of residency at the Memphis Medical

Center. She was assistant director in the Medical Records department. Her notes to David in files that lacked certain forms or signatures began professionally enough, but when she'd written, "How about signing these over dinner tonight? My place. Eight o'clock," he'd rushed through afternoon rounds so he could get home, shower, dress, and arrive on her doorstep fifteen minutes early, wearing the best clothes he could afford as a resident.

She was everything he had ever wanted.

They had dinner that night, then went dancing on the weekend. He waltzed her into his heart, almost without trying. They were married. A year later, Alyssa was born, making their family complete. After the accident, when they'd both been tragically torn away, David couldn't heal. Even five years later, he felt wounded and tender when thoughts of them surfaced.

Marilu and her dance partner approached. She had a sappy look on her face.

"Phillip Warner, I'd like you to meet my uncle, Doctor David Stewart. Phillip has just moved to Germantown from Midtown. He lives only a few blocks from us. He'll be going to my high school."

David shook hands with Phillip, noting a similar sappy expression on his face. "Have you ridden the *Memphis Queen III* before?"

"No, sir. My family has lived in Memphis forever, but we've never ridden the riverboats. I'll have to tell everyone how much fun it is."

It was unfortunately true that many Memphis residents were never involved with the river or the part of Memphis that depended on the river. Memphis had become an "edge" city—most of its citizens living around the perimeter in the suburbs instead of in the interior. Joe had been urging David to move to Germantown for months. It was tempting, but he liked Midtown. Fran had loved it there.

He excused himself. Marilu and Phillip went toward the refreshment table. Lisette had to be among the crowd somewhere. A woman didn't get off a riverboat in the middle of a cruise. Not easily, anyway. And she had to be the only woman dressed entirely in black.

After searching every inch of the boat, he was forced to admit she simply wasn't there. How could she vanish?

Someone might recognize Jacob Morgan's name. He questioned each of the chaperons, the crew and musicians. The General Manager of the Memphis Queen Riverboat Line, a good friend of David's, was on board. The crew had lured him onto this cruise, then surprised him with a cake covered in candles, and a new cap to replace the one he'd been wearing for at least the last six months. David wished him a happy birthday. He grinned his usual "Can you believe it?" grin, then checked the passenger list. Neither Jacob nor Lisette Morgan was listed. He had lived in Memphis all his life but was completely unfamiliar with Jacob Morgan or his daughter. He did remember reading about a company called Morgan Enterprises while at the University of Memphis, but that was in a history course. David thanked him for his help and let him get back to the party.

Even though it seemed pointless, he watched for Lisette the remainder of the evening. She never reappeared.

At midnight, when the *Queen III* docked and everyone prepared to disembark, Marilu and Phillip approached David with dreamy expressions. He knew without asking that Marilu was "in love."

"Uncle David, Phillip has something to ask you."

"Sir, I would appreciate the opportunity to drive Marilu home this evening." He flexed his fingers repeatedly, shifting weight from one foot to the other, digging at his tight collar.

David remembered being that nervous once. And that speech! Did kids even think in such terms as "appreciate the opportunity" any more? Phillip was trying awfully hard. And it would save a lot of time, not having to take Marilu all the way to Germantown.

"I think that would be all right." David glanced at his watch. "Have her home by one o'clock."

Phillip grinned and released a big sigh. "Thank you, Sir. She won't be late. I promise."

"Thanks, Uncle David." Marilu rose on tiptoes to kiss his cheek, whispering, "Dad would never have said I could."

She left so quickly he could only stammer, "Wait! Maybe I should . . . Marilu!" Damn. Joe would probably have his head for this.

She grinned over her shoulder, but didn't come back. Maybe it would be all right. Phillip seemed nice enough. And the memory of Lisette's eyes, her cheeks flushed with embarrassment and indignation, still dominated David's thoughts completely. It would've been a strain to listen to Marilu chatter on and on about how wonderful a certain young man had become over the space of one evening.

And wasn't it interesting how important a certain young woman had suddenly become in his life?

David lay awake for hours that night. Just as he was about to fall asleep—somewhere around three a.m.—he realized he was dreaming. Actually, he floated along in that limbo between sleep and wakefulness where the dream carried him along, but he was conscious enough to be able to watch himself move through it. It was an incredible feeling and quite stimulating, considering the topic of the dream.

He relived the encounter with Lisette Morgan on the riverboat. Every word, every nuance of her expression came back with breathtaking clarity.

Then the dream changed. She stood there, just inside the ballroom door, but this time he forgot about the plant being crushed and didn't turn around. He kept his eyes on her, determined to see where she'd gone.

Everything slowed to a fraction of normal speed. He took a long step toward her, reached for her hand and saw it melt away, along with the rest of her. She faded until, transparent and wispy, she disappeared altogether.

The scene changed abruptly. He found himself outside on the third deck, at the bow railing. The wind had grown colder and stronger. Even docked, a chilling wind swept across the boat. He shivered, then decided to go inside and headed for the staircase where he'd followed Lisette into the ballroom before.

"Doctor Stewart!"

David whirled around. "Lisette?" He hurried toward her. "Where did you go? I looked everywhere for you. You have to tell me where you live. I don't know your father, and—"

"I'll tell you everything. We have to—"

A man's voice interrupted. "Lisa! We're docking! Do you have your things ready? What are you doing out here?" He came up the starboard staircase, a fairly young man with a full dark brown beard, dressed in a formal jacket that appeared to have come from an antique shop. From Lisette's expression, David surmised she knew this man—and didn't like him.

Lisette whispered, "I have to get out of here. Will you take me home?"

He was about to tell her he'd take her anywhere in the world she wanted to go—when the telephone rang. David sat straight up in bed, disoriented, searching for Lisette, then grabbed the phone. "What!"

It didn't take long to determine the call was a wrong number. The caller apologized, he mumbled, "No problem," hung up, then glanced at the clock. Four thirty. He never went back to sleep.

The next morning was foggy and damp. Even with little sleep, David decided to run as usual. He'd always loved jogging through the neighborhood surrounding their home. Now, misty with fog, the frosty breath of autumn left his face damp and tingling with early morning chill. A light breeze caressed the huge brown and amber sugar maple leaves that had fallen onto the lawns. A sprinkling of green grass still clustered about the base of the trees. Soon there would be night temperatures below freezing and much of the foliage would sleep for the winter. David felt most alive and most at peace with himself and the world on mornings such as this one. He would always feel alone and lonely without Fran and Alyssa, but he could sometimes be free of the pain of losing them for at least as long as it took to traverse the area around his home in Midtown.

Memphis held the promise of a gorgeous display of fall colors in a few short days. The ginkgo trees were already resplendent with brilliant yellow leaves, which would fall within a few hours after every leaf had changed color.

David allowed his thoughts to wander back to the brief encounter with Lisette Morgan. He wondered if he actually saw and spoke to her or if he'd fallen asleep and dreamed he'd found her there on the deck. She disappeared so completely it was easy to believe the latter. He almost dismissed the incident as something he'd imagined. It reminded him of the stories he heard from young patients.

As a pediatrician, there was nothing more satisfying than helping a child in pain to feel better and smile again. Having lost his daughter, David felt a keen desire to embrace all children as his own, to somehow fill the void that had opened inside him that terrible day. The children he treated loved to tell stories because he always tried to listen with rapt attention. Above all, he loved the children themselves, and they knew it. He never allowed himself to think he might ever have children of his own again. Until that time—if it ever came—it was enough to be nurtured by the children he helped to be healthy and happy.

David's breath came in heavy draughts, muscles flexing rhythmically, slick with sweat, lungs filled with sweet Tennessee air. One more block to complete one more mile. The promise of a glorious day.

He'd been in Memphis since birth, attended Treadwell High School, then the University of Tennessee. He, Fran and Alyssa had lived in the house he still called home. For him, it would always brim with Alyssa's laughter and the subtle magic of Fran's smile. The memories kept David alive.

When she was three, Alyssa had attended nursery school. Every evening he hoisted her into his lap for a report of her day, complete with paintings, carefully-drawn letters and numbers and, on occasion, a clay or salt sculpture presented lovingly to "Daddy," and cherished along with the child.

The children who came to see Dr. Stewart every day provided the only means available for expunging some of the pain and regret he felt.

He'd known Fran had been having dizzy spells and insisted she have some tests to see why. After the tests, Fran drove to pick up Alyssa, as usual. He'd wondered a thousand times if Fran had any warning before her heart arrested, sending the car crashing into an oncoming city transit bus.

The test results proved she was afflicted with Wolff-Parkinson-White Syndrome. The congenital heart defect could not be cured. Once diagnosed, the rapid heartbeat and occasional fainting could have been recognized and precautions taken. But it was too late for precautions.

Everyone repeated endlessly that he had no reason to feel guilty, but he still had difficulty reconciling himself to losing them and to the loneliness surrounding him.

He'd thought about moving dozens of times but found it impossible. Leaving the house where they'd been a family would be like abandoning them, something he could never do. And he loved the old houses with their covered porches and nostalgic style too much to consider moving to Germantown, even though parts of it were just as old. Joe and his wife, Shawna, loved it there, but David's heart was firmly rooted to Midtown, and there he would stay.

When he neared the front door, sadness came flooding back. Fran would not be there in the kitchen with breakfast ready. Alyssa would not be home from school this afternoon, eager to nestle in his lap.

Gone.

Such a terrible, harsh word. But never would the guilt or the longing be gone. And never the emptiness.

David went inside, straight to the shower. Twenty minutes later, he sat at the table, reading the *Commercial Appeal*, drinking a cup of black coffee, scanning pictures of the dance on the riverboat. There, as brilliant as the morning star, was Marilu, dancing with Phillip, looking every bit the fashionable young woman she aspired to be.

He was about to put the paper aside when something caught his attention. The photographer, aiming at Marilu and Phillip, had inadvertently captured another figure as well.

Lisette. Standing in the shadows.

The features weren't clear, but David had no doubt it was she. The sound of her voice and the perfection of her features came back in a rush of emotion and warmth.

It hadn't been a dream—at least meeting her hadn't been.

He thumbed through the telephone book until he had to admit there was no listing for either Jacob Morgan or his daughter—and no listing in the yellow pages for Morgan Enterprises. One phone call to a J. C. Morgan verified it wasn't the same man. They must have an unlisted number or just a cell phone.

There wasn't a lot of investigating he could do on Sunday, but he had to try. For a reason he couldn't name, he knew he had to find Lisette Morgan again, if for no other reason than to prove he hadn't imagined her.

He spent an hour that afternoon in the main library at Peabody and McLean, searching without success all the telephone books for Memphis and every suburb and town within a hundred miles. He even checked the listings as far away as Little Rock and Nashville. Nothing. Any further search would have to wait until Monday. The clerk at the front desk asked if he wanted to look in the Memphis room, part of the history section. He told her he was looking for someone who lived in Memphis now, but thanked her for the suggestion.

Marilu called after supper to tell him again how wonderful he was and how dreamy Phillip had proven to be.

23

She'd been home at ten of one, earning Joe's approval, and Phillip had asked Marilu for a date the following weekend. Life couldn't be better. He half-listened, thinking about Lisette while Marilu chattered on and on.

He didn't sleep much that night, either.

Monday morning, David called the Chamber of Commerce, the telephone company, and the public utilities, just to see if they had a customer by the name of Jacob Morgan. There were no listings. He had no idea what to do next. He hurried through hospital rounds and got to his office fifteen minutes late.

"Morning, Lana."

"Good morning, Doctor Stewart." She took one look at his red eyes and said, "Big weekend?" David didn't answer. She called the first patient.

He worked steadily until noon, met Joe for potato skins, wild rice and shrimp, downtown at The North End—one of their favorite restaurants—then saw another steady stream of patients until a little after five o'clock.

He always checked with Lana before leaving. She had run the office for the past four years and he depended on her. She could have held him up repeatedly for raises, and he would have caved in and agreed without a single protest. He gave her bonuses twice a year, hoping to keep her working happily for years to come, but that could change soon.

Before Greg Chandler had entered the scene, David had taken her to dinner a couple of times, but nothing had ever come of it. He thought it best to keep their relationship strictly professional. This new boyfriend made it easier—and harder, too. A pediatrician just out of residency, Greg would soon be David's partner, giving David more free time and Greg a chance to establish his practice in Memphis. David had no idea what effect that arrangement might have on Lana's loyalty.

"Busy day." She filed the last of the case folders. "Tomorrow's better."

"When's the first one coming in?"

"Not until after lunch. I decided to give you a chance to sleep late. There were only two in the morning, so I rescheduled them."

"Bless you, my child. Does it show that badly?"

"Let's just say I've seen you look brighter. Get some sleep, Doctor, and don't call me in the morning."

"Thanks. See you tomorrow afternoon." David's only thought was hot water and the Jacuzzi.

At home, he fished the newspaper from its usual resting place in the junipers and went straight to start the water filling the huge tub—a luxury he'd never regretted installing after they bought the house—then to the kitchen to find something to eat. At this rate, he'd be in bed early—barring any emergency calls. He had to come up with a new strategy to find Lisette. Sleep was essential for clear thinking.

He grabbed a cold beer and a chunk of leftover roast beef from the refrigerator, then took everything back to the bathroom and turned on the Jacuzzi. Easing into the turbulent hot water felt wonderful. He lay back and soaked for a while, sipping and chewing, before reaching for the paper.

In the Living section was an article about a riverboat. David read it with interest.

THE NIGHT THE CAJUN STAR VANISHED

Many a ship has sailed from port, continued over the horizon and disappeared forever. Ships have been doing this since sailors first started sailing, and it has occurred in practically every ocean and sea in the world. Possibly the weirdest disappearance of all regards the Cajun Star.

It was considered by many to be the finest afloat on the rivers of America, and families used to drive for miles just to watch the luxurious, palatial boat pass by, with her great paddle wheels churning, fire blazing and smoke streaming from her high smokestacks like black velvet ribbons edged in crimson.

The Cajun Star *left Memphis on November 21, 1885, headed down river to New Orleans. All that evening, she rushed down the great Mississippi toward her port. Passing lesser ships, she saluted them with thunderous blasts from her steam whistle. Then the whistle fell silent.*

Days later, when the riverboat was twelve hours overdue, her New Orleans owners began to worry. They telegraphed upriver for news. She'd last been seen just before midnight on the twenty-first. After that—nothing. A search was started immediately. The riverbanks were examined for wreckage and survivors. People along her course were questioned. Had they heard an explosion or seen a fire?

Nothing. Absolutely nothing! No news of any kind, except from a boy who claimed to have seen the boat explode, and several survivors pulled from the water who told similar tales. But no trace of passengers, crew, cargo or debris was ever found. No explanation of the disappearance of the huge river palace could be offered.

Only "Ole Man River" knows, and he don't say nuthin' at all!

David finished the beer and roast, then washed his fingers in the soapy water. Interesting, he had to admit. He scanned the rest of the article—something about a commemorative dance being held November 21 on board the *Memphis Queen III* in memory of the *Cajun Star*—and found the list of people who had been on the boat when it disappeared. There might be a surname he'd recognize—a relative of someone he knew.

There was nothing unusual until he got to the top of the second column. "Well, I'll be damned." He read it again.

David Ingram Stewart

Someone on the *Cajun Star* with his name. Not just close, but exact!

He shivered. The water seemed to have cooled quickly. He dropped the newspaper on the floor, turned off the Jacuzzi, then stepped out onto the rug. Water dripped onto the newspaper, staining it with dark circles.

He shrugged on a terry robe, released the drain on the tub, retrieved the damp paper and went to the living room. Instead of turning on the television, he read the article again, all the way to the end this time, then went back to the passenger list and read it, name by name. Two entries midway down the second column made his heart pound.

Jacob Morgan

Lisette Morgan Westmoreland

Westmoreland? She hadn't mentioned that name. But it had to be her. No, not her, someone with her name. And her father's name. But, how could that be? Grandparents, maybe? One coincidence could be accepted, but three? Practically impossible.

David scanned the article for the information number at the Memphis Queen Riverboat Line and dialed it, hoping Jim would still be there. An answering machine. He'd have to wait until tomorrow. Damn!

The phone rang just after he hung up. Joe.

"Just wanted to thank you again for taking Marilu to the dance. I hope you weren't too bored."

"Not at all."

"We're having a barbecue at our house. Shawna said to lean on you to come."

"Pass."

"If Shawna asks, I pressured you for an hour."

"Got it. Listen, Joe, I need you to—" He stopped. Joe would think he was crazy. Or would he? Joe was exactly David's opposite in temperament. When they were growing up, Joe had been the aggressive, impulsive brother, always in trouble, while David stood by, innocent, wishing he could be more like Joe. If David told Joe about Lisette—

He responded immediately. "What? Anything. Marilu hasn't stopped talking about 'wonderful Uncle David' since she got home. And that boy who brought her home—the one you know?—I couldn't have picked a nicer kid."

"The one I know? You mean Phillip?"

"Marilu said he's one of your patients. That's why you let him bring her home." Joe hesitated. "That's right, isn't it? You wouldn't have let her ride home with a complete stranger?"

Damn. What could he say? "Not to worry, Joe. Phillip is a fine young man." At least he seemed that way at the dance. And he got her home on time. That said something for him.

Joe laughed. "You had me going there for a minute. Now, what was it? You need me to do something for you? Name it."

"Uh . . . it's nothing, really. I'm glad Marilu had a good time. I think someone's at the door. Gotta go." David hung up, hating to lie, but he had to think about this further before springing it on Joe or anyone. David checked the list again to be sure he'd read the names correctly. There was no mistake.

He sifted it through his mind. There had to be an explanation for those names being on that list.

He struggled with the emotions that had surfaced since meeting this woman. For five years, he'd managed to keep them in check, denying all but the grief that had swallowed him whole. The idea that he might be capable of feeling desire for a woman other than Fran—without guilt—scared him in a way. He could try to forget he'd ever met Lisette, but he didn't want to. Sappy as it might sound, there was a link between them. The list of passengers proved it.

He made his choice, then and there. To learn the riddle of the *Cajun Star*.

To find Lisette.

Chapter Two

Lisette stepped through the door, waited for the handsome doctor to close it, then turned around, intending to take his arm, but didn't see him. Had he stayed outside on the landing? She went toward the door, then swayed, dizzy and disoriented. Andrew appeared at her side. After her husband's funeral, she had intended to leave New Orleans and everything associated with the Westmoreland family, but her stepson, Andrew, had managed to board the *Cajun Star* just as it pulled away from the dock. His presence was repugnant. His behavior after his father's death never could be excused.

"What's wrong, Lisa? You look pale. Did you catch a chill outside in the wind? The night air can be quite cold in November, even in the south." He took her arm and practically dragged her across the room, his fingers pressed to the pulse on the inside of her wrist. As soon as her head cleared enough to stand alone, she pulled away. As always, Andrew's sweaty hands felt clammy against her skin. She shuddered at the memory of those hands on her body, not one full day after his father's death. His insistence on calling her Lisa made her skin crawl. If these people had any idea of Andrew's true nature, they'd gladly help her drop him over the side, into the dark, cold waters of the Mississippi. It would be better treatment than he deserved. As vile as his father had been, Andrew was worse. His black, lifeless eyes peered from beneath unkempt black hair that curled around his ears and forehead. His moustaches, always impeccably trimmed, made his mouth look pouty, but his lips, curled into a permanent snarl, betraying his complete lack of morals or conscience, ruined any chance he might have had to be considered handsome.

"There is no need to simper, Andrew. I am quite capable of standing on my own. I'll thank you to leave me alone." Lisette turned away, trying to dismiss him, but he persisted in following at her elbow.

She recognized practically everyone in the room now. They must have been on another deck when she came in before—otherwise, she really had taken a wrong turn and found a new room. She searched the crowd for the captain. He stood next to the far exit, where he'd been when she went out to get some air—and to get away from Andrew. Why hadn't she seen the captain when she came back inside and found all the strange people? He noticed her attempt to gain his attention and came straight away.

"Is there something I might help you with, Mrs. Westmoreland?"

"Yes, Captain, thank you." Andrew started to protest, but she cut him off. "Please don't interrupt, Andrew. You know how your father always hated when you did that." She almost gasped at the fury in his eyes. "Captain, my stepson is curious about docking procedures. I wonder if you might enlighten him."

He took a long look at Andrew, scowling. They hadn't gotten along well on the trip, thanks to Andrew's arrogance and purporting to know everything there was to know about riverboats. Lisette had called upon the captain before, and prayed now his patience hadn't run out completely.

His scowl changed to a curious smile. "I would be happy to instruct your stepson in the art of docking a riverboat." He turned back to her. "It might take a bit of time."

"That would be splendid, Captain. I knew I could count on you."

The captain took Andrew in tow. She would have to send a gift to the captain once home again. The trip from New Orleans would have been far more unpleasant without his help.

With Andrew safely occupied, for a while at least, she continued the search for Doctor Stewart. All the unfamiliar people had disappeared, along with the doctor and the strange room. She still felt slightly faint, yet completely awake, having no idea where she'd fallen asleep to dream about Doctor Stewart, but she supposed it didn't matter. He seemed so real, yet impossible—because the lighted bridge was impossible, as well as the lighted buildings along the riverfront.

She decided to go back to the next deck, to see if the dream might return. At the door, she waited while an elderly gentleman with a handlebar moustache opened it for her, then went outside. The landing was empty.

She went up the wide staircase to the third deck and stopped at the railing overlooking the bow, where she'd spoken to Doctor Stewart before. Several couples meandered about the deck now, but there was no sign of the doctor. The riverboat eased around a bend in the river. As expected, there was no sign of any bridge ahead, and the only lighted building in Memphis was the Tennessee Brewery. Aunt Portia had written that the Brewery now had its own generator and left the lights burning after dark. Beautiful. The dream she'd had of dozens of buildings lighted along the river had been spectacular, especially the pyramid. If she needed proof she'd been dreaming, that amazing sight certainly provided it. With Mr. Edison's invention of the light globe, it surely wouldn't be long before the vision became reality—except for the pyramid, of course.

Lisette gazed at the river. It was tranquilizing—almost enough to blot out reality. She stood at the bow of the *Cajun Star*, feeling the vibration of the huge paddlewheel dipping rhythmically into the dark waters of the Mississippi. It would be easy to get lost in the fantasy of being utterly alone, responsible for no one but herself.

She closed her eyes, reliving the ordeal of burying her husband one month ago in New Orleans. A vile man, he had treated her with contempt during the eight years of their marriage. Gathering her possessions, arranging their cartage to Memphis, and fending off Andrew's disgusting advances and innuendos in the wake of his father's funeral had made Lisette want to disappear. But Andrew was on this boat, following her to Memphis, where she would face another ordeal. She had no intention of allowing Andrew to stay at the Morgan home.

The wind gusted from the starboard now and didn't seem nearly as strong or as cold as from the larboard. She had learned the terms from the captain when he'd escorted her on a tour of the *Star* the second day on the river. Two years ago, Mark Twain had published a book about the Mississippi and his experiences as a steamboat pilot. Once she reached Memphis, she would buy a copy and learn more about this amazing waterway.

Andrew stood with the captain on the deck below, arms crossed over his chest, his boredom on display for everyone. Shifting position, he happened to see Lisette watching and gave her such a bitter scowl, she turned away immediately.

A shudder of revulsion squirmed through her. Andrew, exactly like his father, knew nothing of tenderness or compassion, having impressed Lisette as arrogant and self-centered the moment they met. Her opinion of him had not changed during the past eight years, and the indignities he visited upon her hardened her heart to any fake tenderness he might have shown on this trip. She suspected, though, the captain had seen through Andrew's charade and knew more of his true nature than he'd admitted.

She pulled a lace handkerchief from the sleeve of her dress and dabbed her eyes and cheeks. Crying would not change Andrew's presence on this boat, her father's condition or the past. She learned long ago that tears were no weapons against fate. Yellow fever had claimed her mother, then her father's health and mind. When the vile disease also killed James, she considered it an ironic gift and determined, after forfeiting eight years to misery and grief, to do everything she could to salvage the potential happiness of the future. Once home in Memphis, she would help Aunt Portia care for her father. Somehow, she would find happiness.

She glanced around, hoping no one had witnessed her distress. Across the deck, next to the railing, stood Doctor Stewart. Was it simply a trick of the moon or yet another dream?

She dabbed at her eyes again and moved toward him. He looked directly at her, through her almost, as though he did not see her at all, and headed toward the stern. He couldn't leave. She had to speak to him. She would ask him to escort her home after the boat docked. Such action was improper for a woman in mourning. Aunt Portia might be mortified by such behavior, but she had to have time to talk to him. Obviously, he was no apparition. She was very much awake and intended to verify everything she remembered about their first encounter. As for the lighted bridge, she would try to gain a logical explanation.

"Doctor Stewart!"

He heard.

"Lisette?" He came immediately. "Where did you go? I looked everywhere for you. You have to tell me where you live. I don't know your father, and—"

"I'll tell you everything. We have to—"

Andrew's angry voice interrupted. He bolted up the stairs toward them, with the captain close behind. "Lisa, we're docking. You don't have your things ready. What are you doing out here?"

She could see Andrew was furious about what she'd done. Without looking back at the doctor, she pleaded with him, "I have to get out of here. Will you take me home?" When she turned for his reply, he was gone.

How could he leave without her hearing his footsteps or seeing where he went? There was no good reason for him to leave so abruptly, without saying good-bye, and no way off the deck except by the stairs on the far side. He had to be on the boat somewhere.

She hurried toward the far staircase, but Andrew caught her before she reached the top of the steps.

"What the devil are you doing? Your behavior tonight has been abominable!" He clutched her arm so tightly, she almost cried out in pain, but bit her lip instead, refusing to give him the satisfaction.

His fingers dug into the tender flesh of her upper arm until fresh tears stung her eyes. "You're hurting me. If you don't release me this instant—"

"Mr. Westmoreland, I'll ask you to step away." The captain's expression broached no alternatives. In another moment, he would be on Andrew like a hawk on a mouse.

Andrew released her, his lips drawing back over his teeth

35

in a gruesome smile. His tone changed when he spoke to the captain.

"No need to worry. I was coming for . . . my step-mother . . . to tell her it's time to prepare for docking." He turned back to her. "Lisa, what must you be thinking? Everyone inside is waiting to tell us good-bye."

"Thank you, Captain, for your assistance. Sometimes my stepson forgets his own strength." At home, she would shut Andrew out of her life forever. She clung to that thought; desperate to believe it could be true.

The captain glared at Andrew, clenching one fist repeatedly.

"I need to get my things from my quarters," she said. "Everything is packed and ready. Captain, would you accompany me, please? Mr. Westmoreland can see to his own baggage."

"I would consider it a pleasure to escort you, Mrs. Westmoreland."

"Thank you."

Andrew didn't like it, but had no choice in the matter. "Very well. I'll wait for you on the dock. We'll go directly home so you can rest."

"*I* shall go directly home. *You* may go directly to a hotel." She pronounced the words crisply and with as much venom as she could muster. Andrew strode off across the deck and down the opposite staircase at double his usual pace.

The captain tipped his hat and followed Lisette down the steps.

"Captain, I wonder if you remember a passenger, Doctor David Stewart. I spoke briefly with him earlier. In fact, he was here when you arrived just now."

"There's no one on this boat with that name, Ma'am. I

would have been alerted to the presence of a doctor. You say you were speaking to him?"

"Yes, but it doesn't matter. I must have been mistaken about his being a doctor." She wasn't, though. Another piece of the puzzle. If she could get home to her father and Aunt Portia, she would somehow make sense of this.

After making sure the Chief Purser had everything well in hand, the captain insisted on escorting Lisette home to Adams Avenue. "Just to be sure you aren't bothered on the way."

Aunt Portia met them at the door with a hug for Lisette and copious thanks for the captain. He handed her baggage through the door.

"I appreciate your help and your kind concern more than you could ever know, Sir. Won't you come in for some refreshments?" Lisette was weary to the point of exhaustion, but social etiquette dictated the invitation.

"No, thank you. I'd best be getting back to the boat now. If you should have any further difficulty with . . . your *stepson* . . . I'll be glad to help in any way I can."

She knew he was genuinely concerned for her safety. If Andrew had behaved himself on the boat, this offer wouldn't have been necessary. It was embarrassing to have drawn such attention to herself while in mourning.

"I'll remember. Good night, Captain."

"Ma'am." He tipped his hat and left.

Only a few seconds passed before she was back in Aunt Portia's arms.

"Oh, child, I didn't think you'd ever get here." Her tears flowed freely down her softly lined face. "I'm sorry about James, and sorry you had to make this long trip, but, praise the Lord, I'm glad to have you home again."

"I'm glad to be here, Aunt Portia."

Her aunt hurried to the kitchen and bellowed at the top of her lungs. "Seth! Seth, where are you?"

In just a moment, a tow-headed boy appeared. "Yessum?"

"Carry Mrs. Westmoreland's things upstairs to her room—you know, the one we cleaned yesterday."

"Yessum." He grabbed what he could and promised to be back for the rest "in two shakes of a coon's tail."

"I swear, that boy will be a hillbilly until the day he dies. Come into the parlor and sit down. I know you must be about to drop with weariness. I swear, I've wished a hundred times—no, a thousand that I could have been with you these past six months, having to care for James during his illness and afterward, with no one but that good-for-nothing Andrew there with you. Did he ever lift a hand to help? I know he didn't. Lord, but I've prayed and prayed for you. Let me look at you. You're tired; I can see that. You need a cup of tea. I'll—"

"It's all right, Aunt Portia. I'm here to stay. You don't have to say and do everything in the next five minutes."

She grinned sheepishly. "Forgive me, child. I've waited so long, so very long—" She gathered Lisette into her arms and sobbed.

Lisette held her, letting her cry until she was spent. Lisette's tears came just as readily. Until now, she hadn't realized how intensely glad she was to be home again.

"Portia? Who is it? Portia, where are you?"

Aunt Portia leaned back. "Oh, dear. I'd hoped to prepare you before—Well, there's no time for that now." She dried her eyes on her apron. "In the parlor, Jacob. Come and see who's here."

Lisette's father stopped at the parlor door and peered in, his expression amused, curious, but little more.

Lisette could hardly breathe. Aunt Portia had written about her father's spells, his failing memory, the weakening of his mind and body since the fever. It was a miracle he still got around as well as he did. Lisette could see in his eyes, in the deep wrinkles which had settled into his face, it was all true, and more. The tightness in her chest proved heartbreak was, indeed, painful.

"Papa, I'm home," she managed to say, the words catching in her throat.

He came farther into the room, studying Lisette as though she were a new species instead of his daughter. "You look familiar, but I don't think . . . I've ever . . ." A light seemed to flicker behind his eyes. "Lisette?" Tears streamed suddenly down his face.

"Yes, Papa. It's me." She held him, cried with him. Oh, God, what happened to this man, such a short time ago considered one of the most astute businessmen in Memphis?

"I thought you were gone for good." He pushed her back. "How old are you, now? Sixteen?"

She tried to smile through the tears. "No, Papa, I'm thirty-two. I've been gone eight long years, but I'm home now, to stay."

An odd look swept across his face. "Home to stay? Well, sit down; sit down. I'm plumb worn out, myself." They sat on the divan next to the front fireplace. He continued to smile in that blank way, nodding constantly.

Lisette glanced at Aunt Portia. Her eyes shone with tears. Looking straight into her father's eyes, Lisette told him, "I had a fine trip, Papa, coming home from New Orleans. The *Cajun Star* is a beautiful riverboat. The staterooms were nice, even though small, and standing on the deck, I met—"

"Want something to eat? I'm starved. Where's Portia? Portia's my sister, you know. Takes care of me and my little girl. Couldn't live without her. Portia!"

"I'm right here, Jacob. Would you like something from the kitchen?" Her sad expression included a smile and a narrow shake of her head.

"Haven't had anything to eat all day," he told Lisette. "Want something?"

"No, thank you, Papa."

He followed Aunt Portia to the kitchen, muttering all the way about empty cupboards.

"There's no food in the house. Can't find anything to eat."

"Now, Jacob, you had breakfast and lunch. Don't you remember?"

"Don't remember eating today. I ate yesterday though. Didn't I? Starving!"

Lisette sat alone for a moment in the elegant parlor, fighting emotion, then, as a distraction, rose and slowly toured the room, drinking in the sight of familiar objects and furniture she'd not seen in eight years. The courting couch, Turkish chairs and sofa brought back wonderful memories of growing up in this house. The Chinese Ceremonial Prayer Chest, inlaid with mythical and realistic animal depictions in mother-of-pearl, had been an antique before it was ever finished, such craftsmanship requiring over a hundred years of painstaking work. It stood exactly where it had always stood, in the corner beside the front windows.

The Chinese screen stood in the far corner, four panels illustrating four seasons—peony for spring, lotus for summer, chrysanthemum for fall and plum blossoms for winter, embroidered with the *Forbidden Stitch*—stitching so small, the women who sewed it often went blind. The screen provided part of the separation between the parlor and music room, where musicians sat during parties and dinners. Even now, birds and flowers on the screen appeared to have been painted instead of sewn. Such a treasure. It had stood in that corner since its arrival when Lisette was six, two years after her mother died. A lifetime ago. Lisette lovingly examined each item in the room. Victorian decor meant filling every inch of space with something pretty, something meaningful, something ornate and expensive.

She picked up a porcelain figurine from the gold cherub table. This delicate, dancing angel had belonged to her mother, Brianna Lisette Durand Morgan. Its eyes were closed, a contented smile gracing its lips and folded wings framing its face.

The soft glow from the pair of fireplaces along the outer wall, crackling, warm and friendly, cast a thousand interlacing shadows throughout the room, soothing her memories, shutting out harsh, painful realities.

Her father's failing mind, his frailty, his helplessness, suddenly overwhelmed Lisette. Still clutching the angel, she sank onto the Oriental rug and wept for all that had been lost. Aunt Portia's hands on her shoulders, lifting, holding her, sharing the grief, soothing with her presence and love, comforted Lisette as nothing else could. She was home. She would help Aunt Portia make her father's life the best it could possibly be for as long as he lived. Home meant everything.

Jacob appeared at the door with something in his hand that he bit and chewed. His fingers were greasy and stained. "Want some? Not the best I ever ate, but pretty good. Don't know what it is."

41

Lisette replaced the angel on the table, pulled a handkerchief from her sleeve and dried her eyes and face. "No, thank you, Papa. Do you know who I am?"

He squinted, pondered, shook his head. "Never saw you before in my life. Staying long?"

She smiled, reached for his hand. "Yes, Papa. I'm staying a long time. I'm Lisette."

He nodded and smiled. "Pretty name. Had a daughter named Lisette. Portia!"

"Yes, Jacob?"

"When's dinner? I'm starved!"

Portia sighed. "We had dinner hours ago, Jacob. You just finished what I'd hoped to save for tomorrow's lunch. Let me take you upstairs. It's time for bed."

"Bed? When's breakfast?"

"In the morning, Jacob. In the morning." Aunt Portia led him to the staircase, smiling at Lisette over her shoulder. "I'll be back soon. If you're hungry—"

"I'm fine. Take your time."

Lisette sank into the overstuffed Turkish chair, closed her eyes, and tried not to think about tomorrow.

A knock at the door.

She went back into the foyer and answered it without using the clear crystal in the stained glass window to see first who it was. She realized her mistake the instant she opened the door.

Andrew.

She tried to close the door in his face, but he inserted his foot and elbowed his way into the foyer.

"You aren't welcome here."

"You told me. I don't have money for a hotel. I used every penny I had buying passage on that miserable boat. You can't expect me to sleep in the street."

"I don't care where you sleep. You aren't staying here. In New Orleans, I had no choice. But, this is *my* house. Get out." She stood beside the open door, her spine as stiff as her resolve.

"Nice place. When I asked for directions to get here, they called this street Millionaire's Row. You never told me your father was a millionaire." He went into the parlor and sat on the Turkish sofa beside the front fireplace, holding his hands out to warm them.

She reluctantly closed the door. The chill night air would overwhelm any warmth produced by the fireplaces.

"Andrew—"

"We're going to have a talk."

"No, we aren't. You're going to leave. My father—"

"Is a doddering old fool. I learned that just after I found out how to get to Adams Avenue."

She burned with shame and anger. How could she evict this obnoxious excuse of a man without help? Andrew wasn't that bright. Surely, she could come up with a way.

"Like it or not, Lisa, you have a responsibility to me. I am your stepson."

A shudder of revulsion shook her. "Don't call me Lisa. Any relationship we had died with your father. I had to endure his treatment of me because he was my husband. You are nothing but an intruder in my home. Leave this house."

"Not until I'm ready. We're going to talk. And we're going to get some things straight between us, right now, so there won't be any . . . scenes . . . in the future, like that one you pulled tonight on the boat. After we talk, you'll understand exactly what I expect of you—and what you can expect from me."

It took every bit of control she had not to scream at him. How dare he speak to her this way? If he thought she would do *anything* because he told her to, he was not only arrogant and repulsive, he was daft, too. If the Morgan family had any influence in Memphis at all, there would not be a person in the city who would hire Andrew or allow him room and board. He'd be forced to go back to New Orleans.

Lisette knew she had to plan carefully what to say—and what *not* to say—and, above all, stay calm. She took several deep breaths, trying to regulate breathing and organize her thoughts.

Andrew went to the front window, pulled the draperies aside and peered into the night. Moonlight filtered through the window, illuminating his face in such a way he appeared demonic.

She drew in a slow breath when she saw how angry he was. She knew he'd been upset, but this look was entirely new. Rage fired his eyes, and his thin lips, tensed into a straight line, made his otherwise passably handsome features downright ugly. She reminded herself to stay calm at all costs.

"All right now, *Lisa.*" Andrew left the window and offered his hand to her. She refused to take it, so he grabbed her wrist and dragged her across the room, throwing her onto the sofa.

"Take your hands off me. How dare you treat me this way? I'll have you horsewhipped." She got up quickly and retreated several steps away, terrified at the change in him, searching her mind desperately for something, anything, to distract him. She had to have help.

"You and I have to get some things straight."

She didn't dare challenge him. Clamping her lips shut, she tried to clear panic from her mind.

Andrew came toward her. She took another step back.

"Stop! If you move another inch, I'll beat you senseless. Do you understand me? Don't think for one minute I wouldn't do it."

She stood still, then spoke in the quietest voice she could manage. "I understand you care nothing for me. You are no gentleman. I'll give you money for a hotel. I cannot possibly think straight with your threats and brutal treatment of me." By virtue of birth, he was supposed to be a gentleman, even though he'd never been considered such in New Orleans. If he ever cared for his father, she might have been able to appeal to that side of him, but they'd hated each other and fought constantly. She knew nothing about Andrew's mother. Mentioning her might lead to disaster.

Andrew smiled, chilling her. Instead of warmth or mirth in the gesture, she saw, rather, a twisted sense of triumph. She felt fear again, more intensely than before.

"I'll give you money for a hotel."

"No."

"Your father would never approve—"

He moved so quickly, she had no time to react. He grabbed her shoulders, then her wrists when she tried to push him away, and with one quick motion, slapped her face so sharply her head pounded, her vision blurring with hot tears.

Terrified, she glared into Andrew's twisted features and saw a side of him more cruel and vicious than she'd ever seen before. His fingers bit deeply into her flesh.

"I have a surprise for you. You are going to invite me to live in this house. I'm going to take over my father's business and responsibilities—and your father's business, as well. You are *not* going to tell anyone about this little talk we're having. If you do, I'll beat you to death and drop you into the river. If you don't believe me . . ." He raised his hand, curling his fingers into a tight fist.

"No! No, please. I believe you. Don't hit me again. Please." The words were bile. Her only choice, though, was to agree with whatever he said, to escape this nightmare by whatever concession necessary.

"That's better. I expect you to listen carefully. Are you listening?"

Bastard. She nodded, wishing with all her heart and soul for a knife or a gun.

"When we are in public together you will tell everyone how happy you are that I'm in Memphis. You will take my arm when I offer it, and you will smile and convince everyone you have full confidence and respect for your stepson and his ability to run Morgan Enterprises. And— are you listening, *Lisa?*—you will say nothing to your father or your aunt. Nothing. Because you are not the only one who will be hurt if you breathe a word of our little conversation to them or anyone."

She felt a different kind of fear now. "What are you insinuating?"

"Your father is not exactly young. A lot of things could happen to a senile old man. And your aunt—"

"You wouldn't—"

"Wouldn't I?" His expression hardened. "Try me. Dear Aunt Portia will go along with whatever you tell her."

What choice did she have?

"I'd like to go to my room now, Andrew." Lisette swallowed hard, despising what she had to say next. "I'm sorry there isn't a room ready to accommodate you tonight. I'll give you money for a hotel. In a couple of days . . ." The triumphant smile on Andrew's face sickened her.

"I knew you'd see reason. I'll be going." The cruelty in his eyes left no doubt he meant every word. "But not until we've gotten to know each other a little better."

He grabbed her shoulders and forced his mouth on hers before she could turn her head. She planted both hands on his chest and pushed hard. "How dare you!"

He hit her again, harder this time, with his fist instead of his open palm. A maelstrom of pain whirled through her. She could scarcely think with the intense pounding in her temples.

"I dare because, in time, I am going to be your husband. As soon as it is socially acceptable, we're going to be married. I'm going to take responsibility for my dear departed father's wife—just as my father asked me to do—and run Morgan Enterprises, since your poor father is too ill and incompetent to do so." He pulled her within an inch of his face, his foul breath hot on her skin. "If you ever push me away again, I promise you won't forget it." He crushed his mouth on hers for what seemed an eternity, his teeth biting into the tender flesh of her lips.

When he finally released her, she pushed past him and ran toward the front door, tears streaming down her swollen face.

When she got to the door, she stood there a moment, her lips throbbing, tasting blood. Swiping at tears, she pulled herself erect, assuming the posture of a well-bred woman, trying to maintain some measure of dignity. She reached into a pocket in her dress, pulled out a small purse, took out several bills and replaced the purse. She purposefully allowed blood to flow from her lip, wanting him to see what he'd done to her. She would not have to testify to Andrew's barbarism. Her blood would tell the tale.

She opened the door and stood there, waiting for him to leave, knowing if she defied him again, he would hurt her worse than he already had.

Andrew took the money. "I'll need more. You can go to the bank Monday." He stared into her eyes. "Good, Lisa. You're learning already."

She didn't respond. He talked animatedly for a moment about how their lives together would be satisfying and productive. He outlined the duties she would have as his wife, emphasizing her role as keeper of the home and children. Lisette shuddered at the thought of bearing this man's offspring. She would rather die than have him touch her again. The cold of the November night, swarming into the foyer, chilled her to the bone.

He went outside to the porch. She immediately tried to close the door, but he blocked it with his boot. "I want to see how much you've been listening." He leaned toward her.

Just as his lips were about to touch hers, she coughed straight into his face. He leaned back sharply, giving her time to slam the door and bolt it. She touched her lips carefully and felt blood, warm and wet on her fingers.

She went back to the parlor and stood for a moment at the window, watching as he walked toward town. With her heart pounding, revenge burning in her like the fires of hell, she vowed to see Andrew in jail before the sun reached its zenith tomorrow.

When Lisette turned from the window, Aunt Portia was coming down the stairs. "Who was that, child? I wanted to come down, but Jacob—"

"It was Andrew." Lisette turned away, hoping to spare Aunt Portia more grief.

"I hope you sent him packing."

"I did. It wasn't easy."

"What a long, trying day you've had. Why not come to bed? We'll take care of that ruffian after a good night's sleep."

"I'll be upstairs in a minute, Aunt Portia." Lisette faced the fireplace, holding out her hands as though warming them. Her fingers were red and sticky with blood. She folded her fingers into fists and found the gesture satisfying.

"If you need anything, child, call me."

"I will."

Aunt Portia came to give her a hug and kiss good-night. There was no way to conceal the injuries now. She cried out at the sight of Lisette's face.

"Your dress! You're covered in blood! Dear Lord—" Portia ran to the kitchen and returned with a damp cloth. Lisette poured out the whole story while Aunt Portia sat beside her on the sofa, cleaning her face and hands. While Lisette talked, Aunt Portia cried.

"So, I coughed in his face and slammed the door."

Portia's eyes widened. "You didn't." She giggled.

Lisette stared at her, completely puzzled. "Aunt Portia?"

"Good for you! I hope you gave him the epizooty."

She tried to smile, prevented by pain in her lips. "You always make me feel better."

She gathered Lisette close and held her, rubbing her back with one hand, stroking her arm with the other.

"Tomorrow, Aunt Portia, I'll decide what I'm going to do about Andrew."

"Don't you mean, what *we* are going to do?"

"I never meant to involve you in all this. If Andrew finds out I told you, he'll do something awful, to Papa or to you. I have to get to the police station, first thing in the morning."

"They'll take care of him." Her frown eased into a smile. "Don't you worry. Even if the officials won't help, I haven't lived all these years with that cantankerous brother of mine without learning a few tricks. Andrew will think twice about what he's done and go home to New Orleans where he belongs. We'll have a party such as Memphis has never seen. Jacob and I always agreed, when the time came, we would have a party. The entire family would announce your engagement. He broke his promise to me when he gave you to James, eight years ago, and you can bet your buttons he heard about it. When you're ready for a new husband, we'll have that party, just as I planned. Andrew won't be anywhere near the Chickasaw Bluffs when the music begins."

"I love you, Aunt Portia. You won't be upset if I wait a while before looking for another husband—if I ever decide to look again?"

"You take all the time you need, child."

Lisette had never told Aunt Portia how abusive James had been. Lisette's letters brimmed with lies, about parties and visits from neighboring women she'd never met. She described wonderful dinners and excursions into New Orleans from their country home, when, in truth, she'd been confined to the house, forced to clean and cook endlessly, with no word of thanks and only the barest necessities begrudgingly supplied. James had never been without money, but, during the eight years Lisette slaved as his wife, she lived like a pauper, along with his two mistresses, who also lived in the house.

When he died, leaving everything to his "beloved wife," a term from a will written years before he married Lisette, she inherited everything, much to Andrew's ire, and spent over three hundred dollars on clothes the day after James died. Thanks to the inheritance, she would never want for anything again, even without the Morgan fortune, but she had to contend with Andrew, who, without her charity, would be destitute. All he had was the deed to the family estate in New Orleans—and the expenses involved with running such a farm. Andrew had neither desire nor intelligence to deal with such matters. He had chosen, instead, to follow her to Memphis, threatening her security.

"Now, child, let's get you upstairs to your room and out of that dress so you can ready yourself for bed. I'll bring you a cup of nice hot chamomile and some teacakes I made today. Tomorrow, you don't get out of bed until you're good and ready. By the time you're up and about, I'll have them locking that scoundrel up and throwing away the key."

"Wake me early. I'll have to show them the bruises as proof Andrew struck me."

Tears came to Aunt Portia's eyes again. "If I'd only come downstairs sooner . . ."

"I don't want you to worry. I know exactly how to take care of this. Now, off to bed with both of us. We'll have dark circles under our eyes for a week as it is."

"All right. Do I need to bring a poultice for your poor face?" She touched her fingertips to Lisette's swollen cheek. "I could kill that man for touching you. He'd better not show his face at this house again!"

Lisette hugged her. "I love you, Aunt Portia."

"I love you, too, child. If you aren't better by tomorrow, I'm taking you to see the doctor."

They went upstairs. Her father's snoring reverberated through the hall from his bedroom on the far side of the wide hallway. The room Lisette would occupy had been her parents'. After her mother's death, Jacob couldn't bear to sleep there, so he moved to the bedroom in the front corner of the house. Lisette's nursery was directly across from her parents' room. Aunt Portia's bedroom was directly across from Jacob, so she could hear him if he called during the night.

Seth had put Lisette's baggage at the end of the cano-pied rosewood bed. She tenderly caressed the sculpted blos-soms on the cartouche-crested headboard. Her mother had loved this bed.

Home again. At last. The tears which came now were happy ones.

"You have a good sleep, you hear?" Aunt Portia said quietly.

"I hear."

"It's so good to have you home again."

After she hugged Lisette again and left, Lisette eased out of the soiled dress, knowing she would never wear it again, and dropped it on the floor in the corner. Rummaging in her bags, she found a heavy flannel nightgown trimmed in lace and pulled it over her head. She'd bought it along with the rest of the wardrobe. It felt heavenly, soft and loose. After wearing her corset all day, she welcomed something less confining. She poured water from a porcelain pitcher into its matching bowl on the sideboard. After cleaning and soothing her face with tender strokes, she slipped between soft sheets and pulled the heavy velvet patchwork quilt up to her neck.

Tomorrow, she would go to the top of the house, to her "secret room," where she'd spent countless happy hours playing as a child, dreaming about growing up and about the man she would someday marry. That dream had been lost. Perhaps, in time, she could recapture it. At home, any-thing was possible.

She must have fallen asleep instantly because her next thought centered on sunlight streaming into the room. Not ready to rise, she turned over and drifted back to sleep.

The dream came softly, tenderly, and she welcomed it.

Chapter Three

David got to his office ten minutes early, feeling strangely restless. He hadn't slept worth a damn—again. The weather mirrored his mood, morning sunshine overcome by low clouds, with rain threatening. The barometric pressure was dropping rapidly. Everyone seemed to be moving slowly—except for Lana, of course.

"Good morning, Lana." He could tell she wasn't going to allow him to be gloomy, and she wouldn't let him escape to the back without a healthy dose of cheer.

"Morning, Doctor. Beautiful day, don't you think? I hope you can make the barbecue tonight. Greg and I are going to announce our engagement." She waited for his reaction.

This development was one reason David had declined Joe's invitation. Lana hadn't been able to keep it a secret, and David suspected everyone there tonight would already have been told too. Shawna was getting the gang together so they could make a formal announcement—and using the opportunity to goad David into making the same announcement about Candy. But it wasn't going to happen. He didn't feel like explaining his personal life to Shawna—again.

"I can't make it, Lana, but you know I'm glad for you."

"I know. We'll miss you." She went back to work. Her engagement to Greg would energize her for weeks to come. She was wearing red this morning, appropriate for her mood. The color complemented her brunette hair and brown eyes nicely. If her smile got any wider, he'd have to do some stitches.

"How does it look today?" He picked up the appointment book. Not too bad.

"We haven't had many sick kids call in today. Mostly routine checkups. If you don't talk a lot, we should be out of here early today."

"I'm not the one who's usually talkative."

"I know. At least that's what you tell me. Ready for number one?"

"Give me a few minutes first." He went to his station to look at the first chart. Debbie Myers. In last week for a cold. Back today with a lingering cough. This shouldn't take long.

Lana called Debbie. He spent less than five minutes, including hearing about Debbie's part in the play they were doing at school which would require her to be in full voice, and was back out in the hall reaching for the next chart when he sensed movement.

Lisette stood at the far end of the hall in the shadows, blinking and frowning, just as she had at the dance, when he'd first seen her in the ballroom. He never took his eyes off her, afraid she might evaporate before he had a chance to speak to her. A ridiculous thought.

"Doctor Stewart?" Her frown eased.

David hurried to where she stood. She wore a long pink-flowered flannel nightgown with hand-crocheted lace at the throat and wrists and more than a dozen buttons down the front. She was barefoot. She stepped into the light and he saw her face. Her cheek and lips were swollen and discolored. Anger instantly boiled inside him.

"What happened? Come in here." He led her into the examination room at the end of the hall just as Lana appeared with the next patient. He motioned for Lana.

She put the boy and his mother in the first room and came on back. "Who's that?"

"Don't call anyone else until I tell you."

Lana tried to peek through the door to get a better look, but he stepped between them, blocking her view. "I'll be there in a minute." He went into the room and closed the door.

Lisette stood by the counter, holding a blood pressure cuff. "What is this?"

"It's for taking blood pressure. Fits around your arm. A sphygmomanometer. Let me look at your face." He had her sit on the end of the examination table, then probed her bruises gingerly, being especially careful not to hurt her. He remembered thinking, last night on the riverboat, how delicate her skin was and how a mere touch might bruise her. This had been more than a touch. More anger built inside him. "Who did this to you?"

She looked away. Tears collected in her eyes. "I shouldn't bother you with it, Doctor Stewart. It isn't your concern."

"Not my concern! Someone struck you hard enough to—" He had to remind himself to be professional. He took a deep breath. "Have you put ice on it?"

"Ice? No. Would that help?"

"Yes. I'll also give you a shot for the inflammation and pain."

Fear appeared in her eyes.

"Don't worry. It won't hurt much—just a prick, actually—and it will make the bruising less painful." He used the intercom and called Darlene to bring the injection.

Lisette calmed somewhat. She appeared curious.

"What is it?"

"I'm wondering where you went after I saw you on the deck of the *Star*."

He had to think for a moment. "The *Star*? You mean the *Queen*, don't you?"

"I've never heard it called the *Queen*. I've ridden twice now, on the *Cajun Star* both times. I saw you on the deck, after the boat docked and asked you to take me home—a thoroughly brazen thing to do, I admit—then you disappeared again. Were you serious about wanting to call on me?"

"Of course." He paused to think. "You saw me on the deck of the riverboat?" That had been in his dream. How could she know about that?

"Yes."

"All right. Let me tell you what happened and you tell me if you remember it that way."

"Certainly."

"I was standing on the third deck by the railing. I started to go back downstairs—"

"That's when I called to you the second time. You didn't hear me the first time."

His heart pounded. "I went to where you were standing."

"You said you didn't know who my father was—"

"I needed to know where you lived—"

"My stepson came onto the deck—"

"And called your name. A man with a beard. With another man right behind him." Incredible!

"The captain, yes. I apologize for Andrew's rudeness."

"He told you it was time to go."

"But I didn't want to go with him."

"Who is Andrew?"

"My stepson." Her expression hardened. She fingered

her cheek. "Andrew Westmoreland."

Rage tore through David like a flash fire. "He did this to you? Or was it your father?"

"Oh, no! Not my father." The tears came back to her eyes. "My father never raised his hand to me, not once in my life. Now, he hardly knows who I am." Her eyes flashed with sudden anger. "Andrew followed me home. I shall report to the authorities what he did to me."

David had to control his rage. It colored his judgment, jeopardizing professionalism. He would deal with Andrew Westmoreland later. "You asked me to take you home."

"Yes. But when I turned around, you were gone. The captain agreed to accompany me."

"You said Andrew followed you home. He did this to you in your own home?"

Lisette hesitated. "It isn't anything you should concern yourself with. I intend to handle the situation myself, with Aunt Portia's help." She looked squarely at me. "Where did you go? Didn't you want to drive me home?"

"Of course I did. I was about to tell you I'd take you wherever you wanted to go—anywhere in the world—when the phone rang."

"The phone?"

"The telephone. It . . . woke me up."

Lisette shook her head. "I don't understand. You were asleep on the riverboat and a telephone woke you? Isn't that the new contraption allowing people to speak to each other, even when they aren't in the same room together? You must be terribly rich or important to have one this soon. It will probably be years before we're able to have one. My husband thought they were ridiculous, but to me such an invention seemed a miracle." She paused. "Why are you looking at me like that?"

How could he explain being dumbfounded at the idea that anyone in this country would think the telephone years away from availability to the general public? He decided to explore this quaint point of view later.

"I didn't mean to stare. You don't understand. I was asleep, dreaming about the dance, about meeting you. I wasn't on the riverboat. I only—" This sounded more ridiculous by the minute. Darlene knocked, then came in with the injection. "You've had injections before, haven't you?"

She shivered. "Once or twice. It isn't pleasant." She appeared really nervous.

"Don't worry. Darlene is an expert. I'll wait outside while she gives it to you, then I'll be back."

He went into the hall. Lana was waiting. "What's going on in there? That woman must have come in the back door. Do you know her?"

"Her name is Lisette Morgan . . . Westmoreland." A bell went off in his brain, but he didn't have time to analyze why. "Start a file. Her stepson, Andrew Westmoreland, hit her in the face—several times, from the look of it. Bruised cheek, split lips—possibly bitten from the look of it. I'd love to get my hands on this guy and—" He saw the look in Lana's eyes and stopped. "Sorry. It infuriates me to see a woman battered."

"I know. I'll get a form for basic info and let her fill it out." Lana went back toward the front office.

Darlene came out, shaking her head.

"What's wrong?"

"I had to give it to her in the arm. She got mad when I suggested it would be better in her hip. She called me a deviant."

He swallowed laughter. "I'll take it from here. Thanks, Darlene."

"Whoever hit her must have been really mad."

"Not as mad as I am."

David went back into the examination room. Lisette stood by the far wall, rubbing her arm.

"I don't know why you have such a woman working for you, Doctor Stewart. She actually suggested—well, being a lady, I can't say."

"Don't let it worry you. That's the way we usually do it around here. It's easier on the patient. Your arm will be sore for a few hours, until the medicine has a chance to dissipate."

"Thank you. Just send the bill to me in care of Jacob Morgan, Adams Avenue, here in Memphis."

"Your father! I've looked everywhere, called everyone I can think to call. No one knows him—or Morgan Enterprises."

Lisette seemed piqued by that statement. "I don't know who you've been speaking to. Anyone who doesn't know Morgan Enterprises must not have lived in Memphis very long. The company was established in 1850 and became one of the foremost producers of arms and ammunition in the South—until the Yankees captured Memphis during the War, of course. Since then—"

"Arms and ammunition?" That would at least give him a lead to follow. "Lisette, I want to see you again. I have patients waiting now, but I could meet you somewhere, or I'll come to your home. Could you give me your address?"

"Address?"

"The exact location of your house on Adams Avenue."

"We live past the Neely home. It might be best if you didn't come to the house. My father isn't well. I wouldn't want to burden Aunt Portia with preparations for visitors."

"Aunt Portia must be a real stickler for southern tradition. Just name a place where I can meet you. Later today?"

"Not today. How about tomorrow?" She thought a moment. "Do you know the Peabody Hotel?"

"Of course. I'll meet you there at noon, by the fountain."

Lisette glanced around the room. "Did you hear that?" She went toward the door, listening.

"What? I didn't hear anything."

"Aunt Portia. Calling me. Is she outside?" Lisette hurried past, the hem of her gown swishing on the carpet. "Aunt Portia? I'm here."

"Lisette, wait." David followed her into the hall, but she was gone. *Damn, not again!* He ran to the back door and outside. No sign of her. Back inside, he searched every room, found Charlie Malone and his mother waiting in Room One, apologized for the delay, and went to the waiting room, full of people.

Lana leaned over the reception desk. "Doctor Stewart? Is there something wrong?"

"Did Lisette come out this way?"

"No, I thought—"

He rushed to the back door for another look. Darlene followed.

"Where did she go? I need more information from her."

"You and me both."

David met Joe downtown for lunch at Sleep Out Louie's. The place was packed. Every one of the tall tables, surrounded by bar stools with long legs, was full, so they sat at the bar and ordered fried catfish po'boys, the special for the day, and two beers. The music was loud, the people were loud—exactly what Joe loved.

"Barbecue. My house. Tonight at seven. Shawna's already talked to Candy. You're to pick her up at six thirty."

"I thought we'd settled this."

"Shawna jumped on me when I told her you couldn't come. What else do you have planned?"

David sighed.

"Uh oh. Trouble in Candyland?"

"We've been coming to this for a couple of months now. Candy wants to get married. I'm not ready yet. I don't know if I'll ever be ready. It isn't fair to string her along. She's a great girl. She'll make someone a wonderful wife."

"Just not you, huh?"

"Not me."

"Don't you think you ought to tell her that?"

"I have. She labels it male PMS and ignores me. I'm not in the mood to hash it out again."

The po'boys arrived. There was enough food on David's plate for both of them, but he decided to give it his best shot. The catfish was delicious and the fries cooked just the way David liked them. Joe didn't waste any time getting started on his.

"Listen, Bro," he said between bites, "come to the barbecue tonight. Afterward, you can tell Candy you've given it a lot of thought, and you're not ready for a commitment. Break it off once and for all. I'll help if I can."

"I've already told her. There's no way you can help. Thanks anyway."

"If you tell her you both need a breather, she may interpret that to mean you're getting ready to pop the question and need a little time to work up your nerve."

"Get serious, Joe. Does that actually happen with men and women these days?"

"Probably not as much as it used to, but sure. You've been sleeping with Candy, haven't you?"

He shook his head.

"You're kidding! Why not?"

"Even thinking about it makes me feel guilty as hell."

"You shouldn't feel guilty. It's been five years. Fran wouldn't have wanted you to become a monk."

"Yeah, I know."

He gave David a look which he recognized as his "Haven't I ever told you?" look.

"David."

Something serious coming. He called him David only when he was serious.

"It's time for you to find somebody else. Fran is gone. If you'd been the one to die, you'd want her to find someone, wouldn't you?"

"We've had this conversation before, remember? Of course I would. As soon as it felt right to her and she didn't feel guilty for sleeping with the guy." The idea of Fran in bed with anyone but him still made David furious. And the thought of sleeping with Candy always made him feel lousy.

He could tell Joe wasn't going to give in on this. David knew him too well. "All right, I'll bring Candy to the barbecue, but tell Shawna this will be the last time, all right? No more calling Candy and arranging dates for me behind my back. I'm going to break it off. As for finding someone else . . ."

Joe nodded, finishing off the po'boy. David had a third left but couldn't eat another bite.

"I'll tell Shawna. But you know what she'll do."

"I know. More blind dates. Can't she give up and let me live my own life?"

"Shawna?"

"All right. I give up. I'll move to Tahiti, where she can't set me up every weekend with her girlfriends who have wonderful personalities and who sew their own clothes."

"Pick Candy up at six thirty. Greg and Lana will be there, so you'll have someone else to talk to. Marilu has invited Phillip. Nice kid. How long have you known him?"

"I can't remember. Good kid. Polite." He'd have to have a talk with Marilu. Tonight.

David got home about five thirty that afternoon. His emotions had been in turmoil all day, thinking about the upcoming confrontation with Candy and about bruises inflicted on Lisette by a barbarian named Andrew Westmoreland. David had wracked his brain, trying to figure out how she could disappear from the office. His efforts to locate Westmoreland had proven to be as fruitless as finding Jacob Morgan—or his munitions plant. Nothing made sense.

Why did Lisette come to the office wearing a flannel nightgown? Barefooted? If Andrew Westmoreland was Lisette's stepson, her husband must be Andrew's father. She'd been wearing black on the boat. Did that mean her husband was dead? She'd said she was living with her father and aunt now. And what about the name she'd used, referring to the riverboat? The *Cajun Star*. He'd have to call the Riverboat Line and ask if their boat had ever been known by that name. Jim would know. Or Captain Dale.

Lisette promised to come to the Peabody tomorrow at noon. He had no intention of allowing her to disappear again. He'd insist on meeting her father, then be sure Jacob Morgan was fully informed about Westmoreland. If he was ill—she'd mentioned something about an affliction—David would offer his services. So many questions. And not one reasonable answer for any of them.

He settled into his favorite chair for a few minutes, a recliner aptly labeled a *Catnapper* when he'd bought it. It was so comfortable he often fell asleep there and spent most of the night catnapping. Tonight, though, he couldn't seem to get comfortable and couldn't relax. In the winter a fire in the fireplace was extremely relaxing. With overnight temperatures hovering in the fifties, it was still too warm for a fire, and he didn't want to listen to music. His mind raged with the memory of Lisette's bruised flesh.

He realized, suddenly, he was out of the chair, pacing from one end of the den to the other, from the bookshelves on the far end to the desk piled high with files he'd brought home, all the way to the kitchen door and back again. This was getting him nowhere. He had to pick Candy up in half an hour. He went to the bedroom to change clothes and wash up a bit before leaving again. Tonight he'd get Joe into the study and tell him everything. David had to confide in someone.

Candy was dressed in blue—his favorite color—wearing Chanel No. 5—his favorite perfume. They made small talk until Joe's house. Once there, David left her talking to Shawna and tried to get Joe alone. Before they could get away, though, Greg and Lana arrived with the grand announcement.

"We're getting married!" Lana's wide grin spotlighted David and Candy. He refused to look at Candy, knowing what he'd see. They congratulated them and held out their glasses for champagne. David took one sip then traded it for scotch and water.

Marilu and Phillip disappeared into the den to listen to what Joe called "their music." David didn't think it half bad, and Joe admitted he didn't, either, but he couldn't let Marilu think her old man liked the same music. She'd be mortified and would find something else he might not be able to tolerate.

The barbecue was great. Joe had grilled sirloins, Polish sausage, and chicken. There was so much pork barbecue in Memphis that the other meats were a welcome change. Shawna had fixed potato salad, slaw, red beans, a green salad and homemade rolls. Everyone ate until stuffed. When apple cobbler was brought out, David begged off for at least an hour. Joe's recliner would have felt wonderful, but Candy suggested they take a walk. Shawna piped her approval and dragged Joe away to the kitchen for a trumped up chore. David doubted Joe would burst her bubble with news of David's breakup with Candy. He'd leave that little task to David.

It was a beautiful night for a walk. In the spring every yard would be resplendent with azaleas and dogwood and a dozen other blooming plants, but there were plenty of fall flowers to complement the yellow ginkgos in November. Joe's barbecue perfumed the neighborhood.

Candy took David's arm. He hadn't thought of it as a possessive gesture until tonight. He had to put a stop to this now. Candy beat him to it.

"David, I think we need to talk about our future."

"I agree."

"You do? You've never wanted to talk about it before."

"I think it's best we understand each other."

She was quiet for a moment. "I don't think I like the sound of that."

"I didn't mean for it to sound ominous. I just think we need to take a breather, that's all."

"A breather? You said that before. We did. You think we need another one?"

She wasn't going to take the news gracefully. If there was one thing about Candy he could bank on, it was honesty, with no punches pulled. At this particular moment, though, he would've preferred calm acceptance. She didn't let him answer.

"You want us to take a breather from what? Each other? What's that supposed to mean, David? I thought we had something special here."

"We do. We did. I'm just not comfortable going any further with it right now, though."

She pumped her chin up and down a few times and pulled her arm out of his. "I see. In other words, you're dumping me."

"I didn't say that. We ought to look at things carefully before we . . . that is, before I'm ready to—"

"I get it, David. There's no need to spell it out for me. You aren't ready to get married because you're still mourning your dead wife after five years. Fine. Do you have any idea how many more years you're going to mourn before you're ready to commit yourself to a new relationship?"

Her remarks about his "dead wife" were uncalled for, in his opinion. He clamped his mouth shut so he wouldn't say something he'd regret later. She saw she'd gone too far.

"David, I'm sorry. I didn't mean that. I thought . . . I guess I was wrong. Let's go back to the house."

"I really need to get home."

"I'll get Shawna to take me later."

They walked back to the house in silence. The minute they came through the backyard gate, onto the patio, David could see in Joe's eyes he knew it was done. Candy disappeared into the house.

"Ready for dessert, David?" Shawna was oblivious to anything but her own agenda.

David declined the cobbler, even though it smelled good, excused himself after asking Shawna if she'd take Candy home later, and left without seeing Candy again.

At home, he realized he hadn't had a chance to talk to Joe and dialed his number.

"What's up, Bro?" He wasn't asking any questions or volunteering any information. David reminded himself to thank Joe sometime.

"Listen, Joe, I have to talk to you. It's important. Remember the woman I told you about—the one I met at Marilu's dance?"

"Have you seen her again?"

"Today. In my office. With her face swollen from her stepson using her as a punching bag. I wanted to talk to you at your house tonight, but—"

"No problem. What can I do?"

"There are some really odd things about this woman. I haven't told you everything, but I want to. I can't find any trace of her, her father, her father's company—she said it dates from 1850—or the stepson who hit her. She said she'd meet me tomorrow at noon at the Peabody. I need to sort things out before I see her again."

"Do you know where she lives?"

"On Adams Avenue, past the Neely House, in the Victorian Village. Must be on the other side of Fontaine House too. It isn't the house in between. I checked. Ring any bells?"

"What's the exact address?"

"Adams Avenue is all she gave me."

"Shouldn't be too hard to find. I assume you've looked in the phone book."

"No listing."

"Been to Adams Avenue?"

"No one by that name in any house for blocks."

"I'll be right over."

"Thanks, Joe."

"Uh, would you mind if I bring Candy with me? I have to take her home anyway. Her thesis was done on Memphis and the Peabody Hotel. I think she went back to the time when the first Peabody was built after the Civil War. If anyone will know this Morgan family, she will."

David thought for a minute. Seeing Candy again so soon could give her the wrong impression, that maybe he was sorry and wanted to make up. He didn't want to do that. "Uh . . . Joe, I don't know—"

"Look, if you're really stuck on this woman from the dance—what was her name again?"

"Lisette."

"Candy will pick up on it. What did you tell her tonight?"

"That I wasn't ready to get married. She wasn't happy."

"Did she cry?"

"Not a tear."

"Then she can't be that hooked on you. She'll get over it."

"Maybe you're right."

"And, happy or not, Candy can help with the history stuff. We lawyers only know about the history involved in lawsuits. She'll be a lot of help, David. If I know you, you'll want to keep things friendly between the two of you. Whadya say?"

He was right. The last thing David wanted was bad feelings between himself and a woman he once thought he might be in love with. "All right. But take her with you when you leave. I don't want any more 'discussions' tonight."

"No problem. We'll be there as soon as we can."

After hanging up, David mulled it over. *Stuck on this woman from the dance.* He hadn't actually come to that conclusion, but now that it had been expressed, he deemed it accurate. Since he'd met Lisette, he'd been taken with her beauty, her grace, her innocence. Yet there was something tough about this lady, too. She wasn't a Dresden doll, to be set on a shelf and admired. There was more to her than beauty or charm.

She'd insisted she would take care of the problem with Westmoreland herself. That took courage, even if it was naive. Surely, with all the publicity about battering in recent years, she knew she didn't have to put up with anything like that.

An hour later Joe and Candy arrived. Candy was polite, but that was all. David had to assume she was still angry but she didn't show it overtly. Maybe she was embarrassed for Joe to know that they'd split up. On the way over, he'd filled her in about Lisette.

"I hope you don't mind my coming with Joe." Candy seemed cool, reserved.

"Not at all," he lied. "I'd forgotten your thesis was on Memphis and the Peabody."

"I've been in love with the Peabody Hotel since I was a little girl. We went by my house on the way to get some of my research sources and information on the important families in Memphis history and the reconstruction of the city after the yellow fever epidemics in the 1870s." She opened a small case and produced a laptop computer David had seen her use a hundred times. "I think I remember a plug on that wall. I hate to use my batteries if there's electricity around."

"End of the couch." The last time she'd been in this house was barely a week ago. She knew where that outlet was. He swallowed his retort and plugged in the cord for her.

Candy booted the notebook-sized computer. It beeped and buzzed, then settled on an island landscape scene. Candy typed for a minute. She typed some more.

While waiting for her to find what she was looking for, David wondered how he was going to tell her tactfully that history wasn't exactly what they needed in this case. Straight out was probably best.

"The family I'm trying to find lives in Memphis now. Maybe I'm slow, but how is history going to help me find the Morgan family?" He tried hard to keep sarcasm out of his voice, but didn't have much luck.

Candy answered, still staring at the screen. "If Jacob Morgan is as important as his daughter seems to believe, and his company has been around since 1850, it might have another name now. We'll work backward until we pick up the name."

"Good idea." It couldn't hurt. And it couldn't hurt David to make nice either. "Thanks, Candy. I'll appreciate anything you can dig up."

Candy hesitated. "Joe told me about her being abused. I'm really sorry, David."

The memory of Lisette's bruises flashed through David's mind. "Let's find out who she is. The more information I have, the better my chances of helping her."

With Candy serving as guide and narrator, they delved into the sources she'd brought, then dialed a library network to see what else might show up. For more than an hour, they found nothing within the past ten years to correspond to the information David had. Working backward in time, he was ready to give up when they reached the forties. Nothing in the past sixty years—then seventy-five. When they got to the turn of the twentieth century, David was ready to quit.

"If we haven't found Morgan Enterprises—"

"Found it."

Joe and David sat on either side of Candy on the couch to see what she'd dug up. Candy didn't let her knee touch David's.

"Morgan Enterprises. Manufacturer of rifles and ammunition. Founded in 1850, prospered until the first part of the Civil War, but ceased production in 1862 after the Union Army captured Memphis. Switched to production of cotton clothing six months later, but didn't do as well. The name change came early in 1886. Westmoreland Enterprises."

"Westmoreland! Are you sure?"

"Do you want to check my work?"

Joe laughed. "Why? It has to be right. The pieces fit, right, Bro? Candy did good." Joe must have sensed the tension between David and Candy. True to form, he was trying to dispel it.

"We're in the wrong century, remember?" David gave him a look he hoped would keep Joe from putting his size eleven foot in his mouth before the evening was over.

"Listen to this, guys." Candy pulled her legs up beside her on the couch, a gesture David knew well. "Jacob Morgan died in 1885 and Westmoreland took over the company. Within a year, the company went into bankruptcy." She set the computer on the coffee table. "He either ruined the company after Morgan died, or took over a failing company and was unable to bring it back. I can't tell from what I have."

"Jacob Morgan? Are you sure?"

"Yep. Here's where it gets interesting. Jacob's sister, Portia, is listed as co-owner and manager after 1873. There was a bad yellow fever epidemic that year. Maybe Morgan

71

caught the fever and his sister had to step in. No way to verify that either. Speculation. There's no wife's name listed, but there is one child. Jacob Morgan had a daughter."

David knew what Candy was going to say, but still couldn't believe it.

"Her name was Lisette."

Chapter Four

"Lisette, wake up!"

Aunt Portia's voice penetrated the fog in Lisette's mind and the residue of the dream. She opened her eyes. "Doctor Stewart?"

"It's time to get up. We have to go to the police station, remember?" Aunt Portia poured water into the bowl on the sideboard. "This cool water should feel good on your face this morning."

Lisette tried to clear her mind. "I wish we didn't have to do this."

"So do I, but it's necessary to keep that ruffian from bothering us again. Get dressed. I'll start breakfast."

Lying there a few moments, Lisette recalled the dream and how concerned Doctor Stewart had been about her bruised face. He had to be one of the kindest men she'd ever known. His eyes had seethed with anger when he heard Andrew had struck her.

She closed her eyes for a moment to clear away the cobwebs. It made no sense to react to a dream as though it were real. The only reality was Andrew.

At the sideboard, she washed her face and noticed much of the swelling was gone. Only the dark blue of the bruise remained. Her lips were still sore, but better. She peered closely into the mirror. The bruises were abnormally better than they should have been. The injection that rude nurse had given her—but she was part of the dream too. Her left arm, where she dreamed the injection had been given, felt sore, tender, just as Doctor Stewart had warned. But none of it made sense. How could her arm be sore from a dream?

She selected a black dress from one of her trunks, pulled it over her head, then buttoned it from waist to neck. The collar was a piece of ecru tatted lace that Aunt Portia had made for her before she'd gone to New Orleans with James. She had moved the collar from dress to dress through the years, attempting to brighten the dull material she'd been forced to use in making her clothes. The collar was a warm reminder of the hours she'd spent as a child watching Aunt Portia tat, listening to stories about her parents.

What would Mother think about all this? Lisette wondered. Her memory of Brianna Morgan was so vague, dimmed by the years and by Lisette's youth at the time of her mother's death, she couldn't be sure any longer if the picture in her mind was real or simply borrowed from the family portrait that had been made the year Lisette was born. Brianna had golden blond hair and incredibly large eyes, which Aunt Portia said were the color of amber. It was easy to see why Jacob fell in love with Brianna at their first meeting. Lisette had inherited her mother's eyes and full lips, but not the blond hair. Lisette's hair was auburn, red-gold in sunshine, a combination of the blond and Papa's once reddish-brown hair.

Aunt Portia appeared at the door. "Breakfast will be ready soon."

"I just have to do my hair." Lisette picked up the brush from the chiffonier and pulled it through the tangled curls with difficulty.

"Let me help. I haven't brushed your hair—"

"—in eight years." It had been one of their special times together. The memory tugged at her heart, just as the family portrait had done. She handed the brush to Aunt Portia. She pulled it through Lisette's hair until it shone like the sunshine streaming through the lace curtains. It felt heavenly to receive this attention after so many years of loneliness and neglect.

"That will have to do for now. You can do a full hundred strokes tonight. I let you sleep longer than I should have. It's past ten already."

Lisette twisted her hair into a long coil, wound it on the crown of her head and secured it with a hairpin, then followed Aunt Portia downstairs to the kitchen for a breakfast of flapjacks and molasses. She had already instructed Seth to ready the carriage.

After they'd eaten, Aunt Portia took their plates to the sink and dunked them into hot, soapy water, scrubbing until they gleamed. "I'll be so relieved when Andrew is locked up and things can get back to normal." She dried the dishes carefully and put them in the cupboard.

Lisette wasn't sure she knew what Aunt Portia meant by "normal," but agreed that having Andrew out of their lives would lift a tremendous burden from her shoulders.

There came a sharp rapping at the front door.

Lisette held one finger to her lips, then tiptoed through the house to the parlor windows and peered around the draperies cautiously to see who was calling.

Andrew.

Aunt Portia appeared at her elbow. "Why, that—"

Lisette shushed her again, then motioned for her to follow. Back in the kitchen, she whispered, worried that Andrew might somehow overhear.

"We have to get to the police station. Is there a way to leave without Andrew seeing us?"

Andrew pounded harder on the door. Lisette feared the

stained glass would shatter in its frame if he continued much longer.

"Out the kitchen door and around to the shed."

"I should have remembered. It's been so long . . . I have to get my wrap. Tell Seth to be ready to leave the minute I get back." Aunt Portia nodded and hurried out the back door, careful not to let it make the slightest noise when it closed.

Lisette hurried back upstairs. There was no sound coming from the front door now. She prayed with all her heart that he'd left. She grabbed her coat, then crept down the stairs, through the hallway and back to the kitchen. When she opened the back door, she pulled too hard, too fast, and it squeaked. The sound seemed amplified to ten times normal. She took care to pull it closed slowly. It made no sound this time.

Skirting the brilliant yellow ginkgos, Lisette tiptoed through the junipers, then, once she'd cleared the backyard, ran to the shed where the carriage was kept. The shed door stood open with no sign of the carriage anywhere.

"Aunt Portia!" she called in a loud whisper.

"Back here, child."

Lisette went around to the far side of the shed. The boy she'd seen last night, who had toted her baggage, sat on the front seat with Aunt Portia in the back. His pale blue eyes gleamed with excitement.

"Hurry, child! I saw Andrew, not a minute ago, walking around the house. If we don't leave now, he'll see us for sure!"

Lisette climbed in, Seth slapped the horses with a buggy whip, clucking his tongue at them, and the carriage jerked into motion. In a few seconds they were into the street. Andrew came running from the back of the house just as they sped away.

Portia leaned forward. "Boy, if you can't make those horses go any faster than that, I'll have your mama whip your behind until your nose bleeds! Now, go!"

"Yessum!" He slapped the horses' rumps again, harder this time. They responded with a faster gait. Lisette breathed a sigh of relief but only for the moment. She had no hopes Andrew would give up so easily.

It took about twenty minutes to reach the station. Seth stayed in the carriage. The minute Lisette stepped inside, she saw Andrew at the counter, speaking to the officer in charge. Her throat tightened and she touched her cheek nervously. He must have had a horse close by to have beaten us there.

"Here they are now, Lieutenant. I told you they'd be along shortly." He took a few steps toward Lisette. "Lisa, how are you feeling after your ordeal? You look absolutely worn out."

She glared at him but said nothing. Perhaps it was fortunate he was here to witness her accusations against him. They could take him into custody immediately. Aunt Portia was already at the counter. Her exchange with Andrew was anything but cordial.

"Stand aside. I don't want you anywhere near my niece ever again, do you hear?"

"I beg your pardon, Miss Morgan. I was just telling the Lieutenant about the intruder you had at your home last evening. He and his men are going to be on the lookout for this scoundrel in hopes you will not be bothered again."

Aunt Portia gaped at him, speechless.

Lisette stepped forward. "Lieutenant, the intruder at our home last evening was Mr. Westmoreland. He forced his way into the house and struck me several times, as you can see by the bruises on my face. I want him arrested." She refused to look at Andrew, feeling her cheeks flame with anxiety and anger. The bruises throbbed painfully.

The Lieutenant frowned. "Well, now, Miss . . ."

"*Mrs.* Westmoreland."

His expression changed to surprise.

"My late husband was Mr. Westmoreland's father. Andrew Westmoreland is, I regret to say, my stepson, which makes his behavior even more reprehensible. I've just arrived in Memphis from New Orleans. My father is ill and I was needed to help my aunt care for him." She nodded toward Aunt Portia. "I did not expect my stepson to leave New Orleans when I did. In fact, I urged him to remain there and see to his father's farming business, but he chose to follow me to Memphis. I'm hoping he will conclude whatever business he may have here and go back to New Orleans where he is needed to continue his father's work."

It was easy to see Andrew didn't like this pronouncement one bit. "There is a perfectly competent manager to see to the farming at home," he said. "I came to Memphis to provide assistance and protection for my stepmother. I am grieved that she has chosen not to avail herself of my help."

The lieutenant cleared his throat noisily. "Well, now, Mrs. Westmoreland, I feel we should get back to the subject of the intruder. Your stepson has given me a completely different account of what occurred at your home. He says he arrived just as the intruder was leaving and that you were hysterical and distraught and mistakenly accused him of being the man who attacked you."

She should have expected such treachery from Andrew. "He is lying. There was no other intruder." She faced Andrew squarely. "He threatened to harm my father or my aunt if I told anyone about his treatment of me. But I am not one to obey cowards who feel they must brutalize women."

Andrew's face reddened. His mouth quivered with un-disguised rage. "I'm afraid Mrs. Westmoreland is still over-wrought from her experience. As I explained before, her attacker grabbed her from behind. The first face she saw was mine. It's understandable that she was mistaken, but I am appalled at her insistence that I was that attacker. During the eight years she was married to my father, I never laid a hand on her in anger. Ask her. She'll tell you."

She knew at that point she was defeated. She could not tell the Lieutenant how Andrew had come to her bedroom repeatedly during the eight years of her marriage, trying to force himself on her, because doing so would humiliate her beyond that which she had already suffered—and would alert Aunt Portia to the fact she'd been lying all those years about the treatment she'd received. Andrew had laid hands on her after his father's funeral, claiming he'd inherited ev-erything—including Lisette—but he knew she would never admit it to anyone. It would ruin her reputation in Mem-phis and any chances she had for social acceptability among Aunt Portia's friends. She had vowed no one would ever know what had happened in New Orleans, the indignities she'd endured. Andrew was forcing her to choose between exposing him and exposing herself.

The Lieutenant waited for Lisette to confirm or deny what Andrew had just said. She had no choice. "The past is past. He accosted me—in anger—last night." She clamped her lips shut, determined to maintain dignity at any cost. She could only hope the lieutenant would see she was telling the truth.

The lieutenant shook his head. "I'm afraid it's your word against his, ma'am. Did anyone see the attacker strike you?"

He peered at Portia expectantly.

Aunt Portia straightened her spine. "I did not witness the actual attack, sir, but my niece was not harmed before Mr. Westmoreland arrived at our home. When he left, her face was swollen and her lips cut and bleeding. There was no other attacker."

"Did you see Mr. Westmoreland arrive?"

Aunt Portia squirmed a little before answering. "No, I did not."

"Then another man could have been there without your knowledge."

"There was no one else!" Portia placed her hands on the counter separating herself from the lieutenant and leaned toward him. "I tell you, this man struck my niece! You must arrest him so he will not harm her again!"

He shook his head. "I can't, Miss Morgan. Without a witness it's her word against his, as I told you. I have no legal reason to detain this man."

Lisette knew there was no use in persisting. She eased Aunt Portia away from the counter. "Well, then, Lieutenant, how do you suggest we protect ourselves from further attacks from this *intruder?*" She glared at Andrew, loathing him, yet fearful as well of what he might do to them for testifying against him.

"My men will try to keep an eye on your home, ma'am. I suggest you keep your doors bolted at all times."

Portia straightened her dress. "You may be certain we shall notify you at the slightest hint of any further intrusion."

Lisette nudged Aunt Portia's elbow. "Thank you, Lieutenant, for your time. I pray we shall not require your services again."

The lieutenant nodded, then turned to Andrew. "My

suggestion to you, sir, is that you finish your business here in Memphis, just as Mrs. Westmoreland said, then return to New Orleans at the first opportunity. Her safety will be of the utmost importance to me, personally, and to the department, from this day onward."

Lisette's spirits lifted. Could it be the officer believed them? "Thank you, Lieutenant. I can't tell you how much I appreciate your understanding in this manner."

"Good day, ma'am. Miss Morgan."

Andrew started to follow them out.

The lieutenant cleared his throat noisily. "Mr. Westmoreland, I wonder if I might trouble you to fill out a report of what you saw last night?" He pulled a sheet of paper from beneath the counter.

"I told you everything. I have business—"

"It won't take long, sir. Fifteen minutes or so."

Lisette smiled and nodded thanks to the Lieutenant. He was giving them time to get home safely. God bless him.

They left quickly. Seth had been watching for them and brought the carriage straight away. Once inside, Lisette took a deep breath. "We're going to have to be careful, Aunt Portia. Andrew will seek revenge for what we just told that officer."

"I know, child. We'll have to be cautious and prepared every minute until that man is gone from this city for good. Let's get home now and see to your father. Seth's mother, Sedonia, can handle him for a short while, but then he decides I'm lost and goes to search for me. When that happens, Sedonia can't handle him at all."

Lisette patted Aunt Portia's hand lovingly. "You've given up your whole life to care for us. I want you to know—"

"Hush, child. I haven't given up anything. You and your

father are as dear to me as any husband and child of my own would have been. Land sakes, child, you *are* my own!"

They held each other for a moment. Together, they would meet Andrew's threats and defeat him if they could. But she knew they would need help.

"Aunt Portia, can we leave Papa alone just a while longer?"

"Why, child?"

"The last time I saw Doctor Stewart, I promised to meet him today at the Peabody Hotel at noon."

"Who is Doctor Stewart? Where did you meet him?"

"On the *Cajun Star*. He was kind and thoughtful, and I think he might help us if we ask him."

Portia tipped up the watch she had pinned to the left shoulder of her dress, opened the cover and read the time with a frown. "It's ten past noon now."

"Then we must hurry." She leaned forward. "Seth, take us to the Peabody Hotel. Quickly!"

"Yessum."

Seth turned the carriage around at the first opportunity and headed for the hotel. Once there, they got out and went inside while Seth went to find a place to wait with the carriage.

The lobby bustled, as usual, with guests and with the riff-raff that frequented the lobby, gambling, drinking and creating an awful din.

Lisette made her way to the fountain, where Doctor Stewart had suggested they meet. Aunt Portia sat down at a nearby table, glancing around the room with a troubled expression on her face. Lisette joined her.

"What's wrong, Aunt Portia?"

"I don't know. Something about this place doesn't feel right. I can't explain it more than that."

"Surely you've been here before."

"Child, I've been in this lobby more times than I could count. Jacob used to meet business associates here. I suggested bringing them to the house, but he said the Peabody was a neutral place where they could talk without being distracted by what he called domestic interference. Most of the time he would come alone, but occasionally he'd want me along. Why, I don't know. I've spent many an hour sitting in this lobby, waiting for your father to conclude a business deal."

"And today?"

"Something isn't right." She hugged herself, as though suddenly cold, casting around for the cause of the odd feeling. "Tell me about this doctor you've come to meet. Is he handsome?"

"Yes. He's traveled all the way to California, just as I've always wanted to do. In fact . . ." She hesitated, wondering if Aunt Portia would find her frivolous if she admitted what had transpired between herself and the doctor.

"What, child? You know you can tell me anything."

Lisette knew it was the truth. It always had been. "He said he would take me anywhere in the world I wanted to go."

Aunt Portia's expression surprised her. Instead of disapproving of the forward remark, she appeared fascinated and touched. "He said that to you? How long had you known him?"

"Hardly an hour. I know it sounds improper for a man to say such a thing to a woman he hardly knows."

"Yet there seemed to be something between you, am I right? Something special?"

She could hardly believe how Aunt Portia expressed the situation so completely in only a few words. "Yes, exactly.

But, a woman in mourning has no business—"

Portia gripped Lisette's hand. "You've suffered enough during the past eight years, having to put up with Andrew. You miss James. No one doubts that."

Lisette didn't correct her. There was no need for her to know James's death had been an enormous relief, and she would never miss him.

"No one doubts you mourned his passing. But did you ever love him?"

Lisette thought about it a moment. Should she admit the truth? She couldn't lie to Aunt Portia any longer. "No. Never."

"Just as I suspected. Although you never said an ill word against him, any man who could raise a son like Andrew would not have been as kind as you indicated in your letters."

She started to say something, but Portia held up one hand and wouldn't let her reply.

"I read more in those sad letters than you thought I would. It's best buried with James. In truth, you've been mourning for eight years—mourning the life you lost when Jacob forfeited your future and your well-being in a game of poker in this very room." Her eyes misted with tears. "Jacob never forgave himself for what he'd done. And I have to admit, I never forgave him either, until you walked through that front door last night."

Lisette's throat tightened. It must have been the hardest thing Aunt Portia had ever done to write cheery letters and never let on she'd guessed what Lisette had not been able to admit.

"It's time for you to stop mourning, time for you to find some happiness. Do you think you might find it with this Doctor Stewart?"

Lisette thought about it for a moment. "I have no idea what his intentions are. To assume, after speaking to him only three times, that he is serious about pursuing a future with me would be presumptuous. He did ask to call on me, though."

"Well, there you are." Aunt Portia smiled and patted her hand tenderly. "If you should find a man with whom you can share the rest of your life—a man who will treat you with respect and kindness—don't let anything stop you. No one will fault you for it. If anyone has the nerve to say a word against you, they'll have to answer to me."

"Thank you, Aunt Portia," she whispered. "I don't deserve you. I only hope my being here in Memphis won't cause us all grief and pain."

Lisette left the table and went back toward the fountain. Aunt Portia was right. Something about this hotel felt different, odd. She turned slowly, surveying the room. No one else seemed to notice how the temperature had dropped in the last few minutes.

Something incredible was about to happen . . .

Chapter Five

"Wait a minute." David held up one hand to stop Joe and Candy. This was happening too fast and getting out of control. "Jacob Morgan and his daughter Lisette lived in Memphis in the 1880s? It can't possibly be the same people I'm looking for."

Joe shrugged. "Candy hasn't found any other references to Morgan Enterprises or a Morgan family with those names. And don't forget Westmoreland."

Candy leaned back. "We're way beyond coincidence here, guys. Too many people with the right names and a business too. I have to admit it sounds like Looney Tunes, but I don't have another explanation."

Joe touched his arm. "Whadya think?"

David's mind was a war. He shook his head, hoping they'd give him some time to absorb, to sort it all out. He paced across the room and back a couple of times, then sat down again. "My impression of Lisette from the beginning has been that she seemed different. She doesn't have a telephone and seemed surprised that I did. Called it a new invention. When I asked if I could call her, she said I could call *on* her. That sounded old-fashioned, but—"

Candy's eyes widened. "Really old-fashioned, maybe?"

"There's more. When I asked her if she worked somewhere in Memphis, she got angry, as though I'd insulted her."

Candy nodded. "In the 1880s, it would have been humiliating for a woman to work if she came from an affluent family. Where did you say she lived?"

"Adams Avenue, past the Neely House."

"Millionaire's Row. The name given to those huge Victorian houses in the nineteenth century. The Neely House has twenty-five rooms and just under sixteen thousand square feet of living space on four floors. That's a mansion in anyone's book. There were several millionaires living on that street. If Morgan lived there, he was affluent all right. Being a millionaire a hundred years ago doesn't really have a valid comparison now, unless you consider the national debt. David, I know this sounds crazy, but—"

Joe stopped her. "Not yet. Let's not jump to conclusions. We sound like Steven Spielberg plotting a new movie. People don't just go from one century to another. Traveling through time is a theory, and that's all."

Candy grinned. "Einstein's theory said that all times exist at the same time. It's like a winding river—the Mississippi is a good example—and all we can see is where we happen to be. The past is just around the bend behind us and the future around the next bend. Getting from one time to the other is the only obstacle. Let's say, just for the fun of it—we can send it to Spielberg later—Lisette somehow stepped from 1885 into our time at the dance the other night."

"She came into the ballroom, looking confused, as though—"

Joe finished it for him. "—as though she didn't recognize anyone and didn't know where she was."

"Exactly. She went back out to the landing. I followed her up to the next deck, asked if I could call her—"

"—then she disappeared when you went back down to the ballroom. That could mean she popped back to her own time again. If she really did come from the 1880s." Joe shook his head. "Are we seriously considering this?"

Candy didn't appear convinced either. "Again, no jumping to conclusions."

Joe picked it up. "Right. Let's examine the facts before we go leaping into la-la land. This requires deductive reasoning and cool heads."

Joe's wanting to stay calm and logical was amusing. Growing up, Joe was always the first to latch onto a harebrained scheme. Now the roles were reversed. David let Joe continue without interruption. For once in their lives, they were in complete agreement. They had to have absolute proof of something this wild or, better yet, a logical explanation within the realms of believability.

Joe did some pacing of his own. "When Lisette called to you on the deck—?"

"In my dream. Which she seemed to know right down to the last detail, as though she'd dreamed the same thing."

"Right. She knew what you were talking about when you mentioned the telephone didn't she?"

Candy this time: "The telephone had been invented by then, but they weren't installed in people's homes until the late eighties, early nineties. Having easy access to one would puzzle her."

"She said it would be years before her family would have a telephone at home."

"There weren't any cars back then, were there? So why did she ask David to drive her home?"

"Come on, Joe," Candy said. "Carriages have to be driven too. Even so, there's still no hard evidence that this woman traveled through time. She may just lead a simple life, home-schooled maybe, old-fashioned and from a family where women don't work outside the home—and don't have telephones because they're outside the service area. There are places like that in the United States today. Places in Tennessee!"

"She's right, Joe. We've jumped to a wild conclusion instead of looking for a logical explanation."

Candy nodded. "The only thing making sense is that we've found ancestors of people who are alive today and who have a thing about family names."

"Except for Morgan Enterprises and this guy, Westmoreland."

Joe sat down again and reached for Candy's notes. "That has to be the biggest coincidence in this story. It's fantastic, but life can be fantastic."

"If you tried to write down real life events and sell them to an editor or a movie producer, he'd scream, 'Coincidence! Contrived!' and laugh at you." Candy chewed on the end of her pen for a moment. "No, I don't think we have a coincidence here." She gathered her notes and turned off the computer. "Let me do some poking around. I could've missed something. I don't have the whole history of Memphis. Just the most important families and their businesses during the time frame I studied. There has to be a logical explanation for all this."

David touched her shoulder. "Thanks, Candy, for all your trouble." She blushed. He withdrew his hand, feeling awkward, like a high school kid on a first date. He knew he shouldn't have agreed to Joe's bringing her. But she'd found Lisette! How could he ignore that?

"No problem, David. It's fascinating. I hope I get to meet this old-fashioned girl of yours someday. She sounds like someone really special. And no one should be mistreated."

"You've got that right. If I can persuade her not to run away again, I'll introduce her to you. Joe, thanks for everything. And thanks for bringing the history professor with you." Looking at Candy this time made the pit of his stomach feel hollow. What was happening? He'd made his decision. Just because she was being so cooperative and helpful didn't change how David felt about her, did it?

"Anytime, Bro. Ready, Candy?"

"Just one more question. Think about the first time you met, David. Did she do or say anything odd about the boat or—"

"She said she'd ridden the riverboat twice." He tried to reconstruct their conversation. The lights! "I completely forgot! She saw the lights on the De Soto Bridge, then asked me when they'd built a bridge over the river. Damn! I'd forgotten all about that."

Candy nodded. "There weren't any bridges over the river at Memphis in the 1880s. Anything else?"

David thought for a moment. "She called the boat a different name. I've lost so much sleep, my memory is mush."

"What name?"

"Damn! How stupid can I get? She called it the *Star* instead of the *Queen*. The *Cajun Star*!" He reached for the newspaper article about the commemorative dance. "The riverboat that disappeared was the *Cajun Star*."

"My God, David. Is there another riverboat in Memphis with that name?"

"Nope." David studied their faces for a long moment. "This is getting creepy, folks."

"Let me do some digging." Candy gripped his arm as she and Joe were leaving. "Ask her what year she thinks it is when you see her tomorrow."

"She'll think I'm crazy."

"She'll be amused. I would be. Good night." She hesitated, then kissed David quickly. When she smiled he felt guiltier than ever.

David waited until they were in the car, then turned off the porch light. He picked up the newspaper article about the *Cajun Star* and reread the names of the passengers. Coincidence? Practically impossible.

The doorbell rang. Candy.

"I hope you don't mind my coming back, David. Joe said he didn't mind waiting a few minutes."

"No, no." She appeared as nervous as David felt. "Come in."

"I know it means a lot to you to find this woman and protect her." She sat on the couch.

"Yes, it does." She had no idea how much.

"Can we talk about something?"

He knew what was coming but didn't seem to have a choice about it. "Sure."

She stared at him for a moment. "Why, David?"

"Why? Why what?" Damn. This was the last thing he wanted to discuss.

"Why did you end it? I thought we had something special. Then, out of the blue, you don't want to see me anymore and won't give any reason. Is it this woman? Have you been seeing her? I think you owe me that much. Surely, after all this time—"

"Candy, it's over. I told you when I first met Lisette—Saturday night on the riverboat. I'd already decided, before I met her, it just wasn't going to work between us. Can't we leave it at that?"

"No. I'll never be able to get past it without knowing for sure what went wrong. I love you, David. I thought we had something worth keeping. I knew you were still hurting—even after all these years—but I was willing to accept that, help you through it. What went wrong?"

He still wasn't sure he knew the answer. "It isn't you, Candy. It's me."

"I don't believe that, David. I can't."

"I'm sorry. There's nothing else to say."

"I thought you loved me." Her eyes were bright, moist.

"I thought I did too." She deserved to know that much.

"What changed your mind? What did I do wrong?" She came to where he was sitting and leaned against him, the way she had since they'd first been dating. He still felt a measure of attraction for her and supposed he always would. It was the same attraction that had brought them together in the first place. But everything was different now.

"You didn't do anything wrong. I just know it isn't right."

"It could be right, David. Give us another chance, please. I know we could be happy. We *were* happy. Is it so wrong to put the past away and get on with the rest of your life?"

"Candy—"

She tried to kiss him. His emotions were in turmoil. He had made no commitment to Lisette, and yet there was something . . .

He stood, moved away. Joe's bringing her here had been a mistake. David never should have agreed to it. Now he'd hurt her again, worse than before. He felt terrible.

She stood with her arms at her sides, stiff, humiliated. "Well, I guess that says it all."

"Look, Candy, I tried to tell you. I didn't want you to be hurt. When Joe brought you over here to help me find Lisette Morgan, he didn't tell you the primary reason for that search."

She didn't say anything, just waited.

As the words formed in his mind, he felt a tremendous sense of relief, as though they'd been there all along but he was too stubborn or too afraid to acknowledge them.

"I care a great deal for her. I know it sounds crazy, since I've known her only a short time, but it's true. It has to do with the part of me that's been missing since Fran died."

Candy's expression had changed to understanding, and possibly even acceptance, probably because he had changed, in ways he couldn't define.

"I don't know what I'll do if I can't find her again. I have to find her."

Candy put her arms around him and held him without speaking for a long moment, then she whispered, "I'm glad, David. You'll find her, I know you will. Then maybe you can be happy."

She left before he could respond. He wondered if he'd ever see her again.

It took him a long time to get to sleep that night. What would he do if Lisette didn't come to the Peabody? The last time he looked at the clock was 1:15 a.m.

The telephone woke him the next morning. "Joe? Did I forget to set my alarm again?"

"Nope. It's only seven thirty. I have an idea. Why don't I go with you to the Peabody?"

David rubbed his eyes and tried to wake up. Another hour's sleep would've felt pretty good.

"Go with me? Why?"

"Well, just to help you keep an eye on things, in case she decides to pull the disappearing act again. She can't very well get away from both of us can she, without one of us seeing where she goes?"

"I suppose not." David pulled his legs around and sat on

the side of the bed. "I don't intend to let her disappear this time."

"I know. If she does turn out to be a time traveler, I want to meet her. Hell, Bro, I want to meet her anyway. Whadya say?"

The old Joe, as adventurous as ever. "Why not. Join the party. I'm going early, about eleven."

"Make it ten forty five. We'll greet the ducks."

David headed for the shower. It would take a substantial amount of hot water to clear the fog from his mind this morning.

By eight thirty he was wide-awake and sipping hot coffee from his favorite mug. Alyssa had made it for him at day care. It was one of those plastic cups with a slot all the way around so a drawing could be inserted. She'd drawn the three of them, a house with windows well above the top of the front door, a chimney puffing smoke, several lollipop trees surrounding the house and a quarter sun in one corner, beaming down on the happy family. How long had it been since David had been that happy?

He pulled into the hospital parking lot at 9:15, made rounds in record time, and left by 10:30, headed for the Peabody. He'd talked to Lana. Greg would take care of his patients this afternoon and tomorrow.

Joe was already there when David pulled in and parked across the street. They went into the elegant lobby together. David never failed to marvel at the intricacy of the decor. A week to go until Thanksgiving, and the staff had already decorated for the Christmas holidays. The Christmas tree on the second floor, overlooking the lobby, twinkled merrily while fluffy green garlands strung with lights looped their way around the elegant railings. The ceiling complemented the festive atmosphere. Stained glass, lighted from above and framed with carved and painted wood, lent Victorian elegance to the tangle of guests and spectators below. The bar was busy serving drinks to those waiting for the ducks to come down from their penthouse roost to swim in the fountain. The baby grand player piano entertained everyone with show tunes and Christmas carols.

David went straight to the fountain. It was impossible to see any of the entrances from this vantage point, but the fountain was centrally located and the logical place to meet.

"Did the hotel look like this in the 1880s?" Joe wondered aloud.

"Similar. After a hundred and twenty years, the decor has changed somewhat, but it was the most elegant hotel in Memphis then, just as it is now. Except for the bar, this area is about the same as it was in the 1920s."

The ducks had become a tradition and permanent residents of the hotel after the manager had placed his live hunting decoys in the Travertine marble fountain in the 1930s. There were no ducks in the fountain prior to that time.

The elevator doors opened at eleven. The ducks waddled out to the "King Cotton March," laughter and applause. Mallards all, they apparently enjoyed the attention of the crowd, strutting up the steps and into the water. The drake immediately chased one of the hens around the fountain, to everyone's delight, honking and splashing. David enjoyed the antics, glancing frequently about the lobby, toward the elevators and shops. There was no sign of Lisette anywhere, but it was still early.

They settled down to wait. David sat at a table beside the fountain. Joe leaned against the wall near the elevators so he could keep an eye on the entrance flanked by bronze statues of two huge dogs. Life at the Peabody continued un-interrupted.

David couldn't sit still. Every few minutes he left the fountain, checked each entrance, studied the faces of tourists, guests and hotel personnel. By a quarter of twelve, he couldn't stay seated at all.

There was still no sign of Lisette at 12:30. David was a nervous wreck. Joe finally intercepted one of his rounds, near the fountain. "Listen, Bro, maybe she couldn't get away. I hate it as much as you do, but—"

"How could you? You don't—"

The quacking of the ducks stopped as though they'd been mechanical and someone had pulled the plug. David took a deep breath. The ducks had vanished—along with Joe.

Silhouetted against sunshine gleaming through windows that hadn't been there before, stood a woman in a floor-length black dress. Lisette.

She searched the lobby until their eyes met. David could see she was breathing heavily, as though she'd rushed to get here. She came toward him tentatively.

He took one step toward her, then another. A poker player, who had appeared at one of the tables, leaped to his feet. "Will Barton, you're a liar and a cheat!"

"Who are you calling a cheat? You sorry, low-down skunk. Step outside and say that again!"

The quarreling gamblers swaggered past Lisette and toward the far exit. David tensed, afraid she would run away or disappear, but she didn't.

"Lisette."

She smiled for the first time. "You came." She hurried toward him.

There, in the center of the lobby, David hesitated, not

knowing what to do. He knew what he wanted to do, but would she object? He decided to risk it.

When she stepped closer, he gathered her into his arms and held her. God, but she felt good. That same perfume—lemon verbena—filled him, made him dizzy. After an instant of hesitation, Lisette tightened her arms around him. They fit together as though fashioned from the same mold.

He stroked the back of her neck, forgetting about her hair coiled with what proved to be a single pin. The pin came loose and her hair spread across her shoulders and down her back like silk. Her breasts, pressed against him, continued to rise and fall, slowing gradually.

"Don't disappear again. Please," he whispered.

"I knew it wasn't just a dream. Your being here proves it." She glanced around nervously. "Andrew could be here soon. The lieutenant won't be able to detain him much longer. He may have seen us come here. We have to go somewhere so we can talk without his finding us. I have so many questions to ask you."

"I'll take you to the ends of the earth and back if that's what you want. No one is ever going to hurt you again, I promise."

Her smile almost broke his heart. He leaned toward her. Would she permit a kiss as well?

Someone touched his arm. "I'm Lisette's aunt, Portia Morgan. I'm pleased to meet you, Doctor Stewart."

Another name from the past became flesh before his eyes.

Lisette stammered, "Aunt P-Portia? I-I, that is—I'm so, so sorry—I forgot." She blushed like a schoolgirl.

Portia smiled. "It's all right, child." Her smile faded. "Oh, dear."

"Dear Lord, no." Lisette's face paled.

"What's wrong?" David squinted against the glare of the windows, then recognized the man he'd seen on the boat. He didn't have to ask Lisette who he was. Andrew Westmoreland. He took her hand and gripped it firmly.

"Doctor Stewart, you don't understand. Andrew has threatened—"

David looked straight into her eyes, then smiled, hoping to calm her. "I promised you wouldn't be hurt again. Trust me."

Westmoreland approached them. "Take your hands off my stepmother."

"Only if she asks me to." David kept his voice quiet and deadly serious. It cut through the silence that had settled on the hotel. Every person in the lobby had stopped to stare.

Lisette took a step forward, still holding David's hand. "This is none of your business, Andrew. Doctor Stewart treated me last night after you struck me." A murmur of shock and surprise traveled through the crowd.

David felt her hand trembling in his. He had to admire her courage, facing an attacker so confidently.

Andrew's face twisted with anger. "You persist with these lies? In front of strangers? We shall deal with this privately. I insist that you come with me. Now."

"No." Lisette lifted her chin. "I'm going with Doctor Stewart. He feels that I need further treatment."

Portia stepped forward. "That is exactly what she needs. Doctor, if you'll accompany us home, you can administer whatever treatment my niece requires."

Andrew glared at Portia until she gasped with what David interpreted as fright.

"This woman is my stepmother and, in time, will be my wife," Andrew said. "She is my responsibility. Thank you for your offer of assistance, Doctor, but no. Whatever treatment Lisa needs, I will personally see that she receives it." His expression left no doubts as to the type of treatment he had in mind.

Saying that Lisette would be his wife made David shake with anger. It took everything he had to control the rage tearing through him.

"She is my patient by her own choice—therefore, my responsibility. Let's go, Mrs. Westmoreland."

David took a step back, intending to lead Lisette to the other exit. Portia followed, trembling visibly. Everyone in the lobby witnessed the altercation without interference.

Andrew lunged at David without warning. Before he could react, Andrew's fist slammed into David's jaw, sending a bolt of pain through his head, almost blinding him. David struggled to keep his balance and his eyes on the bastard, but his legs struck the edge of the marble fountain and he fell backward, into the water. Those watching reacted with shock and fear. Women screamed and ran. Men moved forward as though entering the fray.

When David tried to get up, his right foot slid on the slippery marble and buckled beneath him. Pain shot through his ankle. He slumped over the edge of the fountain, trying to pull himself out. Westmoreland knocked him backward again. There were screams and shouts all over the lobby. Two men grabbed Andrew and pulled him away from the fountain. A uniformed man came running from the front desk.

Andrew managed to throw off the men holding him. With wild rage flashing in his eyes, he grabbed Lisette and dragged her away. Portia, weeping, ran after Lisette. It all happened so fast—

"David! Help me!" Lisette struggled in vain to free herself.

David tried to pull himself upright, but his ankle refused to bear weight. "Lisette!"

"David!" Her voice, strident, hysterical, was the last thing he heard . . . before the ducks panicked and scattered. Feathers flew and water splashed everyone standing nearby. A man from the front desk ran to see what had spooked the birds—and who was sitting in the fountain!

Joe got there first. "David, you're back! I was standing there talking to you and—"

"Damn it, Joe! She was here! Right here! That bastard knocked me into the fountain and dragged her away before I could stop him." He tried to stand, but his ankle, already twice its normal size, sabotaged his efforts.

Joe was helping David up just as the manager arrived, demanding to know what had happened. Joe took a bill from his pocket without looking at it and shoved it at the manager, offering to pay any damages. The manager looked at the money then laughed. "It's going to be a lot more than a dollar. Don't leave this lobby." He instructed a bellhop to watch them, summoned the keeper of the ducks to see to their safety, then went straight to the telephone at the main desk.

"Joe, I have to get back. The ducks weren't in the fountain. They vanished, and then Lisette was there. The shops were gone and the elevators. Don't you see, Joe? It's true. Everything we thought was too incredible—it's all true! I have to get back to Lisette's time. There's no telling what Westmoreland will do to her. I promised she wouldn't be hurt—I promised." David choked on the words. How could he keep that promise now?

Dripping wet, his ankle throbbing mercilessly, dozens of people staring with disbelief and disdain, David knew it was useless.

He'd lost her.

Chapter Six

"David!" Lisette fought Andrew's grip, but there was no loosening his hands from her arms.

Andrew shook her hard, then spoke directly into her ear. "If you know what's good for you—and your father—you'll shut your mouth right now!"

She glared at him, hatred seething inside her. "Make all the threats you like. If you hurt any person in my family, you'll pay for it. I swear it on my mother's memory."

Andrew's eyes glazed over for a moment and his fingers, digging into the soft flesh of her upper arms, loosened.

Aunt Portia appeared suddenly with a large man who lifted Andrew almost off the floor by the shoulders of his coat.

"No one handles a lady that way in the Peabody!" His voice boomed through the lobby.

"Thank you, sir." She grabbed Aunt Portia's hand and hurried toward the far entrance. Lisette knew the man detaining Andrew would not release him until they were safely away. If only they could find David!

Aunt Portia cast about for Seth, motioned for him to come quickly. The carriage pulled up beside them within a minute.

They had only seconds to get away before the Peabody employee was forced to release Andrew. Inside the carriage, she rubbed her throbbing arms. She knew without looking they must be bruised, dark and ugly.

Aunt Portia stared straight ahead, preoccupied. Lisette

saw distress in her eyes and in the way she sat, rigid as a poker, but something else too. Anger? Determination? An odd mixture of emotions struggled in her twisted expression.

Seth had to pull up at the intersection to allow another carriage to pass. Without warning, Andrew ran up to the carriage and grabbed the horses' reins. He breathed hard, still angry, and seized Lisette's arm again. "How dare you—"

"Don't touch my niece." Aunt Portia's voice was so soft now it was scarcely audible.

"Stay out of this, you old biddy. No one humiliates me—"

"I shall do more than humiliate you if you do not remove your hand from my niece."

Something in Aunt Portia's expression or tone of voice made an impression on Andrew. He stepped down from the carriage, mute and seething with rage.

"Seth, we are ready to go home now," Portia said quietly.

"Yessum." Seth retrieved the reins, then coaxed the horses into a brisk walk. They left Andrew standing in the street, scowling.

A wave of relief rushed through Lisette. She put her arms around Aunt Portia. Words weren't necessary. She knew Lisette loved her.

At home, Aunt Portia waited on the front steps, watching for Andrew, until Lisette was safely inside, then she stepped inside and bolted the door securely. After giving Seth instructions to build up both fireplaces in the parlor and to tell his mother to keep Jacob upstairs for a while longer, she addressed Lisette with a kind smile.

"We must tend to your bruises before they get any worse."

"I'm all right, Aunt Portia. What I'd love to have is a cup

of tea." Lisette tried to ignore the throbbing, not wanting to distress Aunt Portia any more than she had already.

Aunt Portia took a deep breath. "Of course. What's done is done. I'll be back in a minute. You rest now."

In the parlor, Lisette sat on the green and gold floral settee, which had belonged to her grandmother, Cecelia Morgan. Aunt Portia had always called it the courting couch. Leaning back, Lisette tried to rest. Within minutes, Aunt Portia was back with the tea. She handed Lisette a cup and saucer, filled it with fragrant tea, added sugar and gave her a spoon. Somehow, the normalcy of stirring tea made Lisette feel calmer. Perhaps everything could be all right again, if she could simply decide the best thing to do.

Her mind was strangely blank after all that had happened. There was nothing left to say or do. It was clear Andrew had no intention of leaving them alone or returning to New Orleans, in spite of the officer's warning.

Shivering, Lisette took the cup with her to the front hearth and stood with her back to Aunt Portia, consumed with the possibilities and alternatives swirling through her mind. She had seen her father do this many times throughout the years. The delicate fragrance and sharp flavor of chamomile reminded her of gentler times. She came to a decision.

"Aunt Portia, there is no excuse for what Andrew did to me today, or for what he did last night. He must be made to pay."

Aunt Portia nodded, squeezing her eyes tightly shut. "I had no idea he was capable of such violence. We have to find a way to—"

A loud rapping came at the front door. Aunt Portia held up one hand. "I'll get it." Her jaw set, she went to the foyer, peered through the clear glass peephole in the stained glass pattern, then turned the knob and opened the door.

"You are not welcome here, Mr. Westmoreland. I suggest you leave immediately, or I shall summon the Lieutenant."

Lisette watched from just inside the parlor door, scarcely a yard from where they stood, yet outside of Andrew's range of sight. She fully expected him to rave at Aunt Portia, but he spoke so quietly, Lisette couldn't make out the words. She had to know what he was saying. One step placed her in the doorway, in full sight of him. Something about Andrew had changed. The difference in him was disturbing. Lisette went to the door, not about to let him think her afraid, even though part of her was terrified.

"What do you want?"

"I came to apologize to you, to your aunt. I cannot expect you to forgive my rash behavior and my totally improper actions. I can only hope you'll hear me out." He dragged his hat from his head, wrung it in his hands and stared at the floor.

Lisette couldn't believe it. Another act. Andrew knew he'd made a fatal mistake at the Peabody, letting everyone see his anger vented on her, and now the weasel was trying to mend the damage.

"Lisette, I think it's time Mr. Westmoreland left."

Lisette couldn't allow Andrew to disrupt their lives again. Until she learned the motivation behind this piece of trickery, she might not be prepared for his next attempt to control them. Perhaps she could use this charade to her own advantage.

"Lisette, please ask Mr. Westmoreland to leave." Aunt Portia was puzzled and agitated.

Lisette hesitated a moment. "I think we at least owe Andrew the courtesy of listening to his apology." She could see

Aunt Portia was completely perplexed by this tact. "Please, make it brief."

Andrew bowed slightly and came into the parlor, bowing past Lisette like a true gentleman. He glanced around nervously, then stood beside the front fireplace.

Lisette seethed again at the memory of his hands on her arms and his fist striking her face. The last thing she wanted to do was offer him a place to sit, but she had to play her part perfectly, or not at all. "Please sit down, Andrew. There—in the corner chair. Aunt Portia, would you get Andrew some tea?"

"Lisette—"

Lisette caught her eye, shook her head, motioned for her to come to the door, then whispered, "Let the heathen hang himself. We know what he is. We won't be fooled again."

"I hope you're right," Aunt Portia whispered back. "I'd just like to send him packing, without so much as a word. It's all he deserves."

"Let's see what the worm has to say for himself. A little humility can't help but do him some good."

"I'll get the tea." She disappeared down the hall.

Lisette went into the parlor and sat on the far side of the room, still nervous about being alone with this miserable excuse for a man.

Andrew perched on the edge of the chair, its legs arranged to facilitate its fitting exactly in the corner. Sitting there, Andrew reminded Lisette of a naughty child, confined to the corner for an infraction of manners. She said nothing, preferring to make him wait.

"Lisette—"

"Not until Aunt Portia returns, if you don't mind."

Andrew nodded curtly. Apparently unable to get comfortable, he went back to the hearth and held out his hands toward the flames to warm them, in spite of his forehead beading with perspiration.

When Aunt Portia arrived with a tray, Lisette took her time serving him, performing as the perfect hostess. Andrew took the offered cup, the tea steaming, sat down, sipped, and let out a cry.

"God Almighty!"

Portia was quick to chastise him. "Mr. Westmoreland, I'll thank you not to blaspheme in this house."

"The tea is scalding!"

Lisette tried not to smile. Aunt Portia had taken revenge on Andrew in such a way he could not accuse her. "We dislike lukewarm tea, Andrew." Lisette took a sip of her own tea, which had cooled to the point she could drink it straight down—so she did. Andrew's eyes widened.

"Delicious, Aunt Portia, as always," Lisette said with a smile.

Andrew set his cup on the turtletop table beside the chair and bolted across the room, stopping just short of the rear door to the foyer, behind them. He took several deep breaths, and straightened his double-breasted jacket over his striped wool trousers. When he turned, his smile appeared somewhat strained.

"Forgive me, Lisette, Miss Morgan. The only reason I can offer for my stupid and frightful actions is the fear of being outcast from this family. Ever since you married my father and he introduced you to me, I have considered it a privilege to accept you as my stepmother. My father was extremely fond of you, and after he suffered the agony of yellow jack, grew increasingly concerned about your welfare after his death. He knew he was dying, Lisette."

Lisette refused, for a moment, to meet Andrew's eyes. It hadn't taken a whit's worth of brain to know that yellow fever had weakened James's heart beyond recovery. She tried to blot out those last weeks, immune to the emotion Andrew was attempting to elicit from her. What was he leading up to?

"When my father knew the end was near, he asked me to take an oath." His eyes actually grew moist.

Lisette thought she might be ill. Andrew had never cared for his father. Repeatedly, after tending to James, she suffered the indignity of Andrew coming to her room, offering "comfort." He'd put his hands on her then too. If James had known what his son had attempted—but it was no more than he had done himself a thousand times. Still, James was a selfish man. Had he known, he would never have tolerated sharing his wife with Andrew. She would have informed James if she hadn't feared Andrew's retribution—and James's accusations that she provoked Andrew's attentions.

Andrew went on after a pause which, she surmised, was clearly meant to evoke sympathy.

"He asked me to take his place, Lisette. As your husband."

Aunt Portia had heard enough. "Liar! James Westmoreland would never—"

"My father was God-fearing. It was in the Biblical sense that he asked this of me. Surely, Miss Morgan, you are familiar with account after account in the Bible of a man marrying his dead brother's wife in order to spare her a life of poverty and misery."

Lisette felt like screaming precisely what she thought about this pompous, presumptuous speech. And she knew Aunt Portia was about to do precisely that. Lisette placed one hand on her arm, reminding her to let Andrew speak his mind. The last words spoken today would be Lisette's.

Andrew turned to Aunt Portia. "I also owe you the deepest apology, kind lady. I have agonized over the pain I've caused your niece. I cannot expect you to forgive me. Just know that I wish with all my heart it had never happened. When it seemed that I would not be able to carry out my father's last wishes, I—"

Lisette could not allow him to say more. "That's enough, Andrew. I think we understand."

Aunt Portia said nothing. Her expression testified she believed none of it.

"You, Lisette, deserve this explanation and the most heartfelt apology of all." He paused, giving Lisette a chance to respond, which she did not. "After promising my father I would do all in my power to grant his dying wish, I was not able to convey that promise to you. I felt it improper to raise the subject during the most painful time of mourning, immediately following my father's wake. Since then I have most grievously betrayed your trust in me. I have no right to expect you to offer me a chance to redeem myself and that trust, but I plead with you to consider giving me that opportunity. I do not expect your decision now. I shall await your pleasure—and I shall abide by your wishes without question." Andrew glanced at Aunt Portia, then lingered when he looked at Lisette again. "Thank you for listening."

Andrew hurried to the front door and out before either of them could respond.

Aunt Portia was first to speak. "If he thinks we're going to fall for that little piece of acting, he's got another thought coming!"

Lisette couldn't believe it! He left so suddenly; she'd had no chance at all for rebuttal. He'd had the last word after all. Andrew had won this little contest, in spite of all efforts for this to be their last confrontation.

Aunt Portia gathered the cups and saucers. "He couldn't possibly be that contrite after treating you in such an abominable manner. He can't be thinking we would even consider giving him another chance?" When Lisette didn't answer, lost in thought over what they were going to do, Aunt Portia added, "Another chance to harm you!"

That brought her full attention to Aunt Portia. "Certainly not."

Aunt Portia released a sigh. "Thank goodness. I thought for a moment you might have been deceived by that heathen."

"Heathen? I wouldn't call him a heathen, Aunt Portia. A bastard, perhaps, but not a heathen."

Portia started at her use of the vulgar word, then laughed aloud. "What are you planning? Even as a child, I could tell when that mind of yours was full of mischief."

"I have something to ask of you. You won't like it."

"What?"

"Give Andrew another chance, just as I am prepared to do."

Portia's jaw tightened. "Never."

"I know how you're feeling now, but—"

Aunt Portia raised her chin defiantly. "Lisette, listen to what you are saying. That—bastard—struck you, then manhandled you. Your arms are no doubt black and blue. If he's capable of doing this to you in front of total strangers, try to imagine what he might do to you in private."

Lisette agreed completely, knowing what Andrew was capable of doing in private, but they had to proceed carefully if they were to arrange the future to best advantage.

"I shall make it clear to Mr. Westmoreland that any violent action on his part toward me, or any member of my family, will be met with the strongest reprisal. I do not think he will dare to raise a hand to me again. The lieutenant was quite specific."

She couldn't depend on Andrew's eloquent apology to represent anything but his own selfish interests. Andrew knew his acceptance into the Morgan family would never take place if he didn't placate Lisette. And she knew in her heart that avarice and greed and desperation had prompted Andrew's pretty words today. Somehow she would have to use that knowledge against him. Otherwise they would never be allowed to live their lives the way they chose— without fear.

David's face caressed her mind like a warm breeze. David would never strike her. She had no real basis for that knowledge, yet it was as secure as Aunt Portia's love. Something about David Stewart was different from any man she'd ever known. And his confession he was willing to take her anywhere she'd like to go . . . and had been so many places himself . . .

"I think I'll go upstairs to rest now. Aunt Portia, could you bring some ice for my bruises?"

"Ice?"

"Doctor Stewart prescribed it for my face. It should work as well on my arms."

"Of course, child. I'll be there in two shakes. You just rest."

Lisette gave her a quick kiss on the cheek. "I know this seems an odd way to proceed, but I hope you'll trust me. I have a plan to hopefully rid us of Andrew Westmoreland forever."

Lisette went upstairs to her room and removed her dress. As feared, her arms were dark with bruising, tender to the touch.

Aunt Portia arrived soon with a clean cloth filled with

splintered ice from one of the blocks in the icehouse. Lisette's plan was forming, bit by bit.

"Aunt Portia, I have to see Doctor Stewart again."

"By all means, we'll see the doctor."

Lisette sat on the edge of the bed while Portia pressed the cool cloth bundle against one arm, then the other. The ice soothed some of the pain away.

She didn't tell her that seeing Dr. Stewart actually had nothing to do with the bruises, although she suspected David would bristle and want to smash Andrew for inflicting another injury on her. The thought of David coming to her defense, offering protection, made her strangely warm. No, this visit would be strictly social. More than anything she wanted to hear all about the places David had been and what he'd seen of the world. And she wanted to ask if he still would be willing to take her anywhere she wanted to go. Did his offer include Aunt Portia and her father? David was not the type of person to turn them away.

"Aunt Portia, I think everything might just work out."

"I hope so, child. I can't bear to see you unhappy."

"I know. Now, listen carefully. I'm going to need your help if I'm to see Dr. Stewart again soon."

Chapter Seven

"Damn it, Greg, be careful!"

Greg Chandler stopped wrapping David's ankle and grinned. "Now, now, Doctor. Your impatient side is showing."

He gritted his teeth. Not one of these people had the slightest idea of what had happened. "All right, I'll try to be still. But you're wrapping it too tight. It hurts, damn it!"

"That's because it's badly bruised. Another round. Lana, hand me that tape, please."

"Certainly, Doctor." Her smile would've brightened the lowest dungeon. If the lights in the dome of the pyramid ever went out, they could hire Lana to fill in.

It made David want to—he kept his mouth shut. If he could just get out of here, there might be a chance to find Lisette. He'd actually been there—in the nineteenth century—along with that bastard, Westmoreland. Just thinking about the way he'd dragged Lisette from the hotel made him want to smash something.

Greg finally finished. The bandaging job looked like a picture from a first aid text. "Stay off of it for at least a week. It isn't sprained, but you could injure it further."

As if David didn't know how to take care of a bruised ankle. Stay off it a week? Until tomorrow, maybe. He let it go, kept his mouth shut, because Lana was still right there, pride radiating from her, along with her perfume, which, for David's taste, was too brash.

Lisette's perfume had been much more feminine and

subtle. Exactly the right fragrance to focus his thoughts on one thing and one thing only. Of course, the atmosphere wasn't exactly conducive to such thoughts. And he hadn't been there long enough to do anything about turning those thoughts into reality.

"David?"

They stared at him. He must have missed something, or said something aloud he didn't mean to say. "What is it?"

"Joe will drive you home."

At least he hadn't embarrassed himself by saying aloud what he'd been thinking. "No! I have to go back to the Peabody. Hasn't anyone heard what I said?"

"We heard, Bro. Come on. We'll talk about it in the car."

Joe offered a hand, but David didn't accept. At the moment he was too pig-headed.

"Okay, show us how big and strong and stoic you are."

"Very funny." The first step on the ankle was murder. The second was intolerable. He'd have to use those damn crutches—at least for the rest of the day. An hour in the Jacuzzi would fix that ankle. Until then? He hated worse than anything having to admit he was wrong, but under the circumstances . . . "I give up. Hand me those damn things."

Lana did so without commenting, giving Greg another smile.

"I'll take care of everything here at the office, David," Greg promised. "No need for you to even come in for at least a week."

"A week! Even if it were broken, I wouldn't need a week to—" Wait a minute. A week without clinic or hospital duties would give him a week to find Lisette. "You know, Greg, I think you're right. Sorry if I gave you a hard time. I'm not used to being the patient."

Greg laughed. "Doctors make the worst patients of all. Relax a little. Take it easy."

David did his best to smile, crammed the crutches under his arms and swung out of the examination room. "Come on, Joe. I'm not sure how crutches and car doors mix." He also wasn't sure how much longer he could perpetuate this charade.

Joe caught him at the front door, opened it, let him go through, then hurried to open the car door too. They stashed the crutches in the back seat.

Joe backed out of the parking space. "I know. The Peabody. You can stay in the car. I'll see if she's there."

"Won't work, Joe. If I'm not there, she's not there."

"I don't get it." He pulled out into traffic, headed for downtown.

David wasn't sure he got it either. "I just know, as odd as it sounds, when Lisette and I are in the same place, we're both there. When we aren't, we aren't."

"Run that by me again."

"Did you see her today in the lobby?"

"Not one glimpse."

"And I disappeared the minute I saw her—the minute she got to the fountain—in her time."

"You still believe you went back to another time?"

"Exactly what year, I can't say for sure. But Lisette lived in Memphis in the early 1800s. She and her father disappeared on the *Cajun Star* November 21, 1885. That would mean when I saw her today it had to be before that. How much, I don't know." He twisted in the seat to face Joe. "Don't you see? She's going to get on that boat and sail down the Mississippi to who knows what. If I can just keep her from getting on that boat—"

"Then what?"

114

David didn't have an answer.

"Then you'll stay there with her? Or bring her back here with you? What if she doesn't want to skip a hundred plus years into the future? What if it's possible for you to come back, but not for you to bring her with you? Are you willing to live in 1885? How would you make a living?"

"I'm a doctor, Joe, remember?"

"A doctor used to prescribing medicines that didn't exist then. What would you do when someone came in with something incurable—which is curable now? Pneumonia? Small pox? Could you stand it, knowing you could save that person if you only had one of our pharmacies on the corner?"

David thought about it. Really thought about it. Joe pulled into the parking area across the street, just down from the Peabody, and turned off the motor.

"I don't know how I'd feel," David admitted finally. "I know I have to find Lisette. Any other decisions will have to be made afterward. This whole deal sounds like something out of a science fiction novel, but I can't justify what I've seen any other way. How do you explain the ducks?"

"You mean no ducks in the fountain when Lisette was there?"

"Exactly. The ducks weren't there until hunting decoys—live ducks—were put in the fountain in the 1930s. Then there's the question of my disappearing in front of your eyes. Explain that for me. And what about the shops? No gift shops, no Peabody ducks in the windows, no T-shirts."

Joe scratched his head. "I can't. If I hadn't seen it—or not seen it—then I'd probably be checking you into the psych ward."

"Exactly. Let's go inside. If she isn't still at the Peabody in whatever year that was, then I can't go to her year and she can't cross over to ours, but I have to try."

Joe's grin spread until his teeth gleamed and he beamed with an expression David knew all too well. Adventure brewing. "Let's do it!"

"Right." David went first to the main desk, clumsy on the damn crutches, and apologized to the manager. Stiff and formal at first, he softened more and more as David talked.

"I'm sorry about your injury, Dr. Stewart," he said finally. "Are you planning another swim in the fountain?"

David had to grin at that. "Absolutely not. I just want to wait here a few minutes for a friend."

The manager bowed his head slightly. "Certainly. Enjoy your stay at the Peabody."

"Thanks." He spotted Joe by the fountain, watching the ducks, and joined him.

Joe grinned nervously. "Gives me the creeps when I think about your bleeping out of the picture. You see that sort of thing on television all the time, but when it happened here I flipped out. My eyes were probably as big as saucers—flying saucers. If one of those babies had landed in the fountain instead of you, I don't think my reaction would have been much different."

They stayed half an hour, sipping a drink, Joe wandering to the entrances and back a dozen times, examining every person who came through the lobby. David knew it was a long shot to expect Lisette to reappear. Westmoreland would never let her come back if he could help it. He might even lock her up. David clenched his fists until his knuckles were white. How could he make good on his promise not to let her be hurt again if he couldn't get into the same century with her? He'd have to find another way. Waiting here until she happened to come in the door could take weeks, or it might never happen again. The *Cajun Star* was set to leave Memphis on the twenty-first of November. He had to find her before then and keep her off that boat.

They'd waited an hour.

"She isn't coming, Joe. I'll have to find another way to reach her."

"How did it happen before, on the boat?"

"I don't know. The second time, though, was in a dream."

"Well, take a nap when you get home. Maybe you'll get lucky."

The absurd notion that David could just take a nap, dream about Lisette and tell her to meet him somewhere seemed foolishly simplistic and absurd. Another equally absurd thought followed. But the whole scenario was absurd. Why not? He picked up the crutches, tested his balance. "Let's go."

"Are you sure, Bro? We can wait a while longer if you want. I'm in no hurry."

"I'm going to take your advice—and see a shrink."

Joe's forehead creased. "I was kidding, David. I didn't mean—"

"I know. I'll explain in the car."

They pulled into the parking lot of Dr. Robert Townsend's office complex about ten minutes later. Bob and David had been friends since college. Of all the people he might talk to about the experiences he'd just had, Bob was second on the list, after Joe.

Joe had been skeptical all through the explanation of what David wanted to try next. Of course, it depended on Bob and whether or not he would believe their story.

"Are you sure you want to do this, David?"

"Hell no, I'm not sure. Can you think of anything better?"

Joe got out of the car. "No, but the last thing I'd want to do is tell a shrink I've been popping back and forth between this year and 1880. He's bound to say, 'How well did you get along with your mother?' "

"Very funny. If that happens, you'll get me out of there before he can have me committed, right?"

"Right." Both of them laughed at that.

David almost reconsidered before going into the office, but he couldn't shake the feeling that hypnosis might be the only way to reach Lisette. No way to know until they tried. Joe would be there to corroborate the story. If Bob Townsend couldn't believe David alone, he'd have to believe both of them.

"Dr. Townsend is with a patient. He'll be free in about twenty minutes. Would you care to wait?"

"Thank you." They sat down. Joe reached for a dog-eared copy of *Sports Illustrated*, the swimsuit issue. David let his mind wander, trying to stay calm. He'd been hypnotized only once, in med school. The hypnotist, the doctor lecturing on psychiatry, had pronounced him a good subject because of his open-mindedness. David guessed that hadn't changed. He was here now because he'd opened his mind to possibilities he'd never considered.

His knowledge of time travel theories was limited. About the only thing he knew for sure was Einstein's theory that all times exist at the same time. The mind was a powerful organ, but could David have disappeared just because he *believed* he'd traveled back in time? Could the whole experience have been an illusion, a hallucination, nothing more than wishful thinking?

Joe bumped David's elbow and pointed to a picture of Rubicon, the hottest model on the runway these days, in the magazine, then rattled on about the Yankees' chances of making it to the World Series this year. David shrugged, didn't comment. Baseball was the last thing on his mind. Even the picture of a sexy model in a gold bikini didn't interest him. Although the thought of Lisette in a swimsuit for the first time brought a smile and a few thoughts he didn't share with Joe.

The receptionist came into the waiting room. "Dr. Townsend will see you now, Dr. Stewart."

They followed her to an office in the rear of the building. Bob Townsend sat at a huge leather bound desk, scribbling in a file. The room was lined with books and an occasional fern or potted plant. The traditional couch sat next to the far windows. David almost backed out, but they'd come this far. The picture in his mind of Lisette in a gold bikini convinced him he had to do whatever he could. Even something this crazy.

"Thanks for making time for us, Bob."

"Come in, David. Good to see you. Looks like you've had a bit of an accident." Bob offered his hand to Joe. "Bob Townsend."

"Joe Stewart. Glad to meet you."

"Joe's my brother, Bob. How much time can we have?"

"Let me see." He pressed the intercom button. "Melanie, is Mr. Cooper here yet?"

"He just called to say he'll be delayed. Shall I call him back and reschedule?"

Bob raised his eyebrows to question David. He nodded. "Yes, reschedule. No calls, please."

"Thanks, Bob. I appreciate your time."

"No problem. My next patient isn't due for an hour.

How can I help? I'm afraid I'm not the best doctor for an ankle injury."

"All part of the story."

Bob leaned back in his chair. His pleasant expression soon changed to deep interest and wonder as David related the details of meeting Lisette at the dance and at the Peabody. Almost immediately he began taking notes on a legal pad, encouraging David to continue, remaining solemn. Not a glimmer of a dubious smile.

"Joe saw the whole thing. I figured you'd be interested in an eye witness."

"You saw him disappear—then reappear."

Joe nodded. "I was looking straight at him. Then he wasn't there. Scared the hell out of me. The next thing I knew, he was splashing around in the fountain, his ankle swelling, ducks flying everywhere."

Bob smiled, then pondered a moment. "All right, David. I have to tell you a fantastic story like yours wouldn't hold an ounce of credibility if you weren't the one telling it."

"I appreciate that, Bob."

"You obviously need my help to contact this woman again, am I right?"

Bob was as sharp a doctor as David had ever known. And open-minded. At the university, they'd considered him wild and crazy. When he'd decided to become a psychiatrist, David had told Bob he'd be his own first patient.

"Hypnosis?"

"Would we have a chance?"

"No way to say until we try."

"Then you'll do it?"

"Why not? I could suggest that you're able to observe people in the 1800s and see what happens. You might tell me I'm crazy, that people can't hop from one century to the next, but out-of-body experiences are one thing science can't explain. Some of it is pure hoax, of course. But I was with a guy once in med school who said he could travel anywhere I told him to go. I sent him to my parents' home, about eighty miles away. He described the furniture, my father sitting in his recliner, my mother talking on the telephone, and even the paintings on the wall and the inscription on one of them. I knew he'd never been to my parents' home. I had no choice but to believe he'd actually left his body and gone there."

"Then you believe it's possible? That guy wasn't going back in time, was he?"

"Not at all. After the session I called my house to see if Mom and Dad were home."

"Were they?"

"The phone was busy."

No one said anything for a moment or two. David released a long sigh. "So, you'll tell me to leave my body and go searching back through time until I find Lisette. Will I be able to speak to her?"

"David, I can't say, and I wouldn't even speculate. Your accounts of seeing her in dreams—and her seeing and speaking to you—are the most incredible parts of the story as far as I'm concerned. If I could guide your dreams—"

"Exactly. Is that possible?"

Bob stood, walked around his desk to the far wall and pulled a volume from the bookshelf. "Dream therapy is well known. As far as guiding the dreamer to address specific issues in the dream, there's a simple method that generally works."

David's excitement grew. He knew exactly what Bob was getting at. "Post hypnotic suggestion."

"Precisely. I hypnotize you, tell you that you're going to

dream about this woman and go to wherever she might be. I can also tell you that you'll return to the hypnotic state during the dream and be able to speak aloud, giving details about the dream as it happens. If you're sleeping close enough to a tape recorder—"

"Or here in this office."

"Better still. We'll have documentation you can listen to when you wake up. If you speak coherently, of course. Talking during sleep is rarely coherent speech."

"When can we do it?"

Bob sat down, still holding the book. "Give me one day to review the documentation. We want to do this right." He pressed the intercom button.

"Yes, Dr. Townsend?"

"Melanie, clear my schedule tomorrow from four o'clock on. Designate two hours to Dr. David Stewart."

"Yes, Doctor."

Bob stood, offered his hand to David, then Joe. "Thanks, gentlemen, for turning an otherwise dull afternoon into something quite extraordinary."

"I can't thank you enough, Bob."

"Thank me day after tomorrow, when we see what we have."

In the car, Joe shook his head and laughed. "I have to admit I never expected him to go for it."

David leaned back, resting his head against the seat. "I knew Bob in school. He was undisputed king of the practical joke, and his jokes always had some psychological theory or dictum as a basis. He'd write up what happened to the victims and turn them in as assignments—case studies."

"Nice guy."

"Yeah. I'll never forget the time he got us all. We'd just

come in from a dull lecture—some professor specializing in . . . I forget . . . and we found Bob upstairs in the frat house, lying in a bathtub, covered in blood. Swear to God, it looked like someone had hacked him to death and dumped the body in the tub. A couple of guys started to gag and vomit, somebody ran to call the police, then Bob sat up and said, "How was the lecture? Murderously boring?"

"I'll bet you wanted to kill him for real!"

"Some of the guys were really mad, but most of us were so relieved we could only laugh. Bob had used catsup and body paint to create the illusion. I never went into that bathroom again without the image flashing through my mind of Bob lying there in all that blood."

"So, what do you think will happen tomorrow? Is this another of his jokes?"

"I don't think Bob would joke about this. And who knows what will happen? The clock is ticking, even though it's a hundred years old. I can't let that bastard hurt her again. And I have to tell her . . ."

Joe waited a moment. "Tell her what, David?"

David laughed, startled by what had passed through his mind. "Never mind. Take me by the library, then drop me off at home. I'll get my car later. I have some reading to do before tomorrow."

At home, David settled into his recliner with a dozen or so books he'd checked out on Memphis history. Before he was ready for bed at midnight, his mind was swimming with dates and facts, some interesting but useless in this situation, others immensely interesting and potentially quite useful.

The yellow fever epidemics were foremost in his mind, simply because of the number of them. Six! Beginning in

1828, followed by outbreaks in 1855, 1867, 1873, 1878 and 1879. The worst was 1878, killing more than five thousand people. This epidemic prompted the state legislature to revoke Memphis's charter in 1879. It wouldn't regain the charter until 1893, but in the meantime, it would become "the cleanest city in the country," and its growth would be assured.

David thought about living in 1885, when the threat of another bout with yellow fever had to be on everyone's mind. Could he stand to watch people die without being able to help them? Even if he were able to take a supply of drugs, they'd eventually run out. There was no way he could vaccinate everyone against the fever. He could at least vaccinate himself, Portia, Jacob and Lisette. A chill ran down his spine when the possibility occurred to him that Lisette might be the one in need of a specific drug— one which he'd depleted helping others—and that she might die, just as Fran had. Could he live with that?

It was a question he'd have to answer before he went any further.

Chapter Eight

They had an early supper that evening, Aunt Portia, Jacob and Lisette. Consumed with questions and problems, she hardly spoke while they ate. Aunt Portia seemed content to let her think, understanding she had to work out the details of a plan to rid them of Andrew for good. She'd told Aunt Portia she had such a plan, but, in truth, it was nothing more than vague wishes that refused to coalesce into a workable scenario.

She concentrated, instead, on the pleasure of sitting at this table with the people she loved, having dinner just as they had years ago. The table was covered with a white cloth, set with Grandmother Cecelia's china and crystal. A huge arrangement of gold mums stood in the center of the table. The gasolier cast a soft glow, softening Aunt Portia's lined face and muting the blankness dominating Jacob's features since he'd come downstairs this evening. The portraits of her grandparents and her mother completed the family and lent such warmth to the room, Lisette found it difficult to swallow the lump in her throat.

The silence apparently bothered Aunt Portia. She fidgeted, then rearranged the food remaining on her plate. Finally, she dabbed at her lips with a napkin and stared at Lisette until she smiled.

"Lisette, you've eaten practically nothing. Are the Boston baked beans scorched? I tried to watch them, but—"

"They're delicious, Aunt Portia. The roast and potatoes are perfect, the beans are perfect, and the apple pan dowdy has tortured me all afternoon with its scrumptious fragrance. My mind is simply full—"

"I understand." She glanced across the table. "Jacob, you aren't eating, either. I swear—"

His eyes suddenly turned back into his head and his back arched so drastically that Lisette feared he would snap his spine. She leaped from the chair, as did Aunt Portia, and together they grabbed him, sagging, and lowered him to the floor, trying to keep his head from striking the edge of the table. By this time, his body shook as though buffeted by a strong wind. His lips were turning blue. A strangling noise came from his throat.

Lisette held his head in her lap and screamed at Aunt Portia to bring something to put in his mouth. A spoon inserted between tongue and teeth brought the tongue back into alignment and the strangling ceased.

Aunt Portia wrung her hands. "Dear God, what is wrong with him? Jacob, can you hear me?"

"It's a seizure, Aunt Portia. There's nothing I know to do except keep him breathing until it stops." She'd seen James in a seizure much like this one, when he was ill with yellow fever. The doctor said high temperatures were the cause, but her father's skin felt cold and clammy. "Get a quilt. And a pillow. We can't let him get too cold."

She hurried away and came back with two quilts which she draped over him. "What else can I do? Tell me what to do!"

"There's nothing else. As soon as he stops shaking—"

He relaxed into her arms. At first she thought he was dead, but his breathing resumed and color returned to his pasty face. She removed the spoon from his mouth. A trickle of blood came from his lip where he'd bitten it. She dabbed at the blood with a napkin from the table.

"Thank the Lord." Aunt Portia bowed her head and murmured a prayer of thanks.

"Help me get him upstairs. Call Sedonia."

Aunt Portia hurried to the kitchen and brought Sedonia and Seth back too. With the four of them lifting, they were able to get Jacob across the room to the bottom of the stairs. It took everything they had to move him, as he was nothing but dead weight in their arms.

"We'll never get him upstairs. We'll have to make him comfortable down here."

"But where?" Portia asked.

Lisette cast about for a good place. "The music room. We'll make him a pallet on the floor. Sedonia, bring more quilts."

"Yes, Ma'am."

"Seth, move the furniture around in there to make a space next to the far wall for Mr. Morgan. Quickly!"

"Yessum!" Seth disappeared into the music room.

The bumping of furniture indicated he had taken the orders seriously. Lisette tried not to think about the scars he might inflict on those expensive tables and chairs. Right now, her father was all that mattered.

The door. The sound of knocking gave Lisette a shiver. She tried to ignore it, but Aunt Portia could not. She opened the door without looking first to see who it was.

Andrew took one look at Jacob lying at the foot of the stairs, his head in Lisette's lap, and bolted through the door.

"Good God, what has happened here?" Andrew tried to take Jacob but she elbowed him away.

"Don't touch him. He's had a seizure. Another could kill him."

Andrew knelt, lowered his voice to almost a whisper.

"Let me help you, Lisette. I can carry him upstairs. Please."

She had never seen this side of Andrew. Under the circumstances, she really had no choice.

"Very well. I'll show you where to take him."

Andrew lifted Jacob and followed her up the wide staircase, being careful to protect him from the banister on the left and the wall on the right. He carried him into the bedroom and waited while she hurriedly threw back the covers. Then, with tender care, he laid Jacob on the bed and bent to remove his shoes.

She stood back and watched while Andrew prepared Jacob for bed. Easing off his jacket, Andrew hesitated before removing the trousers.

"He's my father. I'll be caring for him. Take them off and give them to me. They'll have to be laundered."

Andrew nodded, removed the trousers and covered him to the neck with the sheets and quilts. Then he turned to her. "What else can I do?"

She had no idea how to respond to this behavior. In all the years she'd known him in New Orleans, he'd never had a kind thing to say. His jealousy of her place in his father's life—and the fact that James was not willing to share her favors with his son—had been evident from the moment James had brought her to New Orleans. Andrew had never held his tongue about how he felt. Sincerity or true sympathy were emotions she had considered him incapable of feeling. Could it be she had misjudged Andrew all these years?

"Lisette, is there anything else I can do to help you?"

She gathered her composure. "No, Andrew. But thank you. I appreciate your help more than you know."

"When did this happen?"

"At table. Only a few minutes before you arrived. We

were making a place for him in the music room since we could not get him up the stairs."

"Well, if you should have to move him again, I will gladly help in any way I can. Have you sent for the doctor?"

"No. There hasn't been time. Perhaps Aunt Portia—"

"Lisette! Lisette, the doctor is here!" Aunt Portia hurried into the room followed by a short, round man with a balding pate and thick spectacles. "This is Doctor Samuels. I sent Seth the minute Andrew got here. Oh, Doctor, please tell us he's going to be all right."

Doctor Samuels took one quick look at Jacob. "I'll need to examine him. If you'll all wait downstairs, I'll take care of everything."

They went into the hallway. Lisette lingered at the door for a moment. "If you need anything, Doctor—"

"I'll call you. It won't be long, I promise."

She closed the door. Andrew followed them downstairs. Sedonia was pacing from the front door to the stairs, her face a mass of wrinkles and worry-lines. "Is Mister Morgan going to be all right?"

Aunt Portia hugged her. "The doctor is with him now. We'll know soon. Thank goodness Doctor Samuels lives only four houses away."

Sedonia took Seth and went back to the kitchen, promising to bring tea. Lisette went straight into the parlor and collapsed into a Sleepy Hollow armchair with plush upholstery that made it more comfortable than most of the other furniture in the room. It had always been her favorite place to curl up as a child, to read or to listen to Aunt Portia's stories. Aunt Portia sat on the settee. Andrew paced back and forth a couple of times, then sat down on the Turkish sofa.

For a long while, no one spoke. Lisette's mind whirled

with worrisome thoughts and suppositions. Her father would require more care now than ever before. Remembering when James suffered his seizure and the agonizing weeks afterward, she felt as though someone had constricted her chest with a tight band. The work involved in taking care of a complete invalid was staggering, even when that person was a loved one. Aunt Portia would never be able to manage it, and even with two of them it would take all their time and energies to keep up with the demands of caring for him.

Then there was Andrew. She honestly did not know how to feel about him anymore. He gazed into the fire with the oddest expression. There was no hate there, or anger. He seemed lost in thought, with a sad turn to his lips.

Doctor Samuels came back downstairs just as Sedonia arrived with a tray carrying tea, cups, saucers, and pastries.

Lisette met the Doctor at the bottom of the stairs and escorted him into the parlor. "How is he?"

"The best I can tell, blood vessels in the brain have broken. There's bleeding. In severe cases, holes are drilled in the victim's head to allow the blood to escape—"

Aunt Portia gasped and paled at the suggestion.

"I don't think that will be necessary for Jacob."

Lisette motioned for Doctor Samuels to sit down and offered him tea, which he declined.

"He's already feeling better. Whatever you did when he had the seizure was the right thing. He opened his eyes, followed the movement of my hand, then went to sleep. We'll know more in the morning."

She could not dare to hope it could be over so quickly. "Will he be greatly impaired?"

Doctor Samuels smiled. "You'll see differences, of course. With Jacob's mind the way it was, the only significant change will be in his ability to get around. I would guess he'll need help walking from now on. And his speech may be slurred. In time, it could get better. No way to predict for sure." He handed her a bottle of medicine. She guessed it to be laudanum. "Give him a spoonful of this tonight before you go to bed, and tomorrow morning, noon and night again. It'll help him rest. Don't try to force him to speak or move. His system needs time to recover."

"Thank you, Doctor."

"Call me if he worsens."

Aunt Portia showed him to the door. Now that the crisis was past, Lisette began to shake. Before she knew it, she was trembling all over, then the sobs came as the horror of it all washed over her. Andrew came immediately and drew her into his arms, then over to the sofa. He rocked back and forth, holding her, saying nothing until the weeping was spent and she regained control.

"I'm sorry. I didn't mean to—"

"There's nothing to be sorry for." He released her, then withdrew back to the hearth. "I came to apologize again and ask if you'd decided to forgive me." He glanced at her. "It all seems quite petty in the face of such grave illness."

She realized she was responding to Andrew's words and reminded herself of his past behavior. If she allowed herself to succumb to this new personality, she might let her guard down, with disastrous consequences. She decided to see how far he was willing to go in this little charade—if, indeed, that's what it was.

"My father's illness is unfortunate, to say the least, but we shall cope with it. Thank you for your help." In effect, she had dismissed him. She could tell by the expression on his face he wasn't ready to be dismissed.

"While I'm here, Lisette, perhaps we could talk more

about my father's wishes."

The weasel was showing his true colors. He would take advantage of her distraction with her father's health to attain his own warped goals. If she shouted her indignation and repugnance at his tactics, he might take the revenge he had promised before. She had to be careful.

"My head is aching terribly, Andrew. Can't we please wait until another time to talk? I'm sure Aunt Portia and I have a long night ahead of us." If she had to ask him pointedly to leave, she would. Perhaps he would pretend to be a gentleman for a while longer and leave on his own.

He didn't like it one bit. She could see it in his eyes. The fact that he'd helped with her father had to be viewed through the context of his treachery. She would be grateful for his help but was determined it would gain him no advantage elsewhere.

"Very well, Lisette. I shall call on you tomorrow. I hope your father will be much improved by then and you will feel better as well."

"Perhaps so." She didn't show him to the door. He went on his own, closing it rather forcefully behind him.

Aunt Portia screamed Lisette's name from the top of the stairs.

Lisette rushed to answer. "What's wrong?"

"Nothing's wrong. He spoke to me! It's a miracle!"

Lisette went upstairs, breathing a prayer of thanks, hoping with all her heart this crisis, too, would pass.

Sedonia's sister, Selma, arrived just before bedtime to help care for Jacob during the night. It would seem he had suffered few effects from the seizure and even sipped some broth at Aunt Portia's urging before taking the spoonful of laudanum the doctor had prescribed and falling into a deep sleep. At least they would be able to rest during the night.

Before going to bed, she slipped upstairs quietly to her secret room and stood at the south windows, gazing toward the river. Mist had settled on the surface of the water and among the branches of the maples.

"David, where are you?" she whispered.

Chapter Nine

David could hardly concentrate. The impending hypnosis session that afternoon had him so agitated and anxious he could hardly finish a coherent sentence. It was a good thing Greg was taking care of the office. When Joe came by to pick David up at three in his Jeep Cherokee, his ankle was much better so he left the crutches at home.

"Hey, Bro! Are you ready for the séance?"

Leave it to Joe to turn the whole thing into a sideshow attraction. "Look, Joe—"

"I know. I'm sorry. The idea of your trying an out-of-body experience has me freaked out, that's all. Blows my mind."

"And you don't believe it?"

"Not for a second. But it ought to be one hell of a show!"

David listened while Joe chattered on and on about Shirley MacLaine and Zen Buddhism and a bunch of way-out stuff he'd read about since their meeting with Bob Townsend yesterday. David would never admit to Joe he'd thought about doing similar reading. He couldn't have his brother thinking they were alike after all these years. It could ruin his reputation as a sensible guy. Actually, their individuality was intact. David had thought about checking out books on time travel and past lives and all the new age stuff, but his car was still at the Peabody, so he had to be content with immersing himself in Memphis history. The only books he had at home on any remotely similar subjects to time travel were science fiction novels—not exactly the best sources for a quick study.

As happened more and more these days, his thoughts turned to Lisette. Joe chattered about the "astral plane" and whether David would see it if the hypnosis worked. Assuming, of course, the astral plane could be "seen." Lisette was a much nicer subject to think about.

David knew enough about human development and aging to know she was twenty-eight to thirty-years-old, give or take a year either way. Her desire to travel and see the world was certainly atypical for a woman of the 1880s, but she didn't fit the stereotype of an old-fashioned woman in other ways as well. He couldn't say exactly why, but it seemed that way to him. Something about her made his blood race and his breathing get ragged and heavy. And the desire he felt when he was with her, or when he thought about her, was something new and fiery and completely unique in his life since Fran died. He'd loved Fran with all his heart, and they'd been passionate about each other. But it was a quiet passion. Not like this. With Fran, making love had been warm and secure and homey. With Lisette, he had a feeling it would be more like fire and lightning. Explosive. It was beginning to sound like something out of a romance novel. And what these thoughts were doing to his system were definitely grist for the romance mill.

Since Fran died, he had dated off and on, with no particular interest in any one woman. Shawna had kept him supplied with hopefuls, and a couple of them had been attractive enough that he'd dated briefly from time to time. Then, about eight months ago, Shawna introduced him to Candy. It had taken six months for him to even think about taking Candy to bed. Then, when she initiated intimacy, he was unable to go through with it. He guessed it was because he didn't want casual sex. Only companionship. But Candy had expected more from David than he was ready to give. He had to admit, Candy was beginning to mean too much to him. Then why had he wanted to end the relationship? Something about it wasn't right, but he couldn't pinpoint exactly what. It could be their relationship was too similar to what he'd had with Fran. No explosives.

Making love to Lisette. He tried to imagine it. Would she be appalled at being touched and kissed? Another stereotype. Back then, "decent" women considered behaving passionately unladylike, didn't they? He remembered when she turned to face him on the deck of the riverboat. The image of her hair blowing around her face, high color in her cheeks, fire in her eyes, led David to picture her lying beneath him, her hair splayed over the pillow, his fingers combing the curls, her face flushed with desire.

"Hey, Bro, we're almost there. Are you with me?"

David closed his eyes and took a deep breath. "I'm here. Sorry. Lost in thought. Turn that air conditioner colder, would you? It's hot in here."

Joe nodded and turned the thermostat to sixty degrees. "I don't have to ask what about."

A few minutes later they parked, got out of the Jeep and walked toward the building.

"I just realized you're walking again without the crutches. I thought Greg said you'd need a week on those things."

"Greg was playing doctor for Lana's benefit. I'm fine. We'll pick up my car when we leave here."

"Let me ask you something. When you went back to her time—at the Peabody—was it November there too?"

David hadn't thought about it. "I don't know. There's nothing that says that it has to be November there if it's November here."

"What's the theory we're going on?"

David motioned to the receptionist they'd arrived. "Einstein. All times exist at the same time. Now that I think about it, the Peabody lobby wasn't decorated for Christmas then, as it is now."

"Doesn't mean anything. Commercialism has accelerated the holidays since then.

"You'll have to ask her what day it is—and what year." His forehead creased.

David could tell a light bulb had gone off somewhere in Joe's brain. "What is it, Joe?"

"Where can we find one of those universal calendars? You know, the ones where you can figure out which day of the week any particular day was on—or will be on."

"Encyclopedia maybe? Almanac? What are you thinking?"

"Well, the riverboat that disappeared—"

"The *Cajun Star*."

"What day did it disappear?"

"November 21, 1885."

"What day of the week was that?"

"I don't know."

"Well, November twenty-first of this year will be on a Saturday. What if—"

"—the *Star* sailed on a Saturday? Is that what you're thinking?"

"If so, then it's probably the same day of the year and of the week in Lisette's time as it is here."

"Joe, you may be on to something. If there's a year in the 1880s that has the same days as 2009—"

"Then we'll know for sure how many days you have before the riverboat sails."

"Joe, you're a genius."

"I've always thought so. Maybe Bob has an almanac?"

David asked the receptionist if she had anything with a universal calendar. She searched a few minutes, then handed him a dictionary with one in the back. They used the formula to find the years with the same layout of days as 2009. It didn't take long.

"Eighteen eighty-five. And today is—"

"November eighteenth. Damn, Joe. That means we have only three days before Lisette disappears on that riverboat."

"You too, remember? That doesn't give us much time, Bro."

"I know. This has to work. If not . . ."

"It will, David. It has to."

"I thought you didn't believe in this new age stuff."

"Hey, I've been known to be wrong once or twice."

"At least."

The receptionist opened the sliding glass window above her desk. "Doctor Stewart, you can come in now."

"Thanks." David laid the dictionary on her desk then followed her to the office with Joe close behind.

"I don't have to come, David. If you want me to wait outside or go on home—"

"Are you kidding? I have to have a witness if we pull this off." He stopped and spoke quietly so the receptionist wouldn't hear. "Thanks for coming, Joe. Really. I couldn't do this without you."

"Anytime. I'm here for you, David. You know that."

"I know." They went back to Bob's office. Nerves hit him again. He needed a distraction. "Hey, Joe. You never told me what Shawna thinks about all this."

"I didn't tell her. She's busy with her thesis. Type, type, type, all the time. I say 'Hi, honey, I'm home,' and she says, 'That's nice, dear.' I say, 'We're having the dog for dinner—roasted,' she says, 'That's nice, dear.' If I'd told her, 'David's going to do an out-of-body thing at the shrink's office tonight'—"

" 'That's nice, dear.' I think it's best we don't tell her."

"Unless it works. Then she'll yell, 'Why didn't you tell me!' Women."

"Yeah." Would Lisette be like Shawna? David had to admit he didn't actually know, but suspected she wouldn't. After a lady-like pause, she'd held him there in the Peabody lobby, the same way he was holding her. No reticence, no reservation. If her aunt hadn't interrupted when she did, he had a feeling Lisette would have kissed back too. It seemed hotter in this building than it had the day before. He'd have to confine his thoughts to a strictly professional level.

Bob Townsend opened the door and invited them to come in.

"Well, this is it, Bro. Fish or cut bait."

"You know I don't like to fish."

"You never catch anything. Fish love to see you coming."

"A perfectly good fishing trip can be ruined by catching something."

Bob indicated the couch to David, a chair across the room for Joe. Nervous chatter ceased. Fish or cut bait.

Bob sat in a chair adjacent to the couch, just out of David's peripheral vision.

"Well, Doc, am I crazy or what?"

"If you're having second thoughts—"

"No, no. Just kidding. I'm nervous, that's all."

"Nervous isn't the word for it," Joe said.

David glanced around in time to see Bob give Joe the quiet sign. David settled back on the couch and tried to relax. He had to be calm and put his mind at rest for hypnosis to be possible at all. The last thing he wanted was to screw everything up by being agitated. He wanted this to work, damn it. Time was running out.

Bob got up, reached for a book of matches lying on the table at the far end of the couch, lit a candle on the same table, then went to the window.

"All right, David, I want you to look at the candle and relax."

David heard the blinds close. The room darkened until the only light was the candle. He stared at the flame.

"Let your mind be still. Think of nothing but the flame. You'll be able to hear only my voice—nothing else. At no time will you be unconscious or out of the hearing of my voice, do you understand?"

"I understand." David felt as though he might be sinking into the couch. The timbre of Bob's voice soothed and simplified everything. David could see nothing in the room but the candle. He didn't want to look away. Everything else seemed to blacken until nothing was visible except the candle's flame. It was extremely peaceful.

"You're becoming more and more relaxed. You cannot separate yourself from the flame. You are the flame."

He felt the warmth of the flame, willingly projecting himself into the center of it. His eyelids felt heavy, but he continued to stare at the candle.

"When I tell you in a moment to close your eyes you will, but you'll still be able to see the image of the flame, even with your eyes closed. Do you understand?"

"Yes." His eyes fluttered closed for a long moment, then back open again.

"I know your eyes are heavy. Close them, and see the flame in your mind."

He closed his eyes, relieved not to have to hold them

open any longer. Heavy. So heavy. The flame continued to flicker. The light and warmth surrounded him.

"Now, David, you're going to dream tonight. About Lisette. In the dream you will be able to talk to her, and she will see you and hear and respond. You will be able to stay with her as long as you continue to dream. Right now, though, you are going on a journey. When I tell you that you can, your mind is going to take the journey while your body rests here on the couch. You'll be able to speak to me, and you'll be able to hear my voice, no matter where the journey takes you or how far away. Do you understand?"

"Yes." He could hardly speak; the relaxation was so complete. It felt wonderful. He wished he could stay this way forever.

"Where you go on this journey will be up to you. You may choose any place—or any time—you want to visit. You may visit Lisette if you wish."

David didn't answer. A vision of Lisette formed in his mind. "Lisette."

"Good. Think about Lisette. Think about where she lives."

"Memphis."

"Think about the year in which she lives. Does Lisette live in Memphis now?"

"No. Eighteen eighty-five."

"Is that the year you dreamed about?"

"Yes. She was on the riverboat. The one that disappeared."

"And you spoke to her?"

"Yes. But the phone rang and I woke up."

"No one will wake you this time. It's all right to visit Lisette now. Go back to 1885 and find her. Tell her whatever you want her to hear. You'll be there as surely as

141

you're here now. Do you understand?"

"Yes."

"It's time for your journey."

Something happened. A separation. Then there was the sensation of weightlessness. David opened his eyes and looked around. There, below him, was Bob, and across the room, Joe. David had never seen Joe look so serious and concerned. And there, lying on the couch, he saw himself. It amused him. What an odd feeling, this sensation of floating—not in some mechanical device, like an airplane, but free flight, with no boundaries and no tethers to hold him back.

He looked above and below, to either side, then straight ahead. He saw Joe and Shawna. Joe's hair was shot with gray. Marilu was there, too, but older. She held a baby in her arms. Someone else was in the room, but David didn't recognize him. Was he seeing the future? The scene puzzled him so he turned around and marveled at the panorama he was about to witness.

There were faces he recognized and some he didn't. Everything changed as he watched. There was no sense of travel or movement. Instead, the landscape below him moved, carrying him into the past. Houses and people were getting younger. The pyramid by the river shrank until it disappeared. The Reverend Martin Luther King Jr. was there, alive and well. Then, farther on, David saw people and places he recognized from Memphis history. A red-haired man was speaking with great animation to a crowd of people. They chanted his name: "Boss Crump! Boss Crump!" Of course! Edward Hull Crump—the man who had shaped Memphis politics for almost fifty years. David had argued with Joe for years about whether Crump had been a positive or negative influence on Memphis. They'd had so many arguments at the North End that the owner had outlawed Crump's name in his restaurant.

The Peabody Hotel shrank, disappeared and reappeared in another location. Then Mud Island disappeared!

David had reached the turn of the twentieth century.

By this time, things were moving and changing so fast, he could hardly stay focused on the faces and buildings flashing past. But then the changes began to slow. David descended among them. He could hear Bob's voice, faint, but clear, at a great distance, telling him to find Lisette.

David saw the *Cajun Star* below appearing out of a bank of mist in a brilliant flash of light and fire. It moved backward on the river, north, toward Memphis, until it eased in beside the dock. David blinked. There, on the first deck, stood Lisette and Andrew Westmoreland. Dear God, no!

"Lisette!"

She couldn't hear. Time seemed to be moving forward again. They left the deck and disappeared inside. Andrew reappeared, without Lisette, and headed for the ramp, but a man stopped him, struggled with him. This new man seemed familiar.

A chill crawled through him. David was seeing himself on the doomed riverboat. The boat left the dock, headed south toward New Orleans. It would disappear forever, into the mist.

David closed his eyes, felt dizzy for a moment. When he opened them again, the riverboat was gone. He went farther into the past, searching the city of Memphis.

David hovered near a huge house facing south. It was four stories, the color of terra cotta, trimmed in gray. He couldn't say how he knew it was Lisette's home. He just knew, even with darkness enveloping the house so completely, muting the colors, disguising details he instinctively knew were there. The arched windows, gray shingles on the roof, and the stained-glass window in the front door were all familiar. Each story led upward to a single room with three arched windows on the east, south and west sides. The house resembled a wedding cake. The only light visible was a dim lamp glowing in an east window on the second floor.

David's heart pounded with anticipation. Would she be able to see him? Bob said she would. His voice was terribly faint now. David could scarcely hear him. How was he supposed to enter the house? Must he stand on the wide, covered front porch and knock at the front door?

Bob told him to enter the room in his mind.

There. In the shadows.

She lay in her canopied feather bed, a velvet patchwork quilt mounded over her, red-brown hair scattered across the pillow, just as David had imagined. If only he could touch that silky hair, feel it between his fingers.

She pushed the quilts back and went to the window. Opened it. Stood there with the night breeze caressing her the way he wanted to.

Fear made him hesitant. Would she be frightened? Or would she think she was dreaming?

Ask her.

Call her name.

"Lisette . . ."

Chapter Ten

After Aunt Portia said goodnight—finally—Lisette couldn't sleep. Images tumbled through her mind like rocks cascading down a steep hill. Andrew's fist against her stinging cheek. Her father's blank face. Tears glistening in Aunt Portia's eyes. The seizure, Jacob's mouth twisted to one side, eyes glazed with pain, then with oblivion. If only David had been there . . .

She thought carefully about Doctor David Stewart. He'd surprised the daylights out of her at the Peabody when he hugged her in front of everyone, even Aunt Portia. Yet, remembering, she could not fault him for his forwardness. He'd been so glad to see her. And it was the first time she'd ever been held by a man and . . .

She frowned, struggling to put into words the way she'd felt. Different than ever before, that was a certainty. Warm. Secure. Loved. But how could he love her when they'd met such a short time ago? She thought about her feelings for him. David intrigued her more than any man she'd ever met. She couldn't wait to see him again. Was that love? Or the beginning of love? Or was it just a normal reaction to being treated with affection instead of cruel disregard?

David was exactly the opposite of Andrew. Where Andrew's eyes were cold and dead, David's eyes softened with emotion when he smiled, and they glistened in the moonlight, and made her want to stare into them for hours. Andrew's touch left her repulsed. David's touch made her yearn to be touched again.

How would it be, she wondered, for David to touch her cheek, her shoulder, the back of her neck? What would she feel if he touched her in other places, where even her husband had never touched her before? As his wife, she expected to be touched by him, but James could never relax around her. Even when they were in bed together, their coupling took only a few minutes. James had never spoken to her during those rough and sweaty couplings, never kissed or caressed her with affection. He claimed his rights as her husband just as he would claim a piece of baggage he possessed.

The hug David gave her at the Peabody proved he would never be nervous about touching her. He would probably want to kiss her too. In fact, she thought he might have, but Aunt Portia interrupted and introduced herself to him. The thought was scandalous. For him to kiss her when they were not betrothed was unthinkable. Wasn't it?

Suddenly too warm, Lisette pushed back the sheet and two quilts and got up to open the window. She gave the heavy frame a sharp rap with the heel of her hand, then lifted it as high as it would go. Pushing her hair back from her face, she drank in the earthy fragrance of the river and was reminded of that night on the riverboat when she met David. The southerly breeze fluttered through the crocheted curtains and shivered around her shoulders. Now the quilts would feel good.

"Lisette."

She drew in a long, slow breath and turned around slowly. Only a few feet away, on the far side of the room, stood David Stewart. She should have been startled but wasn't. It seemed right somehow that he should be here. She was thrilled to see him, even though his presence in her room would give Aunt Portia apoplexy if she knew. Lisette thought about trying to cover herself, but he'd already seen her flannel nightgown in his clinic. The gown covered her as much as any dress.

"Please don't be afraid."

"I'm not. How did you get in without using the door?"

"How do you know I didn't?"

"Because the hinges squeak like a passel of mice in a corncrib no matter how quickly or slowly you open it. And you couldn't have come through the window because I would have seen you. So, how did you get into my room?"

She couldn't help smiling, amused. She'd never allowed any man—not even her father—into her bedroom. In New Orleans she had shared James's bedroom but never considered it hers. The idea of this man being here at exactly the time when she'd been thinking about him was like something from a dream.

Of course. She had to be dreaming. Many times she'd been aware of dreaming while in the midst of some fantastic concoction. Yet, David seemed as real now as he had at the Peabody and at the strange clinic in her other dream.

"I know my being here is hard to explain," David began, then stopped suddenly. "Have I said something funny?"

"I know I must be dreaming. Does that mean I am in control, or does the dream have a life of its own?"

He laughed softly, came around the end of the bed and stopped just in front of her. "I think you'll find I'm very much alive."

Thank heavens this was only a dream. She didn't have to worry about starting a scandal by having a man in her bedroom. The fact such behavior was forbidden made his presence exciting, even thrilling. She would scold herself in the morning.

"Lisette, listen carefully. I want you to meet me tomorrow. Will you do that?"

There was no reason why she shouldn't go along with the dream. "Of course. At the Peabody?"

"Yes, at the fountain."

"I'll try. My father had a seizure at supper tonight. But he seems to feel better now. More at peace. I should be able to leave him for a short while."

"I'm sorry." He frowned, concerned, then his expression changed. His jaw tightened and he frowned again. Anger this time.

"What's wrong?"

"Is Westmoreland still bothering you?"

So that was it. "He tried to convince me he was sorry for hitting me and promised never to do it again. Perhaps he means it, but I don't think so. He wants to marry me."

David's face turned red. He closed his hands into tight fists.

"I could never marry him, David."

"Listen to me, Lisette." He took a step closer and put his hands on her shoulders.

His touch caused exquisite tingling, just as she'd imagined it would.

"Men who abuse women don't just stop doing it. You can't believe anything he says. I know what I'm talking about."

She shivered from the brisk night breeze, which was stronger now, and from his hands gripping her shoulders. She could actually feel each of his fingers through the flannel, warm and intense.

"You believe me, don't you?"

"Of course. You're a doctor. You know about such things."

With feather-lightness, he stroked her bruised cheek. "I

hate the idea of that man touching you ever again."

"I pray, too, that he never shall." Once more, she felt flushed and alive. David's hands, so soft and gentle, and his eyes, burning with concern and something else she could not identify, warmed her as no quilt ever could. "Doctor Stewart, I feel as if I'd known you much longer than a few days."

"Call me David, please."

"Very well, David. It is my dream, after all. Tell me about the place where I saw you in my last dream. The clinic. Is it here in Memphis?"

"It's in Memphis, but not the Memphis you know."

"Is there another?"

He took her hand and led her to the window. "What do you see?" He pulled her back against his chest with his arms crossed in front of her. She placed her hands over his and laced her fingers with his. He smelled of some wonderful cologne, making her dizzy and warm again. "What do you see?" he asked again, brushing his lips across her cheek.

"Memphis, of course."

"In what year?"

"You must be joking. You certainly know as well as I do what year it is." This dream surprised her. She never would've imagined such a question.

He turned her around so they were face to face. "Indulge me."

His eyes were the color of the sea. "Very well. It is Wednesday, the eighteenth day of November, in the year of our Lord, 1885."

He appeared excited, almost agitated. "Then it's all true."

"Really, David, why would I lie to you? Even in a dream?"

Still holding her, his arms around her back now, his thumb tracing lazy circles up and down her spine, she felt light-headed.

"Only three days until the *Cajun Star* leaves for New Orleans."

"Why is that important? Are you leaving on the *Star*?" She shivered again with the thought of not seeing him again. He couldn't leave now. They were just getting to know one another.

David released her, closed the window, then stared into the night for a moment. "Lisette, I don't know how much longer I'll be here tonight. If I disappear in front of your eyes, don't be frightened."

"Why should I be frightened? It's only a dream."

"Yes, a dream. Even so, you must come to the Peabody tomorrow."

"What time?"

"Ten o'clock. I'll have something to show you."

"Can't you show me now?"

He shook his head. "I didn't bring it with me tonight. But I'll have it tomorrow."

"What could it be to cause you to be so serious?" She felt bold and trailed her fingertips down the line of his jaw; she saw him react to her touch with what could only be desire. It made her breathe faster, sent new warmth all through her body. Never in her life had she elicited such a response from a man.

"It's a newspaper article."

"How interesting. Tomorrow, then."

"Now, you must get some sleep so you'll wake up in the morning in time to meet me at ten."

"How can I go to sleep in a dream?"

"Just try." He fingered errant curls at her temples, reminding her he was seeing her for the second time with her hair loose, in nightclothes. He held her face between his hands as though he were holding a priceless gem. "I wish I could stay. I don't want to leave you."

"Do you have to go? There are so many questions I want to ask."

"Ask me tomorrow. I don't want you to dismiss this as something you imagined." He pulled something from his pocket with paper inside, tore off a sheet, and took a pen from his pocket unlike any she'd ever seen. He wrote something on the paper. "A reminder. So you'll know it's real." He placed the paper on the table beside her bed, laid the pen beside it, then stared straight ahead for a moment, his eyes glazed as though in deep thought. "He's calling me back. Not yet! A few more minutes!"

"Who? I don't hear anyone—"

Without warning, he pressed his lips to hers, astounding her completely. If awake, she would have been obliged to slap his face, but since it was only a dream, she circled his neck with her arms and returned the kiss. It was disturbingly delicious and gave her such an extraordinary feeling, she gasped when his mouth moved to the slope of her neck. His hand at her nape massaged and caressed, then worked downward, pressing her against his chest, circling on her back. Then his mouth settled on hers again and his tongue parted her lips. Her response came so swiftly, she moaned. Pleasure and desire moved through her and into him, then back again. She threaded her fingers through his hair, along his scalp and felt him tremble. Eager to experiment, she touched her tongue to his lips, then pushed into his mouth, and heard him groan.

She felt almost faint. He looked straight into her eyes and whispered, "I came through time for you, Lisette."

All pretense of a dream vanished. "You're real. And you're here in my room. It isn't a dream, is it?"

David hesitated before he shook his head. "The only part resembling a dream is the unhappy fact that I can't stay with you. You're very much awake, just as I am. I don't want you to dismiss everything that's happened here, thinking it isn't real."

"I should order you from my room before Aunt Portia discovers you're here." Please, God, let Aunt Portia be sleeping, she prayed.

"Are you going to do that?"

"No. Not unless . . ." She felt absolutely daring and touched her lips to his again. He leaned forward, but she leaned back, teasing him. He smiled.

"Unless what?"

"Unless you refuse to kiss me again before you have to go."

"I could never refuse you anything."

Her knees felt weak. She sank onto the side of the bed, bringing him with her. David took his time, just as she hoped he would. His hands roamed over her body, scarcely touching, yet leaving a trail of warmth wherever his fingers explored. She abandoned all thoughts of what was proper and gave herself completely to the sensations streaming through her. Never had she imagined kissing and touching could be so intoxicating, so addictive.

He became bolder in his exploration of her body. His hand slipped inside her gown—when had he released all those buttons?—and caressed her bare breasts. She thought she might faint, her breathing had become so erratic.

David's lips on her eyes, shoulders, mouth, his hands stroking her breasts, left her breathless and anxious for more.

David withdrew suddenly, easing away, worry creasing his forehead, his eyes glazed again.

"What's wrong? Did I do something to displease you?"

He recovered quickly, smiled and kissed her again, as passionately as before. "You could never displease me, Lisette. But I have to leave now."

"Leave? But you can't! How can you just leave after kissing me, touching me this way?"

"He's calling me back."

"Who is calling? There's no one else here."

"Be at the Peabody tomorrow morning at ten o'clock. I'll explain everything then."

There seemed to be nothing she could do to change his mind. Her throat tightened. "I don't understand any of this."

"You will tomorrow. Promise you'll come, then close your eyes."

"I promise. David?"

"Yes?" He stroked the hair back from her face, his touch so gentle she could scarcely feel his fingers against her cheek.

"How can I be sure you'll come back?"

"When you close your eyes, I'll meet you there."

She kissed him, desperate to keep him from leaving. When she opened her eyes, he was gone. She tasted the salt of her own tears.

Chapter Eleven

"Damn it, Bob! Why did you have to call me back? I was there! I can't believe—"

"David, calm down. I'll explain—"

"You'd better have a damn good reason—"

"You stopped breathing."

David halted his tirade and took several deep breaths. "Completely?"

"Damn near it, Bro."

He looked at Joe for the first time since Bob had brought him out of the trance. Joe's face was so pale, and David realized he must have been in real jeopardy for Joe to be that spooked. David tried to stand, but swayed with a sudden bout of dizziness. Bob grabbed his arm and lowered him back to the couch. He dropped his head between his knees and tried to regulate his breathing. The trance must have taken him deeper than any of them expected. But he'd made it. No matter what had happened, it was worth every precious minute he'd spent with her.

"Now, David, I want you to relax and listen to the tape."

"The tape?" He'd forgotten. When he sat up, the dizziness came back.

"If you aren't going to keep your head down, then lie back on the couch until you've had a chance to recuperate."

He did.

"I have to tell you, David, I never expected this harebrained scheme to work. When it did—and your breathing and vitals diminished the farther back in time you went—I wondered if I was going to be able to bring you home again." He went to a cabinet behind his desk, pulled out a bottle of brandy and three glasses and filled each of them halfway. Joe took one. Bob handed another to David. "Here. Drink this."

He sipped the brandy, which burned its way to his stomach, and pivoted on the couch until he was flat again. He had to admit it felt better than having his head swim like a drunken sailor.

While the tape of the session played, David relived it in his mind, supplying Lisette's voice where blanks occurred on the tape. By the end, his voice was so weak he could see why Bob and Joe had been insistent on calling him back. Did that mean he was close to the point of no return? Was that possible? What would "the point of no return" be? Death? Permanent residence in the nineteenth century? Joe's voice was on the tape too, with language unusual for him. Frantic and insistent. Thinking he was about to lose a brother.

"That's when we lost contact. You stopped talking—and your respiration was down to four a minute." Bob leaned back in his chair, reached for his brandy and finished it, then steepled his fingers.

"Four?" Incredible. When he kissed her—and she kissed back. Damn.

Bob leaned forward. "David, what happened after that last part on the tape? You almost didn't come back."

Joe got up, cleared his throat noisily. "I think I have a good idea. You were close to her. Weren't you?"

"Not as close as I wanted to be."

Bob went to his desk. "I'm not sure planting that suggestion about dreaming was such a good idea, David. To tell you the truth, I'd be afraid for you to go under again

155

without someone there. I'd like to erase the suggestion."

David sat up, testing his equilibrium to see if the dizziness had passed. "It isn't necessary. She's going to meet me at the Peabody tomorrow at ten. It was on the tape, remember?"

Joe dragged a chair closer to the couch and sat down. "Are you sure she'll believe it enough to come?"

"I wrote her a note so she'd have proof I was there. I used the back of a deposit slip and a ballpoint pen. There's no way she can explain that away." He gave Bob a hard look, wanting him to believe this had actually happened. "I was there, Bob. Body and soul. How is that possible? I never believed I'd be able to touch her and have her feel it. I figured I'd be like a hologram, you know? Form but no substance. But there was plenty of substance. It doesn't make sense, does it?"

"No, but who am I to question the power of the human mind? In another moment we might have lost you. You might have been lost to this century—"

"—alive in hers? Is that what you're saying?"

"There isn't a rational explanation for what just happened, David. It's my feeling that your mind created the whole thing. You imagined you were there, you imagined her, everything. I have to say that's what happened, because my training doesn't support any other conclusion. It's impossible to confirm you actually went back in time. It's entirely feasible you fabricated everything, and you've been fabricating since the first time you saw her."

David bristled at the implication he was hallucinating. "I know the difference between real and imaginary. I don't buy it."

Bob removed his glasses, pulled a handkerchief from his pocket and cleaned the lenses. "Frankly, neither do I. You aren't the hallucinatory type. Everything you've told me goes beyond anything I've ever dealt with. I don't know what to say."

"If you could see her—in the flesh—would you believe it then?"

"Of course. We can't all hallucinate the same thing. At least I don't think we can. Not without some outside stimulus to prompt a simultaneous illusion."

"Mass hypnosis."

"An interesting theory, but not very workable. Especially among doctors, who are typically more skeptical than the average citizen."

"We have to have proof."

"Exactly."

Joe hadn't said much. He stood up, his face oddly blank.

"What is it, Joe?"

"Look over there and tell me what you see." He raised one arm slowly, indicating.

"Lisette." David hurried to where she stood.

Bob put his glasses back on. "My God."

"David?" Lisette took one tentative step forward, slumped into his arms, then disappeared.

"Damn!" Joe slammed his fist onto Bob's desk. "Did you see that? It was her! It was really her!"

Bob sat down, pulled open the bottom drawer of his desk and lifted out a tape recorder that was still running. "We'll see."

David stared at the second machine; surprised Bob would tape them without disclosing the fact. "You were using two recorders?"

"I usually do. When a patient gets nervous about being recorded, I just turn that one off. This one runs all the time. Doctors don't have perfect memories, after all." He ran the tape back. They all listened. And stared at each other when a fourth voice came from the tape. One word. "David." Clearly a woman's voice.

"She was here." David felt strangely calm. Now that they had confirmation, everything became clear.

Bob nodded. "She must have fallen asleep and followed you back to this office. Seeing you, David—"

"—was enough to wake her up. She really was in my arms, Bob, for just an instant."

"All right, gentlemen. We have a whole new ball game." Bob advanced the tape to the point where he'd stopped it before, punched the record button and replaced it in his desk. "Where do we go from here, David?"

"To the Peabody."

By the time David got to bed that night, he was exhausted. He tried to settle down, to visualize everything going well tomorrow, yet a thousand questions continued to plague him. What would happen to Lisette if he couldn't contact her again? Would his name disappear from the passenger list of the missing *Cajun Star*? What if David had never seen that article?

As his mind weaned itself from the third degree, Bob's voice echoed, "You will dream about Lisette."

David closed his eyes, relaxed, and let the dream come.

A moment later, he opened his eyes and recognized the velvet quilt he'd seen on Lisette's bed when he'd been there earlier. She lay there asleep. He could see only what the moonlight illuminated, streaming through the window onto the bed. A glimpse of red-gold hair and lace about her neck.

David sat on the edge of the bed, content for the moment to watch her sleep, then touched her cheek with one finger, moved a strand of hair back from her face. She stirred, but did not wake up. He touched his lips to hers.

When her eyes fluttered open, she wasn't startled or afraid. Instead, she surprised him. She lifted the covers and shifted over in the bed, making room.

David unbuttoned the shirt of his pajamas, took it off and draped it across the end of the bed. The pants followed. He eased in beside her.

"David, are you real?"

"I don't know. Are you?"

She smiled and pulled the gown over her head. It floated to the floor. He reached to touch her, caress her, and she came willingly into his arms, kissing with enthusiasm and passion, moaning softly when he bent to kiss her breasts. She seemed to be starved for affection and tenderness and he did everything he could to prolong and enhance, stimulate and elicit from her the exquisite and magical sensations of making love. His only wish was to bring her pleasure. And she brought him pleasure in return.

He could tell she wasn't used to experimentation, yet she warmed to the idea and explored his body with her fingers, making the most delightful noises when her touch brought a sigh or a moan from him.

David suspected she'd never been touched lovingly before, so he took his time, letting her get used to the idea of hands exploring her silky body. By the time he probed and caressed that most intimate place, her breathing had deepened and the noises from her throat told everything about what she was feeling. She pressed against his hand, laced her fingers through his hair and pulled his mouth to hers. He accelerated the pace and felt her stiffen. Her back arched, her lips grew slack. When she relaxed, he slipped inside her. She matched the rhythm, her legs around him, her mouth on his neck, his chest, his mouth. He couldn't wait any longer.

Afterward, they lay in each other's arms, her lips full from their kissing, her body warm and fragrant with love. They drifted into sleep, her head on his shoulder, his arms holding her close.

When the first rays of dawn woke him, David reached for Lisette, but she wasn't there. The movement of his waterbed told him he was home again. He didn't want to disturb the remnants of the dream, but he had to get ready to meet her at the Peabody.

When he got out of bed, he realized he was naked. His pajamas were lying on the foot of her bed! It wasn't a dream! David laughed aloud and headed for the shower.

By the time he left the house, he was ready for anything. He wanted to get Lisette out of the hotel lobby immediately to avoid anyone who might interfere. He knew they had to stay together. Somehow, the link between the centuries depended on their proximity to each other. That thought brought a smile. Staying as close to Lisette as he had last night would be a pleasure.

Even if he could get her into this time, he knew she wouldn't abandon her home and family so quickly—and neither would he. The conflicting possibilities whirling in his brain overlapped and struggled until he was almost crazy.

At the Peabody, Joe and Bob arrived at 9:30. Joe had brought a digital camera.

"Sight seeing?" David asked with a smile.

"Hey, Bro, I intend to photograph anything that happens."

"And if I disappear?"

"I'll take pictures of the ducks."

David wished, in a way, that Joe and Bob hadn't come, but there was no diplomatic way to tell them to stay away. Depending on what happened, they might prove indispensable if Westmoreland showed up. Could he cross into 2009 with Lisette if Andrew happened to be standing close enough to her, David wondered? Joe hadn't crossed over, that first time at the fountain, so David doubted it.

Nine forty five. There was no sign of her. Then, at 9:50, the lights blinked out, then back on. He glanced quickly at the fountain. The ducks hadn't arrived yet. The elevators were still there, the gift shops. No changes. Except for a woman standing at the gift shop window, peering at a Mallard decoy in a display.

Bob saw her just after David did and alerted Joe. David approached her carefully. He would have known this woman even if she hadn't been wearing a maroon and gray striped polonaise dress brushing the floor around her feet.

"Lisette?"

She whirled around. Her eyes brightened as she smiled. Then she blushed to match her dress. "Doctor Stewart."

"David, remember?"

She extended her right hand, holding a piece of paper he recognized as the note he'd left in her room. Her cheeks blazed. "Could you possibly know what is written on this paper?"

"On one side, it has my name and address printed on a bank deposit slip. On the other side, it says, 'Peabody Hotel. Ten o'clock. David.' I left it on the table beside your bed last night."

"The first time you came to my room."

"Yes. The first time."

"The second time, you left your . . ." She blushed.

"Pajamas."

161

"Yes." Her eyes glistened with the same passion he'd seen in them the night before.

She took several steps closer, then saw Bob and Joe. "Oh! You're the gentlemen I dreamed about." She appeared confused and troubled to be seeing dream people in the flesh.

David took her gloved hand and squeezed it. He had to touch her. "You must have followed me home."

"Excuse me?"

How could he put it? "It doesn't really matter. Lisette, this is my brother, Joe Stewart."

Lisette offered her hand to Joe. "I'm delighted to meet you, Sir."

Joe took her hand lightly. "You have no idea how glad I am to meet you, Miss Morgan." The grin on his face widened as he gawked at her.

"And this is Doctor Townsend."

Bob nodded, touching Lisette's fingers for a moment, obviously fascinated. "Miss Morgan. Welcome to Memphis."

She gave a nervous laugh. "Considering I have lived in Memphis all but eight years of my life, I nonetheless appreciate your greeting, Dr. Townsend." She looked at David, her expression soft, her skin flushed and rosy.

David wanted to take her in his arms, kiss her until she was breathless, but there was much to tell her, and they were far from alone. "Lisette, we must go somewhere we can talk and not be interrupted."

"You were going to show me something. A newspaper article?"

"Soon."

"David, maybe we ought to—" Joe began.

David silenced him with one look. "Nothing will happen

as long as Lisette and I are together. Please, Joe."

He nodded. "If you need us, we'll be right here."

"Thanks." David took Lisette's arm and headed toward the staircase. There was a room on the second floor displaying memorabilia depicting the history of the Peabody. If there was no one else there, it would be a perfect place for them to talk.

A group of teenage girls came downstairs just as they started up. They were wearing jeans, turtlenecks, shirts, and sweaters. Lisette stared at them with amazement. "David, those women are wearing men's trousers!" she whispered.

David hurried her upstairs and to the Memorabilia Room. It was empty. "Lisette, I know this is going to be a shock for you, but bear with me. I'll explain everything."

"What's going to be a shock? You mean women who dress like men? It's scandalous, to be sure, but I promise you I am an educated person, thanks to Aunt Portia. I'm not as naive as you obviously think I am."

"I didn't mean to imply that you were naive. Just don't be surprised if you see some strange things. After all, this isn't 1885, you know."

She stopped stock-still. "What are you talking about—not 1885?"

"Come inside. I think you'll find this room interesting." He closed the door, hoping no one else would come in.

She went all the way around the perimeter of the small room, studying the displays. The oldest was dated in the twenties, as far as David could tell from a quick sweep.

"David, all these things are from the future."

"Your future. My past."

He halfway expected her to be frightened, but her reaction was closer to amazement and curiosity instead. They sat at the end of the conference table that took up the center of the room.

"All right, tell me what you're feeling."

She stared for a moment, glassy-eyed, then her expression brightened. "This has to be another dream. I can't find any other explanation for it. I'm imagining all of this—and you. Is that it, David? Are you nothing more than a figment of my imagination?" She touched his face with her hand. "Was last night only a wonderful dream?"

He kissed the palm of her hand, using his tongue, just as he had in her bedroom when their bodies had been more like one than two. Her eyes widened, then narrowed. Her lips parted just a fraction.

"I promise you I'm real, and this is no dream. I'm going to tell you something hard for you to believe, but it's vital that you do."

She nodded, waiting.

David marveled and thrilled at her ability to cope with what had to be an unbelievably jolting experience.

"When I first met you, on the riverboat—"

She nodded.

"You came into the ballroom and didn't recognize anyone, isn't that right?"

"How did you know?"

"I guessed. You stepped from your time," he paused, hoping she would understand, "into my time."

Her eyes narrowed. "What do you mean, your time?"

"Lisette, do you remember, in your room last night—" The blush was back. "—the first time—when I asked you to tell me the year?"

"It was a silly question." She paused. "At least it seemed silly then. Should I be asking you the same question now?"

So sharp. Her mind was whirling now; he could see it in

her eyes. "The year where we are right now is 2009."

She said nothing for what seemed a really long time. "Two thousand and nine."

"Just as you did on the riverboat, you've come into the future more than a hundred and twenty years." He let the information sink in slowly before continuing. "When I met you at the Peabody, and in your room last night—both times—I traveled back through time from 2009 to 1885." He let her consider it, saying nothing more until she was ready.

Lisette stared at him for almost half a minute. "Why do women wear men's trousers in 2009?"

He burst out laughing. He should have known she would focus on something intensely interesting to her, as a woman.

"Did I say something funny?"

He apologized for laughing. "They aren't wearing men's trousers. Women wear pants and jeans all the time in 2009."

"I see." She straightened her spine.

"Just wait until you see what women wear in the summer, when it's hot. When they go swimming."

She didn't say anything, then leaned suddenly toward him and whispered, "Did you really . . . that is, did you kiss me last night, or did I dream it, the way you said I dreamed about your brother and that doctor?"

"I made love to you. And you loved me right back." The blush again. "I'd like to make love to you again."

"Right here?"

"I'd rather take you home with me first."

Lisette's eyes twinkled. "Well, then, I suppose—"

He didn't wait for her to finish before kissing her as he'd wanted to since she appeared in the hotel. When her arms came around him, he gathered her as close as he could manage with all the clothing she wore. What a difference from last night, with only her nightgown—and then nothing at all—between them. She obviously wore a corset and who knew what else beneath that dress.

Lisette tried to pull back, but he whispered, "It's all right. Do whatever you want to do."

Her eyes widened just before they closed and her mouth opened beneath his.

Chapter Twelve

His mouth on hers felt exotic. His tongue knew such interesting things to do, and the feelings running through Lisette made her want to shed her corset, get rid of all these clothes, and love David the way she had last night. Never, in eight years of marriage, had James given her any pleasure when he'd taken his privilege. He'd never touched her the way David had, or kissed her much, and never, never, had he expected her to enjoy what they were doing. He'd just ordered her to "hang on," and told her, "This won't take long." And it never had, thank goodness.

Last night, she'd forgotten everything she'd been taught about how a lady should not enjoy or participate in such activities. Thinking about how she'd behaved should make her want to hide her face in shame, but she couldn't be ashamed of giving and receiving such pleasure. It made David so happy when she responded. She had learned things about a man's body she'd never known. Suddenly, seeing David again meant everything.

"You're smiling." He kissed her lightly, then waited.

"I'll tell you later. When we're alone again."

"I can't wait."

"Should I read the article now?"

David pulled it from his shirt pocket. "Before you read this, you need to know when it was published. It was in last Sunday's *Commercial Appeal*."

"*Commercial?* When did the paper add that word to its title?"

"I don't know. What was it in 1885?" He handed the article to her.

"The *Appeal*." She unfolded it carefully and read the headline. " 'The Night the *Cajun Star* Vanished?' But David—"

He motioned for her to read.

Her heart beat faster as she read about the *Cajun Star* disappearing without a trace. "David, this can't be the same riverboat—"

"Read the whole article, then we'll talk about it."

She read to the end. "I don't understand. The *Cajun Star* is going to disappear after it leaves Memphis on the twenty-first of November and never be found again? That's ridiculous! What's going to happen to it?" Her mind jolted. "I mean, what happened to it? It's hard to remember where we are—when we are."

"No one ever knew or found out. It doesn't matter, not really. Since we know it's going to happen."

"What difference does it make to us? It's unfortunate, of course, for those who will be aboard, but—"

David took her hand. His eyes were gentle and moist, his smile apologetic. Why had he become so melancholy?

"We know the boat is going to disappear. It gives us the advantage. Did you read the list of passengers?"

"No, should I?" A shiver of fear darted through her. "I'm on the list, is that what you're telling me? I can't be. I won't be on the *Cajun Star*. I just arrived in Memphis. Why would I be leaving?"

David took the article and pointed to two names. She couldn't believe her eyes. Her name and her father's!

None of it seemed real. Not this place, or this article, this strange room with artifacts from the future—her future. The only thing real was David, holding her hand, waiting for her to digest these incredible facts. He must have known how difficult this would be to accept. She couldn't accept it. She had no plans to be on the *Cajun Star* when it left Memphis a few days from now. The idea of her father leaving—but not Aunt Portia—made even less sense. It had to be a mistake.

David pulled her into his arms and held her for a moment. "You don't have to be afraid. I'm going to be there with you."

She pulled away. "With me? But you—" He pointed to the article again. She read the name beneath his finger. *David Ingram Stewart*. Dear Lord, no. "You'll be on the boat, too? I don't understand why any of us would be on that boat."

"Neither do I, but it's obvious that something is going to happen to make us board that riverboat. We'll have to leave the boat before midnight." He stroked her arm then tilted her chin upward. "I promised you were not going to be hurt again. Remember?"

"But David—"

"Do you believe something has brought us together? It can't be coincidence. People don't travel through time for no reason. Last week if you'd told me I'd be going back to 1885, I would've suggested counseling with Doctor Townsend."

David was trying so hard to help her understand. "Yes, I believe there's a reason for all that's happened, even though I don't understand what it could be."

"I'm sure we'll figure it out eventually."

"I think, instead of worrying about the future, we ought to decide how to get through the next three days." Andrew's face flashed through her mind, but she didn't mention him to David. "Right now I should be getting home.

Caring for my father is a full-time job. I must be there to help. With this new illness—"

"I wish I could help."

"David, that would be wonderful! I'm sure doctors have found cures and treatments for all sorts of things in a hundred years."

"You can't imagine."

"You'll have to tell me everything that's happened between 1885 and 2009."

"I'll bring you a book—a history of the United States from the Civil War on."

"That would be wonderful. A book that tells about the future. What a novel idea."

He frowned. "Some things will disturb you. Wars. And a depression that crippled the country."

Did she want to know these terrible things to come? "Surely there were good things, too."

"Men have walked on the moon."

"On the moon! David, you can't be serious. It's impossible to go to the moon."

He grinned. "It happened in 1969. 'One small step for man, one giant leap for mankind.' Neil Armstrong."

The idea of someone actually walking on the moon made all of this seem like something from a Jules Verne novel.

David gripped her hands tighter. "I want to go home with you. I can't stand the thought we might be separated and not be able to find each other again. When we learn why all of us are going to be on the riverboat, maybe there will be something I can do to change it."

"Of course. You may stay at our home. As long as you don't leave the house, you won't need different clothes or money—which I'm assuming is quite different now from the money we have. If it's changed as much as women's clothing . . ."

"You're incredible, Lisette. If I didn't know better, I'd say you were raised in modern day Memphis, just down the street from my house."

What on earth did he mean by that? "I assume you're complimenting me. Thank you. I suppose."

"You aren't going to have any trouble at all skipping a hundred years into the future. You'll love all the freedom you're going to have. And," he squeezed her waist, "you're going to love not having to wear all those clothes."

Lisette sat up straighter. "With women wearing so little clothing, it's no wonder that men—" She started to say men were lustier and more playful in bed, but she still wasn't used to being that frank. Surely propriety wasn't one of the things that had been discarded, along with most of the clothing she was used to wearing. Or, for exactly that reason, maybe it had.

"No wonder men do what?"

"Never mind. I'll tell you later."

"When we're alone? I can hardly wait. I'm betting you can hardly wait to get out of that awful corset. As you saw, women dress comfortably now. They don't wear corsets or stays—"

"No corsets? However do they keep their figures?"

"Eating salad. I promise, the first time you wear jeans and a T-shirt, you'll never want to go back to one of these heavy dresses again."

"You consider this dress heavy? Later on in the winter—" She looked away, suddenly overcome with the memory of the newspaper article and that terrible word—"vanished."

"I might not be alive this winter, if the article is true."

"Of course you'll be alive. You'll be here, with me,

wearing jeans and T-shirts and planning where you want to go next." He kissed her quickly. "Listen to me, Lisette. Are you listening?"

She nodded, her mind too jumbled to speak.

"I'm going to take care of everything. You have to trust me."

She had to tell him what was in her heart.

"I love you, David."

His expression was so strange; she couldn't tell what he was feeling. But then he folded his arms around her and kissed her until she felt dizzy with desire. His eyes actually filled with tears.

She couldn't help staring at every person they passed when they walked downstairs. Especially the women. There were about as many wearing dresses or skirts as there were in trousers, but the skirts were shockingly short for grown women. At home, young girls were permitted to wear skirts which were only mid-calf in length, but with leggings. These women allowed their bare skin to show beneath their skirts. And some of the women were as old as Aunt Portia!

David watched her with amusement, laughing from time to time as though it were the funniest thing he'd ever seen. It was certainly the strangest, and in some ways the funniest thing she'd ever seen as well. She could not help gawking when an especially ludicrous example presented itself—a young girl wearing a skirt that did not reach even the top of her knees. What would it feel like to expose bare skin to sunshine and wind that way? She had to be honest and admit she couldn't wait to find out. It would assuredly embarrass her half to death, but it would be thrilling too. Imagine. No corsets. Being able to breathe without stays poking her ribs and making every breath an ordeal.

The shop windows in the Peabody, with their displays of

clothing and toys and all manner of merchandise totally unfamiliar in the 1880s, enticed her inside to buy one of everything to take home and show Aunt Portia. The hats were
extraordinary, the shoes ridiculous, and the odd vehicles
David called cars and buses whizzing past the hotel outside
made her want to ride in one of them. David promised she
would someday.

By the time they got back to the lobby, her head was
swimming from all she'd seen and her dazed mind needed a
rest. But later she'd love to see this new and wondrous
place that seemed as foreign as the pyramids of Egypt. How
much had the world changed in a hundred years?

"David, are there still pyramids in Egypt?"

"Of course. In fact, there's a pyramid right here in Memphis."

"In Memphis? You must be joking." The memory of the
lighted pyramid she'd seen that first night on the riverboat
flashed through her mind. "Then it was real? The one I saw
by the lighted bridge?"

He grinned. "The pyramid here in Memphis is shiny
metal with a glass dome that lights up at night. It's a place
where they wanted to hold exhibits and have examples of
Egyptian art and civilization, but primarily, they have
sporting events. I'll have to take you sometime."

"Sporting events? Like croquet?"

"I'll explain later. Right now, we have to decide what to
do next. We have to be prepared for whatever happens before Saturday. If I don't go with you, I have to hope I'll be
able to find you again, or that we can meet here."

"Why do you think that is?"

"What?"

"That here, in the Peabody, we can go back and forth
between my century and yours?"

"I suppose it's because the lobby hasn't changed a lot. Maybe it's a portal of some kind. A link between centuries."

"I think George Peabody would have approved."

"But he didn't build the hotel, did he?"

"No, his friend, R. C. Brinkley did, in 1868. In 1869, when the hotel was about to open, Mr. Brinkley's friend, George Peabody, died, and so he named the hotel for him. If George hadn't died, it would have been called The Brinkley House. It was enormously expensive to build. It cost a fortune. Sixty thousand dollars."

David grinned. Lisette thought it an odd response.

David waved to his brother and the doctor where they were sitting, sipping drinks, near a piano that was playing without anyone sitting at the keys. Joe approached them first.

"Well, what have you decided?"

"I have to go back with her, Joe."

"I expected that. I think you need to prepare a little first."

"We can't take a chance on being apart. My feelings are stronger all the time that we'll not have this separation problem after the twenty-first."

What an interesting idea. "You mean after the riverboat disappears?" That thought had not occurred to Lisette, but it certainly had some merit.

"Exactly. I think that wherever we happen to be at midnight on the twenty-first is where we'll be the rest of our lives. There's no way to know for sure until midnight Saturday."

"What if that proves to be 1885?" Joe's grin had changed to concern.

Lisette slipped her hand into David's. "It won't matter, as long as we're together." What she saw in David's eyes had to be love. "We must go home now and try to convince Aunt Portia I've been in another century and that we shouldn't get on that riverboat—even though we have no plans to leave Memphis."

Bob broke in. "There may be another link, between the *Cajun Star* and the *Memphis Queen III* the night of the commemorative dance, just as there was before. Joe and I will be on the *Queen*, David. I don't know if we'll be able to help you, but we'll be there, just in case." Bob shook David's hand. "Good luck to both of you."

Joe opted for a hearty hug instead of a handshake. "I love you, David. You know that."

Lisette liked Joe immensely. He seemed to genuinely care for his brother and to wish him happiness. She wished for time to know him better. Perhaps, someday, she would.

"I know. I love you too, Joe. Somehow I'll make this work." David turned back to Lisette. "It's time to go."

She addressed Joe and Bob. "Thank you for everything. I do hope to see you both again soon."

She linked her arm with David's. "How do we get back?"

David gave her a quizzical look. "I don't know. What happened just before you got here?"

"I came into the lobby. The lights flickered. When they settled again, I was standing by that window over there. They seem to love ducks here, don't they?"

David smiled and pointed toward the fountain. "Lisette, meet the Peabody ducks. I'm sorry we weren't here to see them come out of the elevator. They live here in the hotel."

Ducks swimming in the fountain! "David, they're charming. What a clever idea." She hurried toward the fountain to get a closer look. A wave of dizziness shimmered through her. The ducks in the fountain disappeared.

"David, what happened to the ducks?" She turned around, searching. The only person in the lobby she recognized was Andrew, coming toward her from where David had stood before.

Chapter Thirteen

"Lisette, stop!" She disappeared.

David sank onto the edge of the fountain and covered his face with his hands, tried to even out his ragged breathing and calm down. If he could just be calm enough, if his heart would stop pounding from the shock of seeing Lisette disappear before his eyes, perhaps he could follow while she was still near the fountain.

Joe and Bob were talking at the same time. How could David concentrate? Somehow, he sensed Lisette had already left the fountain and possibly even the lobby. Had someone been there? Someone she knew? His gut tightened when Westmoreland came to mind. If he hurt her again—

"David, what happened?" Joe sat beside him. David saw a man from the front desk heading toward them. He pulled Joe with him toward the staircase. The man stopped when they left the fountain and went back to the front desk.

"Listen, Joe, I have to follow Lisette—right now. I can't do it unless I'm by myself. Please. I can't lose her now." David hoped Joe would recognize the urgency.

"Got it. What else can I do besides getting out of here and taking Bob with me?"

"I'm going to try to get calm enough to cross over. Get my medical bag so I can take it with me. What I have in that bag might prove invaluable." He left immediately. While waiting, David explained to Bob that he intended to follow Lisette and stay with her through Saturday.

Joe came back, breathing hard. It occurred to David he

might never see Joe again. David embraced him, tried to convey how he felt. "Good-bye, Joe. There aren't words . . ."

David could see him struggling.

"Bob and I will be on the *Queen III* Saturday night. I don't know how we might help, but we'll be there, just in case."

David nodded, his throat tight.

Joe grabbed Bob and they left the hotel. David went back to the fountain and stood for a moment, watching the ducks floating peacefully. He tried to clear his mind of everything but the thought of Lisette and how they belonged together. He pictured the 1885 lobby, ladies in long dresses, men in tall hats with handlebar moustaches. Lisette . . .

He closed his eyes and felt a swimming sensation all around. He opened his eyes and looked for the ducks. They weren't there. Taking a couple of deep breaths, David backed away from the fountain. No one had noticed his appearance. Lisette had to be here somewhere, otherwise David wouldn't have been able to cross over—if his theory was correct.

He recognized her dress. She stood with her back to him, talking to Westmoreland. With as much control as David could muster, he approached them, glaring at Andrew with all the venom he felt racing through him.

"You again," Westmoreland snarled.

Lisette whirled around, then came immediately into David's arms. He thanked God for giving him this chance to make everything right.

"Listen to me, Westmoreland, I don't want you to speak to her or come near her ever again."

She appeared agitated. Was it from crossing over practically under his nose, or could it be something else? "It's Aunt Portia. He came to tell me—"

"What's wrong?"

"Andrew says she's had an accident." Her expression, grim and worried, told David there was more she hadn't revealed. There wasn't time to waste.

"Let's go."

Westmoreland gave Lisette a cruel smirk. "She isn't dead. At least she wasn't when I left."

"I'll deal with you later," David told him and led Lisette out of the hotel. "Do you have a carriage?"

"No. We'll have to hire one." She asked the doorman to get a carriage for them, which he did, giving David a suspicious look. He knew his clothing would have to undergo a complete change, but right now Portia Morgan had to be his first concern. He hoped he had what was needed in his bag. He couldn't exactly order other medications through a local pharmaceutical company.

They reached the Morgan home within twenty minutes. It was a pleasant shock to recognize the house from his hypnotic trance and to know he hadn't invented what he'd seen that night. The terra cotta wedding cake, trimmed in gray, felt like home. They hurried inside. The beauty of the interior took David's breath away. An ornate staircase led to the upper floors. Lisette ran from room to room. Two doors on the left led into the parlor, with the music room behind, while a door to the right of the foyer opened onto what Lisette called the sitting room. It had a roll-top desk and several chairs and bookshelves filled with leather-bound volumes on one wall.

The next door opened into an elaborate dining room with a massive table, eight enormous chairs and, in the center of the table, a gorgeous flower arrangement. On the far wall was a bay window framed with heavy draperies. Numerous portraits decorated the walls. Gold filigree and intricately carved furniture was everywhere. David would have to look at everything later, when they had more time. Right now, their only concern was finding Portia.

"Aunt Portia!" Lisette called again and again.

Still no answer. Lisette rushed upstairs. David followed to a bedroom on the left, at the end of a wide space between the rooms that had chairs and tables and a magnificent Oriental carpet on the floor.

What he saw in that bedroom made him wish he'd smashed the smirk off Westmoreland's face when he'd had the chance.

"Lisette, wait outside for me."

She acted as though she hadn't heard. Seeing her aunt's face, swollen and bruised, her right eye puffed shut, shocked her into silence. Lisette began to cry, then hurried to the bedside.

"What happened? Did you fall? Andrew—" She stiffened. "He did this to you, didn't he?"

Portia moaned, nodding the best she could. David eased Lisette back so he could determine how seriously Portia was injured.

"Please, Lisette, wait outside. I won't be long, I promise. Why don't you make some coffee?"

"She likes tea. I'll make some tea." With tears glistening, she left him to examine the wounds. As he probed gently, feeling to see if any bones had splintered or broken, he spoke softly, hoping to soothe her fears.

"I'm Doctor Stewart, Miss Morgan. We met at the Peabody. Try to relax. Lisette will be back in a minute with some hot tea for you." Portia tried to smile through her pain. "I don't want to hurt you, but I have to see about your bruises. Did he hit you with his fists or with an object?"

"Fists," she murmured.

It was all he could do to stay professional. "All right. Don't try to talk. I'm going to give you an injection for the swelling and pain. You'll feel much better soon, I promise. There's nothing broken as far as I can tell. You're going to be fine."

She clasped his fingers and squeezed, tried to smile again. He could see her relief, knowing he was there to protect them.

Lisette returned with a steaming teapot and three cups on a tray. The fragrance of chamomile filled the room. David motioned her to place the tray on the sideboard, held one finger to his lips and smiled. Portia was already drifting off to sleep. He had to reassure Lisette there was nothing critically wrong. Time would heal the bruises. The memory of fists on her face would no doubt last a lifetime.

Lisette was shaking so badly she almost tripped going down the stairs. When they got to the parlor, she came into David's arms, sobbing, grieving over what had happened.

"Oh, David, how could he do such a thing to her? She's an old woman. She could never hurt him. He threatened to harm her or Papa, but I never believed he could actually do such a thing. I should have known. I should never have left her alone."

David urged her to sit down on a stiff brocade divan. He knew little about antique furniture, but it was obvious every piece in this room would bring a premium in the Memphis he knew. Comfort clearly was not the purpose of this divan, if anyone could call it that. It had only one arm and was barely long enough for the two of them to sit close together.

He rocked Lisette, held her, loved her, knowing she

filled the emptiness he'd lived with five lonely years. He could not bear to lose her the way he'd lost Fran. He would not lose her, damn it! Even if he had to stay in the nineteenth century for the rest of his life.

"What are we going to do about Andrew?" Her eyes brimmed, cheeks wet and flushed red from weeping.

"I'm going to take care of him." There had to be policemen in this city. If they would not do what was necessary to stop this man from terrorizing this family, then David would. "Have you been to the police?"

"Yes. The lieutenant told Andrew to stay away from this house and everyone in it, but Andrew has no more regard for the law than he does for our right to live in peace."

"He's about to learn. He won't come near this house after I explain things to him." David knew he'd made a similar promise before but had not been here to enforce it. Now Andrew Westmoreland would have to get past David if he were to hurt anyone in this family again.

"I would love to believe that's true, David, and I know it will be, as long as you're here. But what if we get separated? What then?"

He had no answer for her. She knew she would be on her own if he weren't here to protect her. He hoped she wouldn't see the worry surrounding him like a shroud.

After several moments, she took a long, deep breath, as though she'd come to a decision. "David, I've been thinking of a way to rid us of Andrew for good. It involves the *Cajun Star.*"

She went across the room toward the most beautiful teakwood chest he'd ever seen. The inlaid mother-of-pearl ornamentation was exquisite. There was no doubt Jacob Morgan's business had made him a millionaire. Every item in this room was proof of it. She caressed it as though it were an adored member of the family.

"The article you showed me stated that the three of us disappeared on the *Star*, isn't that correct?"

"Yes." What could she be thinking?

"Well, then that's exactly what we're going to do."

"Lisette, you can't be serious. Our goal is *not* to board that riverboat, remember?"

"But what if Andrew thought we were boarding and later believed we'd disappeared along with everyone else? He wouldn't follow or bother us ever again, simply because he would assume we were dead—drowned, or blown up or whatever is going to happen to the *Cajun Star*."

"Are you saying we'll board the *Star*—"

"Not necessarily. Only if we have to in order to maintain the charade. We only have to make Andrew believe we were on board for us to be rid of him for good."

"Then what?"

She circled his waist with her arms and lay her head against his chest. She felt so good nestled against him he almost dismissed conversation in favor of carrying her upstairs to bed for hours of lovemaking.

"We could start new lives somewhere else. You, Aunt Portia, my father and I."

This was exactly what David wanted to do, but never expected her to agree. "I didn't think you'd want to leave this house and your life here."

She held him tighter and he guessed it caused her more pain than she admitted.

"If I could be certain Aunt Portia and my father would be safe from Andrew forever, we would gladly go with you into your world, even though it would break my heart to leave our home. Losing you would be worse." He saw love in her eyes and had no doubt they were destined to spend the rest of their lives together.

"If I can't bring you with me into my world, I will gladly stay here, in yours. I won't live without you, ever again."

Her kiss told more than any words. Somehow they would find a way to be together.

Later they went back upstairs to check on Portia. She opened her eyes, smiled, and asked them to come in. She said she felt much better, that the pain wasn't as bad. She was drowsy but glad to see them.

Lisette told her they had a plan for escaping Andrew.

Portia listened while David read the article, which he had in his wallet, then waited while Lisette explained again what she proposed they do. Portia was silent for several moments before responding. David could see both medications he'd given her were taking effect. Now that the pain was subsiding, she would drift into a deep sleep.

"A week ago, I would have pronounced you daft. But after what I've seen and what Lisette has told me, there's very little which would surprise me anymore." She glanced around the bedroom, her eyes settling on various items. The room was filled with ornate furniture of a dozen different styles and cluttered with hundreds of small items, each unique and, he guessed, special in some way to the members of this family.

"I would not leave this house for any reason—save keeping Lisette and Jacob safe from this heathen. If this is what you truly want, child, I shall do everything in my power to help make it so." Her eyelids drooped and she licked her lips as though they were dry.

"It's the injection I gave her," David told Lisette, who seemed alarmed. "Let her sleep. She'll be up and around in the morning. We can discuss it then."

Lisette brought Portia some tea, helped her to sip it, kissed her forehead, tucked the quilts around her chin, then followed David into the hall. They left the door ajar so they'd be able to hear if she called.

"Where is your father?"

Lisette seemed startled, then a bit guilty. "I forgot all about him. Sedonia watches him when Aunt Portia is away. His room is there." She pointed to the room straight across from Portia's bedroom.

He opened the door carefully. Jacob Morgan snored loudly, oblivious to everything going on in the household. David went quietly to his bedside, determined his sleep was natural and breathing regular, then went back to the hall, closing the door behind him. "He's fine. Would Sedonia be downstairs somewhere?"

"I don't know. I haven't learned her schedule yet. Let's look in the kitchen."

There was no one else in the house. Lisette shivered when they had to conclude Andrew had come here, attacked Portia, then left—all while Jacob slept in his room.

A tow-headed boy appeared at the back door.

"Seth, where is your mother?"

He came into the kitchen. It was easy to see he'd been crying. "Ma's hurt. A man came to the house, told her to leave. When she said no, that she had to stay with Mr. Morgan, he hit her in the face, cut her cheek. Her lip's as big as a goose egg. Why did he hit her? He said he's gonna be master of this house 'fore long."

Lisette gathered the frightened boy into a tight embrace. "He is never going to be master of this house, Seth. Take us to your ma. This is Doctor Stewart. He can help her feel better." They went to a small house behind the main house, which Lisette called the servants' quarters. Sedonia lay in bed, moaning, holding a bloody rag against her cheek.

"Lisette, get a clean cloth and some water to wash away the blood." She went to the kitchen. "Now, Sedonia, let me see your face." Luckily, it wasn't serious. A swollen lip and a cut across her left cheekbone. David cleaned the wounds, applied some salve and gave her an injection for swelling, identical to the one he'd given to Portia earlier—and to Lisette two days before. His anger for this miserable waste of skin had changed to cold resolve that Andrew would never lay his hand on Lisette, or any woman ever again.

Sedonia cried, "I'm sorry, I'm so sorry," over and over. Lisette reassured her it wasn't her fault and that David was here to protect them. Glancing at Seth, David wondered if the boy would be the next target. Or would it be Jacob?

Back in the main house, there seemed to be nothing more to do. They were both exhausted.

"Lisette, you should get some sleep. In the morning, after we find some appropriate clothes for me, I'm going to the police station and file charges against Andrew for assault and battery. I'll get an injunction against him—a peace bond—that will land him in jail if he comes within a mile of this house or any person in it. If he shows up, I'll see him in jail before the day is out. He won't harm anyone again. I made that promise to you before. I'm sorry I wasn't able to keep it." The words almost choked David. "This time I will."

Lisette's smile brought tears to his eyes. Such strength in a woman who'd been battered was unusual. What she said next stunned and saddened him.

"I've been treated like a poor house slave for the past eight years, David. These days with you have been the happiest of my life. I shall never forget the joy you have brought me. Tonight I want you to hold me and love me. And this time I want to wake up in your arms."

He couldn't answer; his throat had tightened so much. He lifted and carried her upstairs and lay beside her on the narrow bed.

Chapter Fourteen

With the sun still hours away from streaming through the lacy curtains in her bedroom, Lisette watched David sleep and thought about the first time they'd loved in this bed. She turned over carefully, not wanting to disturb him. His hair, rumpled, falling over his forehead, and his mouth, open slightly, his lips slack, enhanced the beauty she saw in him. The covers had slipped from his bare shoulders. It was cold in the room so she pulled the sheet and quilts around his neck and felt warmth within herself from the gesture. What was it, she wondered, that elicited this response in her? She loved him and wanted to keep him warm and safe within her arms. It involved mothering, though she would never confess to David that she felt motherly toward him. After making love last night, they'd talked and talked into the wee hours of the morning. He had confided in her about losing his wife and daughter, and their tears flowed freely and together, bonding them as nothing else could. He'd come to the conclusion only weeks ago that no matter how much he cared for another woman, no one could ever take Fran's place. At that, Lisette almost burst into tears, fearing he was telling her good-bye.

But then he kissed her so tenderly she knew they were joined somehow, through the river of time, and there was a reason for their finding each other that night on the *Cajun Star*. He'd called the riverboat—the one he said was much smaller than the *Star*—the *Memphis Queen III*. He promised she would someday meet the captain and crew of the *Queen*, just as she had gotten to know the captain of the *Star*.

He told her about Captain Dale Lozier, the owner of the Memphis Queen Riverboat Line, and about its manager, Jim, who helped him search for her after she disappeared. Lisette laughed at that, for it was David who disappeared! Someday she might be able to meet these people, if it proved possible for them to go back to that marvelous time.

If they couldn't go there, if David had to stay with her, here in the year 1885, she wondered how that would change him. Regressing this far into the past, where technology would not catch up for decades to what he knew to be fact, would have an enormous effect on him. How could he cope with living without the miraculous machines he'd told her about? Refrigerators, microwaves, television sets, DVDs. She hadn't been able to absorb everything he'd told her. And air-conditioning. Mercy, how wonderful it would be to stay cool in the summertime, even indoors, and warm in the winter without having to burn coal or wood, tending fireplaces throughout the night.

When the Union army captured Memphis, Morgan Enterprises had been closed and most of their servants had to be dismissed, leaving those chores to the family. Her father had shouted at the Yankees, "If I cannot manufacture arms for the South, then I will manufacture nothing at all!" It was only the dwindling of the Morgan holdings that persuaded him to begin the manufacture of cotton clothing. Not nearly as lucrative as munitions, but income just the same. Jacob would have died of shame if they'd lost the house.

The Morgan home. Practically a member of the family. How could she leave it to an unknown fate—or to Andrew? How could she allow anyone to live here, to eat from the china, sit in her favorite chair, sleep in this very bed, if not a member of the Morgan family or a close friend? The thought made her chest tighten and brought hot tears to her eyes. Yet, that was the plan. If only she could save the house, take it into the future with all of them, then her life would be perfect.

David stirred beside her, uncovering his shoulders again. When she tried to cover him, his eyes fluttered open and he smiled.

She kissed him before he could say a word and he pulled her into his arms. She marveled again at the feel of his bare skin next to hers, her breasts pressed against his chest, her legs twined with his. She felt him against her, rigid with desire. Her cheeks flushed.

"No you don't," he said. "No more blushing just because we're naked in the same bed."

"But David, I'm not used to such intimacies."

"You'll get used to it because it's going to happen every night for the rest of our lives. Touch me."

She looked away, but could not keep from smiling.

"Lisette, you touched me last night. In fact, you—"

"Don't say it aloud, for pity's sake, David. What if someone were to hear?" She couldn't admit to him that saying aloud what they'd done made it somehow less precious. By keeping it unspoken, it became a wondrous secret between them, a secret they could share without words.

He laughed at her modesty. In truth though, she would not take back a single one of the deliciously naughty things they'd done last night.

"Touch me." This time there was a whisper in his voice and fire in his eyes.

She reached for him, her breathing coming faster when his mouth found hers and they made love again, giving real meaning to those words for the first time in her life.

Before long she ceased worrying someone might over-hear and gave herself to him, body and soul. David's mouth on her body left her breathless, craving more, shocked yet delighted by the level of pleasure he brought to her. She had been raised to think such pleasure a sin, but there could be no sin in loving another human being the way she loved David. The way he loved her.

When his tongue caressed that part of her which no one else had ever seen or touched or caressed before—not even her husband—she thought she might drown in pleasure. Then he was inside her, filling her completely. They be-came one person, joined not only body to body, but heart to heart and soul to soul.

Afterward, lying in his arms, she did not want to leave this bed, this room. If only reality could dissolve and leave only love and pleasure behind.

David kissed her, then slid out of bed. Seeing his naked body sent a shiver of embarrassment and excitement through her. Never had she seen a man completely naked before. It was truly startling and quite stimulating. The shivers continued, in places she would never be brazen enough to name. He saw her watching and grinned, pulling on his trousers.

"I hope you like what you see. You're stuck with me."

She giggled at the thought of being truly stuck to David and marveled at the fact she wouldn't mind it in the least.

"Aw, now, don't giggle. Don't you know it isn't polite to laugh at a naked man? My feelings . . ."

"David, come back to bed."

"In a minute. Nature calls. You do have indoor plumb-ing in this house, don't you?"

"Of course. We'd be primitive indeed not to have indoor

plumbing. The water closet is down by the kitchen."

"The kitchen."

He stayed gone a few minutes then returned, shed his clothing, and dived beneath the covers she held up for him. His skin was like ice. She shivered when she enveloped his body with her arms and legs in an attempt to warm him.

"Did you stand naked in the water closet?"

"It's a good thing I didn't. Parts of me might have frozen and fallen off."

"David! What a thing to say." Feeling naughty, she grasped him firmly, verifying his joke wasn't based on fact. His prediction might have come true if he'd stayed gone much longer.

"That feels wonderful. I'll be warm again in no time."

Feeling adventurous, she moved her fingers up and down and in little circles and heard his breathing change, felt his skin warm beneath her fingers. It was softer than any skin she'd ever touched, and loose. Sliding it back and forth seemed to please him immensely. Before long, he turned toward her to reciprocate.

It was another hour before he drifted back to sleep.

When she tried to get out of bed without disturbing him, he awoke. "I told you about my past last night. Now, I want to know more about you. Tell me about your life in New Orleans."

She couldn't help frowning. Thinking about her life with James was something she tried not to do anymore.

"I'm sorry. Maybe I shouldn't ask. You don't have to tell me if you don't want to."

She knew suddenly she wanted to tell him. It was important for David to know her completely before they made a commitment to each other for the rest of their lives, something she hoped with all her heart would happen soon.

"It's all right. I want to tell you. It isn't a happy story, though."

He settled against the pillows and waited for her to begin. She knew exactly where to start.

"My mother died of yellow fever when I was four-years-old. My father was devastated and never talked about her again. I suppose it was too painful for him. Everything I know about my mother and my grandparents I learned from Aunt Portia.

"She gave up her chance to have a husband and children of her own to live with us and care for me, but she's told me a thousand times she wouldn't change her life for anything. Her parents were some of the first people to settle in Memphis, in the 1820s. Memphis was advertised—"

"You mean in the newspaper?"

"Exactly. Judge John Overton published a piece in the *Port Folio* in 1820 to entice people to come to the Bluff City, where Wolf River emptied into the Mississippi—the fourth Chickasaw bluff. My grandparents, Joseph and Cecelia Morgan, came here from Philadelphia looking for new opportunities and the chance to make a difference in this country. Later on, they founded Morgan Enterprises and lived very well indeed. This house was built in 1850. Some of the furniture in the parlor was my grandmother's."

David grinned and snuggled closer. "I don't know a lot about antique furniture—to me, everything in this house is antique—but I know enough to see there are different styles and patterns, indicating different decades and different families."

"Yes, different styles and families. Every piece has its own story. It would take a year to describe the significance of every piece. And new things are added all the time. There are things in the house now I'd never seen until I returned from New Orleans."

"You'll add more things, now that you're back."

"If I get to stay." The possibilities fluttering through her mind like a flock of birds were obviously flying through David's mind as well. He kissed her hand and stroked her fingers affectionately while she told him about the Morgan family.

"There were only two Morgan children. The first was my father, Jacob, then Aunt Portia. They were loved and spoiled and told repeatedly how lucky they were to be growing up along with Memphis. They had to have been the happiest family in the world, according to Aunt Portia, at least. My father learned about Morgan Enterprises from the time he was old enough to tag along behind my grandfather. He took great pride in the family business and helped to accumulate the wealth my grandfather envisioned and worked toward.

"My father met my mother in New Orleans and brought her home to Memphis after their wedding. She was Brianna Lisette Durand of the French aristocracy, classically beautiful, with blond hair and startling blue eyes. My father was so proud of her, he took her everywhere with him, introduced her to all of his most powerful friends, involved her in Morgan Enterprises as much as she would allow. I was born fifteen months after they were married. Aunt Portia said my mother refused any more involvement with the business after that, wanting to devote every minute to me. I wish I could have known her." Lisette stopped talking, lost in thought for a moment.

"What happened to her?"

"Yellow fever—another of those terrible epidemics. Memphis has been plagued with them since the inception of the city. Aunt Portia tended my mother while she was ill,

194

treating her with laudanum. The doctor was so inundated with sick people; he was never able to come to the house. Aunt Portia used cold cloths, ice baths, everything she could think of to get the fever down. My mother was unable to keep the tiniest bit of broth on her stomach. Before too many days passed, she was too weak to fight the fever. She died in my father's arms." The image of that scene always caused Lisette's throat to tighten. David waited patiently, gripping her hand, until she was able to continue.

"He almost grieved himself to death, he loved her so. He refused to even speak her name for years."

"Who cared for you?"

"Aunt Portia never moved out of the house. She felt it was her duty to care for her brother and niece. And that's exactly what she did. Until this very day."

He drew Lisette into his arms. The memories, so bittersweet, seemed even dearer now that she had shared them.

"How did you end up married and in New Orleans?"

"Another gift of the saffron plague. Nine years ago my father also contracted yellow fever. They called it the saffron plague because of the yellow cast to the skin it caused. He didn't die, but in some ways it might have been kinder if he had. His mind was affected by the high fever. He simply wasn't the same person he'd been before."

"In what way?"

"He couldn't concentrate for any length of time. They noticed it first when he would go to his office at Morgan Enterprises. He'd be adding a column of figures and suddenly leave his desk and the building and be gone for an hour."

"Where did he go?"

"We didn't know until one day we were contacted by the

authorities to fetch him. He'd gotten into a brawl at the Peabody Hotel with some gamblers. We learned later he'd lost almost five thousand dollars playing poker."

"That was a lot a money back then."

"It was a terrible loss, even to a business as successful as Morgan Enterprises. Remember, I told you the company closed in 1862 after the Union soldiers took Memphis. By 1866, most of our savings were depleted. Believe me, we felt the loss of that money keenly."

"After that?"

"We kept him home, or tried to at least. He was failing rapidly by that time. He couldn't be trusted to run the business. So, Aunt Portia took over."

"Portia ran the company?"

"Don't be fooled by her, David. She's exceptionally bright and resourceful. Of course, we couldn't let many people know she was running the company. No one would have trusted her to do things as well as my father. But she did. In fact, the company prospered more than it had in years. But then, my father's heart had been in the manufacturing of munitions. Not cotton clothing."

"So Portia ran the business, Jacob stayed at home. What did you do?"

"Helped care for my father, when he'd allow it. We tried to keep him out of the Peabody and away from gamblers, but from time to time he would leave the house after dark without our knowing and reappear in the morning, all his money gone, sometimes bloody from a brawl."

She paused, thinking. She had come to the most painful part of the story. It would be the first time she'd told anyone what she'd endured in New Orleans.

"How did you end up married to Westmoreland?"

"My father was at the Peabody, playing poker with a

'gentleman' from New Orleans who was in Memphis on business."

"James Westmoreland?"

She nodded. "When Papa ran out of money—by then we didn't let him have a lot to carry around—he bet my hand in marriage on two pairs—fours and deuces."

"He used you as a bet in a poker game?" David sat up straighter. She could tell he was as incredulous such a thing could happen as she and Aunt Portia had been when they learned what Jacob had done.

"James was holding three tens. He came to the house with Papa, ordered me to gather my things and be ready to leave Memphis at dawn the next morning."

"He couldn't have expected you to actually marry him!"

"Of course he did. He'd won fairly. There were witnesses to the game. Since I was unmarried, I had no choice but to honor my father's bet. James seemed a decent man at the time. My only hope was to be treated with dignity."

"Were you?"

"At first, perhaps. While we were on the *Cajun Star*, he was civil enough. We had little to say to each other."

"What happened when you reached New Orleans?"

"I barely saw the city. We went straight to his plantation. At first glance the house was beautiful, but signs of neglect became evident. The closer we came, the shabbier it looked. Inside, it was a complete shamble. I learned, eventually, from a servant girl in the kitchen, that James had adored his wife and the house had been well kept and a happy place while she was alive. She succumbed to the fever two years before my arrival. James had not allowed anyone to do repairs or even clean more than the floors after her death. His depression turned him into a bitter man, incapable of loving anyone ever again."

"What about Andrew?"

"While Mrs. Westmoreland was alive—I never learned her given name—she protected Andrew from his father, who never cared a whit for him. After her death, James had no use for Andrew whatsoever. They avoided each other, never speaking. I learned, again from the kitchen servant, Andrew had never done one lick of work around the place, that he spent most of his time in town spending his father's money. Why James allowed it, I never knew. I finally decided it had something to do with Andrew being the only child they'd ever had. Perhaps she'd pleaded with James before she died to take care of the boy. I could only guess. Since I had reddish-brown hair, everyone knew at a glance I was neither French nor Cajun. It made me what they called 'an American,' and therefore an outsider. I asked several times to be allowed to learn French but no one was willing to teach me. It made me even more of an outcast. That, and the fact . . . that we weren't legally married." Lisette's face burned with embarrassment.

"He didn't marry you? I can't believe—"

"He did after several weeks. He told me on the boat that I was his wife, even though we'd not be getting a preacher to say so, but I couldn't bear the thought of living in sin. I pleaded with him constantly to make our marriage legal. Eventually, he gave in. We summoned a priest to come to the house, but James was drunk when he arrived and practically unconscious. The priest suggested that Andrew 'stand in' for his father in the ceremony. Andrew even signed the marriage certificate. At least we were married."

"How did Andrew treat you?"

"With contempt. He'd adored his mother. I was nothing more than another mistress, added to the others in the household."

"He kept mistresses at home?"

"Two of them. James had brought both of them home at once, about a year before. He told me he had no intention of getting rid of them. He showed me his bedroom, told me to be there every night at ten, then stowed my things in a box in the corner. I longed for a room of my own, like Marie and the other girl. I can't remember her name. It was French and hard to pronounce. They spoke nothing but French. It made it easier to tolerate their presence, passing them in the halls every day and sitting at table with them in the evenings."

David got out of bed and pulled on his funny blue pants again—the ones he called jeans. Then he pulled a soft shirt over his head called a T-shirt. When laid flat, it resembled the letter T.

"Where are you going, David?"

"Nowhere. I just can't sit still, thinking about that man bringing you into a home where you were going to be his wife, then making you put up with two mistresses. Why did you stay?"

"What else was I supposed to do? Where could I have gone? James had taken every bit of money I'd brought with me from Memphis, claiming everything I owned was his. Legally, that was so. If I'd tried to leave, he would have beaten me senseless. I wasn't there long before I knew he was capable of such brutality." She closed her eyes, remembering that awful night.

David sat beside her. "You don't have to tell me if you don't want to."

"It's all right. I want you to know. I've never told anyone. It's time."

He nodded and kissed her. She took a deep breath. "When Marie said something he didn't like one evening at dinner, he dragged her out of the room by her hair, ordering us to stay where we were. We listened to her screams while he beat her mercilessly. We were told, when he returned to the table, no one was to touch her or talk to her until tomorrow."

"That sorry bastard! What happened to her?"

"We heard her moaning and crying, hour after hour. A few minutes after midnight, I persuaded the kitchen servants to help me. We tended her bruises and bathed away the blood. James heard and came storming downstairs. I told him we had complied with his orders—it was 'tomorrow.' He didn't say anything, just scowled and went back upstairs. We helped Marie into bed. She didn't come out of her room for more than a week and never raised her voice to James again. After that day, I was treated better by Marie and the other girl and all of the house servants. I suppose the incident had proved to them whose side I was on."

David was so angry, Lisette stopped for a moment. This was a side of him she'd not seen, even when she'd told him about Andrew's striking her. He stared out the front window for a long time, muscles twitching in his jaw, his lips pressed tightly together. When he finally turned to look at her again, she saw anxiety in his eyes.

"Did he ever beat you like that?"

She hurried to reassure him. "Not that severely. I did everything James asked of me, even when it humiliated or embarrassed or shamed me. I never gave him cause." She didn't mention the dozens of times James had cuffed her with the back of his hand, or shoved her down the stairs. David had heard enough. It was in the past, or would be as soon as Andrew was out of her life forever.

David held her. His arms felt so good. She pressed her face to his shoulder.

"Tell me the rest. I want to hear it all."

"Are you sure?"

"Yes. How did James die?"

"Yellow fever. The epidemics were as bad in New Orleans as they were in Memphis. He came down with the fever and lived another three months. I tended him, with help from the others, while Andrew strutted around, thinking he'd become master of the house and lands. He assumed, as I did, that he would inherit everything when his father died."

"But he didn't?"

"It came as the biggest shock of my life. The day James died, the man who had always kept the books for the plantation told me James had made out a will years ago, when his first wife was alive. He never changed it after her death. In the will he left the land and the house to Andrew but all the money to his 'beloved wife.' Even though I was not the wife mentioned in the will, I was still his wife, so I inherited the money."

"How much was there?"

"One hundred and eighty-five thousand dollars. I couldn't believe it. The sad part was that Marie and the other girl got nothing. When James died and they heard about the will, they came to me, ready to spit at my feet. I gave each of them twenty-five thousand dollars. They had endured James's ill temper a year longer than I had. I thought they deserved something for it. They hugged and kissed me, then left. I never saw them again."

"What about Andrew? Why did he follow you to Memphis?"

"Because James left him no money with which to run the plantation. In the will he said something to the effect that Andrew had never worked a day in his life. If he were to have anything at all, he'd have to work the land. He specifically stated in the will that Andrew was not to receive one penny of the money left to his wife."

David smiled for the first time since she'd begun talking. "How did Andrew take it?"

"He ranted about what a horrible bastard his father had been—excuse the language, but that's what he said—smashed a good bit of furniture, which could have been sold for enough to run the place for several years, and stormed out of the house. He stayed gone three days. When he came home . . ." She didn't want to tell David this part. There was no telling what he might do the next time he saw Andrew.

"When he came home?"

"He'd been drinking until he couldn't walk without staggering. He told me he was master of the house and everything in it and that included me. He dragged me upstairs." She couldn't say it. From the look on David's face, she knew she didn't have to. She squeezed her eyes tightly shut for a moment, trying to push the memory away. "I fought him. He beat me until I was almost unconscious. By the time I was fully awake again, it was done and he was gone." She tried to swallow the anguish and humiliation choking her.

David's expression was a mixture of hatred, rage and grief. He held her so tightly she could scarcely breathe.

She heard the tears in his voice. "What happened then?" He took several deep breaths.

"I waited until he left the house, then locked every door. I expected him to come back, but he didn't. He stayed away until two days before I was to leave New Orleans for Memphis. When he came to the house, he wasn't drunk or abusive. He asked for my forgiveness and promised he'd never lay a hand on me again."

"You didn't believe him!"

"Absolutely not. Just as I didn't believe him when he came here the day after he struck me and asked for forgiveness. I know what he wants, David. If I were to marry him, he'd have the money and Morgan Enterprises, and I'd be penniless and dependent upon him for everything."

"Doesn't he know you realize that?"

"I don't know what Andrew thinks about anything. I just know I want him out of my life forever. If that means disappearing with the *Cajun Star*—"

"And leaving this house?"

Her throat tightened with the thought of losing her home. "If that's what it takes, then that's what we'll do. I don't see that we have any choice. Even if you and I manage to cross to your time, I couldn't leave my father and Aunt Portia here to contend with Andrew. And there's hardly a way to bring the house with us, is there?

David's expression changed again. His eyes widened and he gazed across the room for a moment, obviously in deep thought.

"David? What are you thinking?"

"There might be a way to do what you just said."

"Bring the house with us? That's impossible. Isn't it?"

"Maybe not. We don't have much time. Are there some clothes in this house I could wear? What size is your father?"

"He's not quite as tall as you are. He lost a lot of weight after the fever. You might be able to wear some of the clothes we bought for him after he got well. Where are you going?"

"We. I'm not ready to go anywhere without you. Not yet. You mentioned your father's accountant. Did he also have a lawyer?"

"Several. Do you want to talk to them?"

"As soon as possible. They probably don't work on Saturdays."

"They work whenever we need them. For what they've earned working for Morgan Enterprises they wouldn't dare turn me away. What do you want them to do?"

"You'll see. Let's take a look in your father's closet."

Chapter Fifteen

David tried on several of Jacob Morgan's suits and finally chose what Lisette called a double-breasted frock coat with striped wool trousers and a top hat to match. The leather boots with shiny toecaps were a half size too large, but he was able to lace them tightly enough to keep them on his feet. Lisette combed his hair "stylishly," and he was ready to go.

She wore a burgundy wool dress, trimmed with embroidery and brocade, with a matching hat trimmed in feathers and ribbons. She seemed nervous for some reason. David asked why.

"Because I'm supposed to wear black, mourning for an entire year after James's death. But Aunt Portia told me she thought I had mourned long enough."

"I agree. He kept you prisoner and abused you for eight years. You should wear red, for celebration."

"You really think so?"

"There's no need for you to mourn that man another day. It's time you focused your attention on love." He gathered her close. "My love. For you."

She pressed her lips against his, opening her mouth for the kiss. His body tensed with desire for her again. But they had important business to take care of. A crazy idea had been born in his mind. He only hoped he could pull it off.

They took the carriage to the lawyer's office at the corner of Jefferson and Main. Seth drove the horses while Lisette and David sat in the back, holding hands like teenagers. He couldn't see enough. Even at three miles an hour, it all went by too quickly. There were buildings he recognized from the Memphis he knew, only they were new and beautiful. There were buildings which had fallen down or been replaced that he'd never seen before. The churches were magnificent—the Calvary Protestant Episcopal, St. Peter's Catholic, Trinity Lutheran and the first Presbyterian Church—and all existed in Memphis in 2009.

One thing about the city disturbed him. Trash and filth seemed to be everywhere, and greasy, stagnant water. He mentioned this to Lisette.

"The city is much cleaner now than it was."

"Cleaner? It must have been horrible before. It's a wonder people didn't get sick and die from it."

"They did. The noxious fumes rising from the filth caused the yellow fever epidemics. Once we realized that's where the fever was coming from, there was a city-wide effort to clean up the streets, to prevent those fumes from afflicting us again." She saw him smiling. "What did I say that amuses you so?"

"Cleaning up was the right thing to do, but it was done for the wrong reason. Yellow fever doesn't come from noxious fumes."

"It doesn't?"

"No, it comes from a tiny organism, too small to be seen without a microscope. These organisms—people sometimes call them 'bugs,'—are carried by mosquitoes. Mosquitoes breed in filth and in standing water."

"So it was the mosquitoes all the time?"

"By eliminating the mosquitoes' breeding places, you reduced the chances of contracting yellow fever."

She shook her head. "If we'd only known sooner, then Memphis might still be a chartered city."

"Don't worry. Memphis will regain its charter in a few years and will eventually be 'the cleanest city in the country.' Memphis in 2009 is a beautiful city. I can't wait to show it to you."

When they reached the downtown area, he saw the river for the first time. The banks were not the same as the ones he knew. The river was constantly changing but would always retain its majesty. Old Man River never got in a hurry for anyone. It went where it pleased, when it pleased. The faces of people on the banks changed constantly. The river—its soul—would never change.

"David, you look so peaceful. What is it?"

"The Mississippi."

She smiled and kissed his cheek. "It's beautiful. I missed it when I was in New Orleans. So close, yet so far away."

He held her face in his hands, kissed her. "I promise you won't have to leave it if you don't want to, except to travel. You can always come home to the river."

From the way she smiled, he knew it would be difficult for her to leave 1885 because of her home and family. Hopefully, he could make the leaving easier, depending on how cooperative this lawyer proved to be. If only he could contact Joe! He'd know exactly what they needed to do to save the Morgan home and make sure it still existed in 2009.

They arrived at McAllen, Chambers and Rogers just before one o'clock. Louis Rogers, the partner Lisette had always dealt with, was still at lunch, due back any time. While waiting, they talked about twenty-first century Memphis and what she could expect. Computers, education for women—careers for women—all amazed her.

"Remember when I asked you, on the boat, if you worked somewhere?"

That same look of indignation clouded her face. "I couldn't believe you were being so rude."

"I didn't mean to be rude. Women work all the time where I come from."

"Why? Don't they have husbands?"

"Yes, sometimes, but in my century one salary sometimes isn't enough to provide enough money for all the things families want to do, or for the payments they have to make. So, women work to earn extra money, because they enjoy it, because they like contributing something to the place where they live, to make life better for themselves and their families." David could tell this was an entirely new concept for her. He let it soak in a minute.

"Did your wife work?"

"She did before our daughter was born. She was a teacher. Then she decided she'd rather be a full-time mother. When Alyssa was four, we enrolled her in nursery school."

"Children begin school when they're only four-years-old? They're just babies!"

He laughed. "Children grow up more quickly than they used to. In some ways that's good. In other ways, I suppose it's bad. But Alyssa loved going to nursery school. She'd come home every day with paintings she'd done, or something made from clay." His throat constricted until he couldn't talk anymore, his chest tight with the pressure of years of anxiety, so he just smiled.

"Oh, David, I'm so sorry. You miss her terribly, don't you?"

He nodded, still unable to trust his voice.

"Would you like to have more children someday?"

Having another child would make his life complete. There was an emptiness inside which nothing but the laughter and love of a child could fill. He had never let himself think about having another child. He gathered Lisette into his arms and whispered, "Nothing could make me happier. Nothing."

"Then, we shall have as many children as you want, David. Will ten be enough?"

He laughed, relieved to feel the pressure in his chest abate. "Two or three will be plenty."

"A small family, then."

From the way she held him, he knew their "small family" would make her happy, too.

Mr. Rogers returned and invited them into his office.

"I'm so sorry I wasn't here when you came before, Miss Morgan. No, I'm sorry. It's Westmoreland now, isn't it?"

"My husband died. I'm a widow."

"I'm terribly sorry. I hadn't heard." He offered his hand to David. "I'm Louis Rogers."

David shook hands with him. "David Stewart."

"Doctor Stewart wants to speak to you about a most urgent matter. I would appreciate it if you would help in any way possible, just as you always have for the Morgan family." She reached for David's hand. "Doctor Stewart and I are going to be married soon."

"Congratulations! May I be the first to offer best wishes to you both!" He directed his next words to David. "This young lady is her father's pride and joy, Doctor Stewart. I cannot tell you how much he adores her. When she left for New Orleans, it grieved him terribly."

Lisette was visibly moved by this admission. David had no doubts that Jacob, even in his diminished state, regretted his actions. Any father, having committed such an unforgivable sin, would have been devastated. The lawyer rattled on.

"I'm gratified to know that she . . . well, that the two of you . . . that is—"

"Thank you." Lisette sat up straighter, her composure regained. "You have served the Morgan family well for many years. I'm sure that will be the case for years to come."

David could see the statement came with difficulty. Truthfully, neither Lisette nor David could state with any finality what the future would hold. One thing he knew for sure, though. That future would include both of them, either in this century or his own.

Mr. Rogers focused his attentions on David, now that the formalities were out of the way.

"I want to be sure the Morgan home is still here a hundred years from now and the furnishings preserved in excellent condition."

He leaned back in his chair. "What you ask is difficult, Doctor Stewart, but not impossible. Such preservation would cost a great deal of money. The preservation of a home for that length of time—"

Lisette broke in. "How much money?"

"There's no way to say for sure. I would estimate a hundred thousand dollars. The interest that money would accumulate should take care of every eventuality, without having to disturb the principal."

David knew Lisette had at least that much left of her inheritance from Westmoreland. And there had to be money from Morgan Enterprises.

Lisette smiled confidently. "That amount is available now. I had my assets transferred from New Orleans just before I left, coming home to Memphis. How do we handle it?"

He almost did a double take. "You have that much in a

bank account, Miss Morgan?"

"I do. It was my inheritance from the late Mr. Westmoreland. I would gladly invest a hundred thousand dollars to insure the Morgan home's preservation. Can you arrange it for us and manage the account and the maintenance whenever necessary? That is, you and your successors."

Once more, David was astounded at how quickly Lisette had picked up on what he had in mind. But there was one last detail he wanted to include in this arrangement.

"May I speak with Mrs. Westmoreland privately for a moment?"

"Of course. Would either of you care for something to drink?"

"No, thank you." Lisette was clearly anxious for him to leave so David could tell her what was on his mind. After he left the room, she kissed him. He felt her tears on his cheek. "What a wonderful idea. I never would have thought of it."

"I'm glad you approve. There's one more thing we have to do to insure that you'll still own this house in 2009, when we get back."

Her smile faded. "What if we don't?"

"I felt I should ask you before telling Rogers to stipulate in the trust that the ownership of the house be retained by the Morgan family until it passes into ownership of Lisette Stewart, or . . ."

She stared at him for a long moment. "Or your brother, Joe. Is that what you're thinking?"

Incredible. "Exactly. I'll write to Joe, tell him what we've done and that the house will be his in 2009 if we can't get back. He'll make sure the Morgan home is never sold or the contents divided. This law firm will keep the letter, pass it through the firm and deliver it on the date I specify. This will probably be the most unusual request Rogers has ever received. He'll take care of the letter and the house, which will remain just as it is now."

"Forever." Her bottom lip quivered but she surprised him and laughed. "David, I love you so much. You have no idea what this means to me."

"I think I do. In the short time I've been there, I've fallen in love with the Morgan home. If we can save it, we must." He kissed her again. "I love you, Lisette. Just the minute we're settled, I want to marry you."

Mr. Rogers knocked lightly. They invited him in. After hearing what they wanted to do—David didn't mention the letter—he called for his secretary. She took notes for a document to be drawn up immediately.

"We have to sign tomorrow." David had to give him credit. He didn't ask why.

"Certainly. We'll have it ready for your signature by ten o'clock tomorrow morning. If that isn't soon enough—"

"That will be fine." They shook hands. After more congratulations from his secretary and the other lawyers of the firm who came to tell them good-bye, they left the office.

David had never seen Lisette so calm and serene—and happy—as she was at that moment. He longed to share that serenity. The *Cajun Star* sailed tomorrow evening at six o'clock. If he only knew what to expect when they boarded that riverboat.

Back at the Morgan home, Lisette went to check on Jacob and Portia. David settled himself at the desk in the sitting room, intricately carved and immaculately polished, and thought about sitting here again a hundred years from now. Barring natural disasters, the fund Lisette had established would provide more than enough money to keep the property intact and maintained.

He found paper and a quill pen. After one scratch, he went upstairs to his medical bag and found a ballpoint clipped to his prescription pad. Back downstairs, he began to write.

November 20, 1885
Dear Joe,
You will receive this letter on November 21, but 124 years later—if this lawyer does as I ask. The Cajun Star is scheduled to leave Memphis tomorrow at 6:00 p.m. Lisette and Jacob Morgan will pretend to board the boat, as will I. Our plan is to trick Andrew Westmoreland into believing Lisette, her father and I are lost, and will, therefore, pursue us no further. He mistakenly believes he will be able to take over the Morgan home and all of Lisette's assets, including Morgan Enterprises, by virtue of his relationship to Lisette, but we have taken steps today to make sure this doesn't happen. Along with this letter you will receive documents and instructions for the administration of a trust fund set up today to insure the protection of the Morgan home. I hope and pray nothing has happened to the house between now and the time you receive this letter. If necessary, I'll stay with her and we'll care for the house as long as we live. There are many variables, especially concerning Portia and Jacob Morgan. If necessary, I'll write additional letters, to be delivered to you later on, so you'll know what happened and what to expect.

There's no way to tell you, Joe, how much I love you. I could never have asked for a better brother or a closer friend. Remember all the good times we shared and know that I always envied your adventurous spirit and your foolhardy craziness. You did everything I always wanted to do. Thanks for a million laughs and enough scares to last a lifetime.

I have to tell you this, just so you'll know that all I've done is worth the price I may ultimately be required to pay. Lisette is everything to me. I can't live without her. Please understand, if I can't come back, I'm happy here with her and I regret nothing. Tell Bob how much I appreciate his help.

I guess that's about it. Tell Shawna and Marilu I love them, too. Try to explain why I didn't have time to tell them good-bye in person.

One more thing. Check the history books and the genealogy charts for Stewarts born after 1885 in Memphis, Tennessee. I think you know what those children will mean to me.

Always,
David

David read through the letter, decided he'd said all there was to say, folded the fragile onionskin paper carefully, then found an envelope in the second drawer. He sealed the flap, addressed it to Joseph Ingram Stewart and slid it into the lapel pocket of Jacob Morgan's suit. With a sigh, he went upstairs to find Lisette.

She was in Portia's room, sitting beside the bed in an ornate chair that David suspected would be as uncomfortable as that funny little divan in the parlor. If they were to live in this house, either now or a hundred years from now, at least one comfortable chair would have to be added. Portia was saying something about her parents and the early days of Memphis.

"Come in, David." Lisette pointed to another chair across the room and motioned for him to bring it close to the bed. "I told Aunt Portia we're going to be married, and she was about to tell me something that happened between her parents when she was a little girl."

David pulled up the chair, sat down, surprised the chair wasn't nearly as stiff as he'd expected, and listened with interest. For a few moments, at least, the difficulties facing them could be ignored in favor of sweet memories.

Portia's voice was stronger now, and her bruises were fading. He thought about giving her another injection, then decided to save the medications for emergencies. The thought of depleting them made him slightly panicky.

Portia pointed to a rock on the crocheted doily covering the bedside table. "Hand me that rock, child." Holding it, she reached for Lisette's hand, a gesture he suspected was a tradition from Lisette's childhood.

"You listen carefully, David. This story is for you, too. My father adored my mother, but he had a rather gruff way about him at times. When I was four or five-years-old, and Jacob a year older, Mama fixed something for supper she'd never fixed before. I can't remember what it was. When Papa sat down and tasted it, he said, "I'd sooner eat rocks!" and stormed away from the table.

"Jacob and I sat like statues in our chairs, terrified to say a word. Mama didn't say anything, either. The three of us ate supper in silence. We were scared spitless. We ate every bite on our plates, told Mama it was real good, and ran straight to our rooms.

"The next evening, just before supper, Jacob and I hurried to the table. We couldn't wait to see what would happen. Papa came to the table as though nothing had happened. Mama came from the kitchen with the huge cooking pot, the one she used to cook beef stew. The smells coming from that pot made my mouth water. "She set the pot in front of Papa. He said grace and opened the lid. The steam smelled heavenly."

"What did Grandpapa do then, Aunt Portia?"

She smiled, making them wait a moment longer. "He picked up the big ladle, then stirred through the pot. The pleased expression on his face changed to a frown. When he raised the ladle, we strained to see what was there. The gravy-coated lump on the ladle was bigger than any meatball Mama had ever made, perfectly smooth and about the size of Mama's pincushion. When Papa put it into a bowl, it made the oddest clinking sound, not like anything cooked! Papa went right on ladling until we all had a bowl with three or four lumps, covered with thick brown gravy.

"I spooned one of the round objects into my mouth." Portia nodded. "In the most delicious brown gravy my mother ever made, before or after that day—rocks."

Lisette shook with laughter—and so did David.

"I knew it!" he said, wiping his eyes. "What happened then?"

"No one said a word. Mama smiled, passed around bowls of mashed potatoes and snapped beans, a plate of hot, flaky biscuits, then spooned gravy from the rock stew onto her potatoes.

"Jacob and I did the same. Everything was delicious, and we even licked the gravy off the rocks. Papa did, too, without a word. After supper was over, he got up from the table, said, 'Cecelia, that was the best gravy you've ever made,' and went to the parlor for his after-dinner cigar.

"Jacob and I helped clear the table. Mama washed and dried the rocks carefully, then put them away in a cabinet, as though they were part of the china dishes. He never said another bad word about Mama's cooking."

They all laughed together and David made a promise to

himself to bring this lady with them into the twenty-first century if he possibly could. Joe would love her. David already loved her. And he knew without asking, Lisette would never leave Aunt Portia alone, at Andrew's mercy. If they were to be happy and secure, in whatever future awaited, it had to be a future without Andrew Westmoreland. The idea of their running away and leaving Andrew here, while the four of them started new lives elsewhere, grated on David, even with the Morgan house protected. There had to be another way.

Lisette touched his arm. "David? What are you so deep in thought about?"

"Nothing. Just thinking about eating rocks. Will you ever serve rocks for dinner?"

She grinned mischievously. "Not if you don't ask for them."

"Believe me, I won't."

Portia's eyes drooped.

"We need to let Aunt Portia sleep."

Lisette gave him the strangest look.

"Did I say something wrong?"

"No, not at all. I think she'll be pleased to have you call her Aunt Portia. After all, she'll soon be your aunt, too."

That idea pleased him. He replaced the chair and noticed for the first time its legs were arranged so it fit exactly in the corner, facing into the room.

"What an odd chair. What's it called?"

Lisette smiled. "It's a corner chair."

He felt foolish. "A perfect name for it. I don't dare ask why it's made that way."

"When soldiers were on duty, they often had to sit in the corner. Being able to face directly out from the corner made their sentry duty easier."

Every piece had a story. It could take years for him to hear them all.

In Lisette's bedroom, they undressed and got into bed. She came into his arms, resting her head on his chest.

"Tomorrow is the day," she said softly.

"Yes. November twenty-first. 'The Night the *Cajun Star* Vanished.' "

They lay for a long time before she whispered, "Love me, David. This could be the last time."

Chapter Sixteen

The next morning David asked Lisette to list every piece of furniture and décor in the house—a gargantuan task, considering the Victorian decor. Aunt Portia insisted on helping her, stating she'd felt much worse during the yellow fever epidemic that afflicted Jacob. David said this inventory was essential for the house to be preserved exactly as it was, without anything "borrowed" or stolen during the next hundred years. Lisette used the odd pen he'd left on her bedside table the night he'd appeared in her room. He called it a ballpoint, named for the tiny ball on the end of the pen point which turned, pulling ink from the barrel of the pen downward so the ink would flow continuously onto the paper. It was quite ingenious.

David was a treasure house of information about inventions that were commonplace in his Memphis, yet completely unknown in theirs. Movies, for instance. She could not imagine being able to capture on a screen the actions of people in a room. Yet David said it was done all the time, with video cameras and DVDs. Or was it DDVs? She couldn't remember. It excited her and made her eager to visit his Memphis. Seeing such wonderful inventions, riding in cars and vans and airplanes—flying machines!—would be as fascinating as traveling across the country as she'd always longed to do.

David said it was possible to see the entire world without ever leaving the parlor, with an invention called the television. He talked about satellites, machines orbiting the earth—a mind-boggling notion that left her astonished every time she thought about it—bouncing electrical signals from one place on the earth back to another place in less time than it took to blink. They had to be powerful, extraordinary things.

Writing with the ballpoint pen was an adventure. What other marvelous things would she see and do if they actually made it to his world?

She continued writing, glancing at Aunt Portia from time to time. What would Aunt Portia think of such inventions? What of her father? As addled as he was now, would he even know he'd been transported into the future more than a hundred years? Undoubtedly not, so it wouldn't be traumatic for him to do such an unbelievable thing. Aunt Portia would be as enthralled as Lisette to experience such an adventure, though. As a child she'd asked questions by the thousands but Aunt Portia never grew impatient. "How can you learn if you don't ask questions?" she would say, and "The only stupid question is the one you don't ask."

David was equally eager to answer a thousand questions about the Memphis where he lived and prone to ask the same number of questions about this Memphis. How could the two cities be so different, yet in other ways so much alike? It would seem things change while people stay much the same. No matter what age a person lived in, or what sort of machines and progress might be available, human nature remained constant. People would always want the same things: food, shelter, warmth when it was cold, to be cool when it was hot, and the freedom to be happy. It was their freedom Andrew had threatened this past week. Yet, for an entire day they hadn't heard from him at all. Rather than feeling more at ease because of his absence, Lisette felt apprehensive, knowing he'd never give up so quickly. He had to be planning something.

"The gilt curio cabinet, the Medallion table, the boulle table, and the Canova statue, 'The Kiss.' " Aunt Portia glanced around the parlor. "That seems to be everything."

"We have to give this list to Mr. Rogers today when we sign the papers. There may be time later on to list anything else you think of."

Aunt Portia motioned for Lisette to sit beside her on the settee. "Child, does this doctor of yours know what it would mean to me for this house to be loved and cared for through the next century and beyond?"

Lisette kissed her cheek, which was almost back to normal. David's medicines were miraculous. "I'm sure he does. Did you hear him call you Aunt Portia last night?"

She nodded. "It made my heart flutter to hear it. Are you going to marry him?"

"Yes. I know it seems terribly sudden."

"True love is always sudden, child. When Jacob saw your mother for the first time, her golden hair gleaming in the New Orleans sun, he whispered, 'Portia, do you see that woman? I'm going to marry her.' He did, too. When he gained an introduction, Brianna blushed like a rose. I knew then he was right. They were meant to be together. Just as you and Doctor Stewart are meant to be together."

"Don't you think you could call him David?"

"You don't think he'd mind?"

"I think he'd love it."

"I would, indeed." David came into the parlor. His smile enhanced his handsome features, which, to Lisette, were the most alluring, kindest features she had ever known.

She went to meet him. He kissed her, right there in front of Aunt Portia, but Lisette didn't mind. She could tell from Aunt Portia's smile she approved.

"Please, Miss Morgan, call me David."

"Only if you'll call me Aunt Portia."

He went to where she sat and looked carefully at her face. "You look as if you feel better this morning. I'm surprised to see you up and around so soon."

"I have a wonderful doctor."

"How is the inventory coming? Are you going to be able to finish by noon?"

"We just did. Aunt Portia has been helping me. I couldn't have done it without her. We started upstairs, where there were fewer pieces and left the parlor until last. Listing every last piece would take days, I'm afraid."

"I wish I'd brought my video camera. We could take pictures of everything. Best inventory you can make when time is short."

"A camera? Do you own one, David?"

"As a matter of fact, I own several. I have a thirty-five millimeter camera, a video camera, and a digital camera that transfers pictures into a computer or a printer." She frowned. "I'll explain later. Someday, you'll be using every device I've told you about. You too, Aunt Portia."

She smiled but didn't seem overly excited. "What's wrong? Are you feeling ill again?" Her face appeared to be flushed, as though she might have a fever.

"No, child. I'm fine. I just wish we could live here in this house, as we have for more than thirty years and not have to worry about riverboats or heathens or inventories."

David sat next to her. "I have an idea how we may be able to grant your wish." He looked at Lisette before he spoke again. She had no idea what he was about to say.

"I haven't discussed this with Lisette. It occurred to me late last night. What if the four of us were to leave Memphis before the riverboat leaves here tonight? We've insured the safety of the house. Andrew won't be able to touch it after we're gone. We'll go to the Peabody, hold hands, think about Memphis in 2009, and leave. Your house will be waiting for you, only more than a hundred years older. There would be some differences, I'm sure, but if all goes well, you'll still be home."

A rush of apprehension overwhelmed Lisette. "David, that would solve practically everything. Why does the idea frighten me?"

"Because leaving the place where you grew up, where you've lived practically all your life is always traumatic and difficult. The Memphis where I live is so different, it might as well be another city altogether. Another world. I think you'll love it, though, once you've had a chance to get to know it."

"I know you're right." She still felt anxious, but didn't voice it. "Why haven't you mentioned this before?"

"Because I felt there was going to be a reason why we were compelled to board that riverboat tonight. As far as I can determine, that reason simply doesn't exist."

"Won't it change history if we don't disappear with the boat?"

"Not if we disappear into 2009 instead."

What he said made sense. Still, it frightened her to think they might be challenging time itself. David went on, trying to convince them.

"Wouldn't it be wonderful, Aunt Portia, to live in a beautiful city where yellow fever is a thing of the past, and where there are medicines to cure diseases that kill people now?" he said, with pride in his voice.

Aunt Portia gasped. "You mean you actually have medicines to cure yellow fever?"

"Not only to cure it, to prevent it with a vaccine that

makes a person immune for about ten years. Where I live, no one has to live in fear of cholera or yellow fever, smallpox, pneumonia or diphtheria."

Tears glistened in Aunt Portia's eyes. "A miracle. It sounds like heaven."

David laughed. "Well, not exactly heaven, but I think you'll enjoy living there. I'm not sure how we'll all cross into 2009 at the Peabody but we've already accomplished the impossible."

"After what we've seen in the last week," Lisette said softly, "I think I could believe almost anything."

She could tell Aunt Portia was tired. The inventory and such challenging ideas were taking their toll on her. "Let me help you upstairs. David and I will take the list to Mr. Rogers so he can put it with the trust. I'll get Sedonia to come into the house, in case you need anything. She's already back to cooking and cleaning. David's medicines have worked a miracle on her, just as they did with you."

"Yes, a miracle." She gave David a long look. "We only need one or two more, isn't that right?"

His answer was a hopeful smile. They helped Aunt Portia upstairs and back to bed. Lisette worried about her. The beating she'd taken from Andrew had depleted her energies severely.

Back in the hall, Lisette whispered to David, "Is she really going to be all right?"

"In time." He rummaged in his pockets, looking for something, then frowned when he didn't find it.

"What's wrong? What are you looking for?"

"I've lost the newspaper article—the one about the *Star*."

"It's probably in Aunt Portia's room. You read it to her last night."

He smiled. "You're right, I'm sure. Last night we were still on the list. I have no idea what might happen if we don't board the *Cajun Star* at six o'clock this evening. To keep history as close to right as possible, I think we should cross over at the Peabody when the boat sails."

"If only we could warn the captain."

"I'm not ready to change history that much. There's no telling what the consequences might be."

She didn't say anything for a moment. David asked what was on her mind.

"I've been thinking all morning about Andrew and the fact we haven't heard from him. I can't help but think he's up to no good. Yet there's no legal way he can get to our money, the business, the house or any of it. Why doesn't he go back to his plantation in New Orleans and try to make a success of it?"

"Because that would be the logical and honorable thing to do. He doesn't strike me as being particularly honorable about anything he does."

"So, what is he planning? Where is he? I gave him enough money for two nights in a hotel, but that's all. He doesn't have enough money for return passage to New Orleans. I'd gladly pay his way, though." A thought struck her. "David, I think I've got it!"

"What?"

"I'll offer to pay Andrew's passage to New Orleans on the *Cajun Star*. I'll offer him enough money to run the plantation for a couple of months. There won't be any need for all of us to go if we can just get Andrew on that boat." The thought of luring Andrew to his death troubled her, but she hadn't been able to come up with another plan. If Andrew's death meant freedom for her father and Aunt Portia, then she could learn to live with what she'd done.

He didn't answer.

"What's wrong? Don't you want to be rid of Andrew for good?"

"Yes, but is this the way? Sending him off to an unknown fate? If the boilers are going to explode on the *Cajun Star*, I don't know if I could wish such a death on anyone—even a bastard like Andrew. I read about the *Sultana*."

She had also heard about the explosion of the *Sultana* and shuddered, thinking about the terrible destruction of boat and passengers, the disastrous result of putting too many people on one vessel. She pictured Andrew on a boat destined to such a fiery death and squeezed her eyes tightly shut at the vision.

"Tell me, David, what else we can do."

"I don't know, but let's keep searching for an alternative plan. When I became a doctor, I swore to save human life, no matter whose life it happened to be." He looked away, struggling.

She knew then what she'd have to do if they were unable to cross to David's century. But she would do it—not David. She could not ask him to break his oath as a doctor. If it came to that, sending Andrew to his death would be her doing and hers alone.

"It's almost eleven o'clock. We should go to Mr. Rogers's office to sign the papers and deliver the inventory."

David seemed agitated, obviously concerned about the short time remaining before the *Cajun Star* departed Memphis this evening and about her suggestion. She wouldn't mention it to him again.

Lisette told Seth to hitch the horses to the carriage. Aunt Portia was sleeping peacefully while Jacob ate some sort of mush Sedonia had cooked for him, muttering between bites how "starved" he was. Lisette almost wished Sedonia and

Seth could come with them, but David had already thought about them. They would instruct Mr. Rogers, in the event Jacob, Aunt Portia and Lisette were no longer available to occupy the house, that Sedonia and Seth would be hired as caretakers and allowed to live in the Morgan home for the rest of their lives with a stipend from the trust. This solution made perfect sense and satisfied Lisette's desire to provide for them after they'd helped the Morgan family for so many years.

At the lawyer's office, Mr. Rogers greeted them with a broad smile and all the papers he'd promised to have ready. It took only a few minutes to sign everything. David asked him to add a page concerning Sedonia and Seth. He had his secretary prepare the extra page, and it was also signed. The inventory was added to the bundle.

"I have one other request," David told him and pulled an envelope from his pocket. "I'd like for you to arrange to deliver this letter to my brother, Joe Stewart."

"Of course, Doctor Stewart." He glanced at the address on the envelope, then frowned. "I'm not familiar with this street, or this town. Is it near Memphis?"

Lisette didn't understand what David was doing. How was it possible to send a letter to Joe? "David, when is the letter to be delivered?"

"On November 21, 2009."

Mr. Rogers's jaw dropped with surprise. "I'm sorry, Doctor Stewart, but did I hear you correctly? 2009? Your brother?"

"Yes, my older brother. You'll hold the letter in this office as long as the firm does business. If the firm closes, you'll arrange for another firm to hold the letter until November 21, 2009. On that day, at noon, the letter will be delivered to Joe Stewart, at that address in Germantown, a suburb of Memphis. I promise you; he'll be there to receive it."

To his credit, Mr. Rogers responded professionally.

"Certainly, Doctor Stewart. Is there anything else we can do for you today?"

David was grinning from ear to ear. "I think that's every-thing. It's been a pleasure doing business with you."

"And with you, Sir. I have to tell you, we haven't had a client with such entertaining requests in quite some time. I wish I could be the one to deliver this letter to your brother." He paused, pressing his lips together for a mo-ment. "Perhaps, Sir, if you wouldn't mind, that is, you and I might discuss this further over a drink at the Peabody some evening. I'd like to hear more about your brother and where he lives."

David laughed and shook his hand. "I'd like that. Maybe we can do it sometime."

Mr. Rogers looked at Lisette. "Will there be anything else, Mrs. Westmoreland?"

"That's all for today, I believe. Will you be available later in the day, in case Doctor Stewart thinks of something else he needs?"

"Absolutely. Don't hesitate to call on me. Good day to you both and congratulations again."

On the way home, David bought Lisette an ice cream and told her about a place in his time with more than two dozen flavors, all of which were available for tasting before having to make a selection. She thought he must be joking, but taken along with all the other fantastic things he'd told her, she decided to reserve judgment until she could see— and taste—for herself.

Back in the carriage, David asked Seth if he would take them on a short tour of the downtown area.

David tried to absorb every sight and sound possible. He believed they were actually going to leave Memphis this evening and return to the time he called "home." For all their sakes, and his happiness, she hoped he was right.

By the time they got back to the house, it was almost two o'clock. Only four hours until the *Cajun Star* would sail. Inside, the first thing she noticed was her mother's angel, lying on the floor, broken into more than a dozen pieces. Sadly, she knelt to gather the remnants of the porcelain beauty. "Sedonia? What happened here?"

There was no answer. She ran upstairs, David right behind her, to Aunt Portia's room. She wasn't there. David looked into her father's bedroom.

"He isn't here either."

"Where could they be? Where is Sedonia?"

Lisette could hear Seth downstairs, calling his mother with no answer. David and Lisette went through the kitchen, outside to the servant's quarters. No one. Even Seth seemed to have disappeared.

"David, where is everyone? We had the carriage. They couldn't have gone somewhere without us."

Seth came to the back door of the main house. "A man is here to see you, Ma'am. He says he knows where everybody is."

Lisette hurried past Seth to the foyer. Standing there, with a wicked smirk on his face, was Andrew.

"Where are they? What happened? Did my father have another seizure?"

"He didn't have a seizure, but Auntie Portia almost did. They're alive and well, along with that ridiculous woman. What was her name?"

"Sedonia," Lisette murmured, barely able to speak at all.

"Yes, Sedonia. They shall stay alive and well as long as you do what I tell you."

David was to the point of explosion. She put one hand on his arm, terrified. "Let's sit down and talk about this like sensible adults," she said carefully. "David, let's hear what Andrew has to say."

"I'm not about to sit down and discuss anything with this miserable excuse for a man."

"David, please—"

"Westmoreland, you will tell me, this instant, where Jacob and Portia Morgan are, and then you will disappear from this city forever. Where are they?"

The cold glint of hatred in Andrew's eyes pierced Lisette's heart like a dagger. He smiled, knowing he had the upper hand.

"I think not. Actually, it's probably a good thing you're a doctor. The Morgans are going to need your expert care. If you ever see them again."

"You sorry bastard!" David lunged at Andrew and seized him by the throat. Andrew grabbed David's arms, trying to dislodge him, but David's anger made him too strong to overpower.

"David, no! We can't accomplish anything this way. David!" She grabbed his wrists and tried to make him see reason. They had to listen to Andrew's demands. Otherwise, she might never see her father and Aunt Portia again. "Please, David, let's listen to what he has to say!"

David stopped his attack, breathing heavily, his face brilliant red. Lisette thought for a moment he might be having a seizure, but he finally controlled his rage. She whispered frantically. "He has them, David. We have to listen. We have to."

Andrew rubbed his neck, coughing and choking. If he

left now, they might never see Aunt Portia or Jacob alive again.

David finally took a deep breath and expelled it slowly. "All right. We'll listen to what the bastard has to say. But hear this first, Westmoreland. If you harm either of those people, I'll see you rot in jail for the rest of your life."

Andrew's face paled a little, but he continued to smile in that cold, calculated way.

"We'll see who rots. And where." He stomped off into the parlor and sat down in the Turkish chair. David and Lisette sat together on the settee.

"All right, Andrew, we're listening. Where are my father and Aunt Portia?"

"Somewhere safe, with two friends of mine and Sedonia to see to their needs, of course. But, the question is not where they are now, but where they'll be tonight."

"Where?" She could hardly speak; her breath came so shallow. She continued to hold David's hand tightly, hoping he wouldn't lose control again.

"On board the *Cajun Star*, of course, bound for New Orleans."

She couldn't believe it. "You're going to put them on the riverboat? Why?"

"I'm surprised you haven't already guessed. But then, you thought you were the only ones privy to the fate of the poor old *Star*." He reached into a pocket of his coat and pulled out a piece of paper. It took only a few seconds for Lisette to recognize it. The newspaper article. She felt all the color drain from her face. The expression on David's face startled her. There was something in his eyes she didn't recognize.

David stretched his legs and leaned back. "So what? You found a novelty newspaper I bought from a street vendor.

And you believed it? You surprise me, Andrew. I never thought you were the type to believe such nonsense."

Andrew clapped his hands slowly and sharply. "Bravo, Doctor Stewart, for such a grand performance. You forget, I witnessed one of your little disappearing acts in the Peabody Hotel."

David's expression changed again. Lisette could tell he knew he'd soon have to confess the truth.

"Andrew, none of this makes any sense to me," she said, trying to keep her voice steady. "Tell me how this involves my aunt and my father. You know I'll do anything to get them back, safe and sound. What is it you want?"

Andrew's eyes narrowed, as dark as pitch. "That's quite simple, my dear. Or, should I say, my dear *wife?*"

She could not have grown colder more quickly if someone had dropped her into the icy waters of the Mississippi. "That is one thing I will never be."

"But you already are. You married me eight years ago in New Orleans. Surely you haven't forgotten. It was such a touching little ceremony."

She hurried to correct this vile lie. "David, you know it isn't true. I told you about Andrew standing in for his father at our wedding."

Andrew leaned back, thrusting his legs forward and crossing them at the ankles. His pose struck fear in her because it demonstrated complete confidence. "Who stood beside you at the altar? Who promised to love and cherish you, until death should part us? And who, dearest Lisette kissed your lips when the priest pronounced us husband and wife?"

She couldn't answer. Her throat constricted with anxiety and fear, making speech almost impossible.

"And who signed the marriage certificate—with his own

name, which happened to be the same as his father's?" Andrew pulled another piece of paper from his pocket and slung it into David's lap. "Read that, Doctor, and know the truth. It states quite clearly that James Andrew Westmoreland—that's me—married Brianna Lisette Morgan, the lovely lady sitting beside you, on the twenty-fifth day of July, 1877, in New Orleans, Louisiana, Father Pardieu, presiding, witnessed by Marie LeBlanc and Genevieve Lamont."

Chapter Seventeen

David focused on Westmoreland. "This isn't going to work. We'll fight you. The priest will testify to the truth."

"Fight all you want. That old priest is dead. Died just after the ceremony, God rest his soul. While you're trying to prove me wrong, Lisa will have to live without dear Papa and precious Aunt Portia. By the time you concede defeat, I won't be responsible for the shape they'll be in. You will. Poor Jacob. We had to drag him to the carriage. Auntie Portia could hardly walk."

Lisette closed her eyes. David knew this was killing her.

"Listen to me carefully." Andrew took his time, enjoying the torture he was inflicting. "You're going to board the *Cajun Star* this afternoon at half past five. It's leaving the dock precisely at six o'clock, according to the chief purser, and won't wait for anyone. If you try to leave the boat before it sails, I promise you'll not see Jacob or Portia Morgan again."

It was all David could do not to slam his fist into that smug expression. He reached for Lisette's hand. Her fingers were curled into a tight fist. He managed to loosen them enough to hold her hand. He had to shake Andrew's confidence.

"Just because we get on that riverboat doesn't mean you're going to be able to make this scheme work."

"Oh, I think you're wrong." He shook the article at David. "This says you're wrong."

"That says nothing. We don't have to stay on that boat after it leaves Memphis."

"How are you going to get off? Hand everyone a life board and hope they can hold on long enough in that cold water to be rescued? I doubt Jacob will be up to this little plan. Dear Aunt Portia certainly won't. But I suppose you can try."

David looked at Lisette. "No lifeboats?"

She seemed puzzled, shook her head. Clearly, there weren't lifeboats on a riverboat. David had assumed every boat carried lifeboats. A twenty-first century assumption. The bastard was right. There was no way Jacob or Portia could survive clutching a life *board*, immersed in the river.

"All right," David told him. "We'll be on the boat at five thirty. How do we know you'll bring Jacob and Portia Morgan to the boat and that they'll be in good health and unharmed?"

"You don't. But you have no choice in the matter. You'll have to trust me." He laughed raucously, crumpled the article in his fist, then slung it into the fireplace where it burst into flames, curled and blackened.

David felt Lisette trembling. He had to get Andrew out of this house so they could devise some sort of plan to counter his offensive against them. If David could find Jacob and Portia before five thirty and release them, he'd have Andrew arrested for kidnapping and extortion.

"I want to see Jacob and Portia. Let me examine them."

At first he shook his head and laughed, as though David were crazy to expect such privilege, but then he sobered and contemplated. David held his breath. Could he actually be considering it?

"Please, Andrew. Let David see them. You don't want to be responsible for their deaths. You're a liar, a cheat, and a man who abuses women, but surely you aren't a murderer as well."

Silently, David praised her courage.

Lisette took a shuddering breath.

Andrew's lip curled in a cruel smile. "All right. I'll let the good doctor take at look at them. But only him. You, dearest Lisa, are not to leave this house for any reason. If you do, I'll know, and you'll never see them again."

"I promise. Thank you, Andrew."

"Get my medical bag. Upstairs."

She ran to fetch the bag and brought it back to the parlor in less than a minute.

David kissed her, trying not to let her see his doubt. "I'll be back soon. Don't worry. I'll take care of them." She nodded, trembling like a leaf in the wind. David went to the front door. "Let's go, Westmoreland."

"Of course. You're anxious, I can see. Remember, Lisa, not one step outside this house." He pointed across the street. A heavy-set man stood there, watching the front door.

"Stay here, Lisette. Lock the doors." David strode down the walk to Westmoreland's carriage, praying the Morgans weren't already dead or injured beyond recovery. If Andrew actually took David to see them, he'd be the most astonished person in Memphis. He had to be on the alert every moment. Maybe Andrew would slip up and tell him where they were before it was too late to help them.

The driver took them to the Peabody Hotel.

It was the last place in Memphis David needed to be, but if Jacob and Portia were there he would have to chance it, and stay well away from the fountain. He glanced at his watch: 2:45. Andrew had been smart to wait so late to pull this stunt. David only hoped he'd have a bit of luck in finding the Morgans quickly so he could get them out and away, back home with Lisette. He had no idea how he was going to accomplish such a feat.

Inside, he followed Andrew around the edge of the lobby toward the staircase, being careful not to step on even the perimeters of the carpeting in the fountain area. He felt nothing strange, no tingling sensations, no light-headedness, nothing to indicate he was about to be zapped back into 2009 without warning. He couldn't remember feeling any of these things before but had to be alert to anything out of the ordinary.

Andrew stopped at the staircase with a blank expression on his face, as though thoroughly bored. David couldn't believe he could be so nonchalant after kidnapping two people. He left the staircase and wandered over by the fountain. David glanced around, expecting to see men closing in. But criminals were seldom as clever or as organized as they were in movies or novels. This was Andrew. From what David had learned about Andrew, he was probably smart enough to dream up a scheme like this but more than likely too lazy to attend to details. David would have to outsmart him at his own game.

Andrew left the fountain, still grinning, walking back toward the staircase.

"Quit stalling. Are they upstairs?"

"Did you think I had the resources to stash them here, at the most expensive hotel in Memphis? I'm surprised at you, Doctor. We're here because it's time for you to go back where you came from."

David sensed movement, hesitated a fraction of a second too long. Two men grabbed him from behind. One of them clubbed him in the head. David struggled through the pain to stay conscious. He managed to see enough to gain his bearings. They were dragging him toward the fountain.

He struggled harder, yelling for someone in the lobby to

help. The hoodlums twisted his arms behind him so tightly he couldn't get any leverage or traction toward regaining his feet. Not one person stepped forward to help.

Andrew was laughing, pointing at the fountain, shouting orders to the men who held David.

If only he could break free, but these men were huge. He knew from their grip on his arms he could never overpower them. His knees were against the marble.

"Back you go, Doctor!" Andrew's fist caught David's jaw, then he pushed hard against David's chest.

David landed with a splash in the cold water. Andrew's laughter echoed through the lobby. People seemed to be everywhere, rushing to see what was happening, yet no one was willing to get involved. Gamblers, hotel guests, personnel from the front desk, ran toward him.

A uniformed man from the front desk hauled David up from where he sat, completely drenched. One of the Peabody ducks pecked at his heels while another flapped crazily toward the bar, panicked. Two girls in Daisy Dukes and tank tops laughed and pointed.

It took a lot of talking to convince the manager he wasn't jumping into the fountain as part of a publicity stunt or something just as hare-brained. Two policemen arrived, hauled David off to the station, questioned him, then gave him a citation for disturbing the peace and suggested he go home and change into more suitable clothing. Jacob's suit was shrinking so rapidly, David felt as though his body was in a vice. Within a few minutes, the trouser legs had risen above his calves and the sleeves of the coat to just below the elbows. If he hadn't been so angry, he would've felt ridiculous.

The clock at the station said it was four o'clock. He had only two hours left and no way to tell Lisette what had happened.

David called Joe at home, then at his office, where he was catching up on work he'd missed this past week chauffeuring David around, and told him to come fast. Joe tried to ask about a letter he'd received earlier today, but David put him off, promising to explain everything later.

The thought had occurred to David that Andrew was now free to kidnap Lisette as well. David had played right into Andrew's hands. He'd underestimated him with disastrous results.

Joe got there ten minutes later.

"Hey, Bro! I didn't expect to see you again so soon. And certainly not at the police station." He came toward David with his arms wide, ready to hug, but David waved him away.

"There's no time for that now. I have to get home and into some different clothes."

Joe took a look at the shrinking suit and stifled a grin. "You do look pretty strange, all right."

"Where's your car?"

"Right outside. You're going to get the seat all wet. Maybe we can get a plastic bag or something for you to sit on."

"There isn't time. I'll pay to have the upholstery cleaned. We have to go right now. Back to the Peabody."

He held up both hands in mock fear. "Whoa! You convinced me. I assume you're going to tell me what's been happening on the way to your place?" He dug in his pocket. "And I can't wait to hear about this little jewel." The yellowed envelope in his hand had to be the letter David had given to Rogers.

Incredible. The fact it had survived didn't surprise David. Joe's receiving it an hour after David gave it to Rogers would require some thought when there was time.

"I didn't expect to get back so soon."

"Uh, David, about what you wrote—"

"Later, okay?" Sometimes, Joe's tendency to talk more than listen could be a real pain in the butt!

David stood by the fountain for fifteen minutes but nothing happened. The lobby was full of people. He couldn't just tell them all to clear out so he could be alone! He finally gave up. There had to be another way for him to get back to 1885.

On the way to Midtown, David told Joe everything that had happened. The car hadn't even rolled to a stop in David's driveway when he opened the door and got out. He had to use the extra key, buried under a rock in the backyard, to get in. He went straight to the shower. By the time he got out, it was five o'clock.

He put on a suit and tie since the dance on the *Memphis Queen III* would undoubtedly be formal. Joe was in the kitchen, helping himself to a beer when David came into the living room.

"Tell me again what happened, David, in detail this time. To tell you the truth, I didn't understand half of what you told me on the way. Where is Lisette?"

"Being kidnapped."

"Kidnapped?"

"Andrew Westmoreland tricked me into the Peabody, then dumped me into the fountain, and here I am. Lisette doesn't know. I left her at home, alone. Stupid, I know, but necessary under the circumstances. Westmoreland kidnapped her father and aunt this morning. He's putting them on the *Cajun Star* at six. He wants all three of them to disappear with the boat. Got it now?"

"Wait a minute. Westmoreland knows the boat is going to disappear? How did that happen?"

"He found the newspaper article about the dance to-night. Do me a favor; find the number for the Memphis Queen Riverboat Line for me. I have to call Jim and make sure he'll let me go on that cruise. Bob is coming, isn't he?"

"Last time I checked, he was." Joe flipped through the telephone book, found the number, dialed, then handed David the receiver. He got the after-hours recording, listened, then dialed Jim's extension number.

"This is Jim."

"Jim! David Stewart. Can you handle one more on that cruise tonight?"

"Sure."

"You're going to ride the boat tonight, aren't you?"

"Yep."

"When do you plan to cast off?"

"Six sharp. We'll be back about midnight. This is a long one. We usually do three hours. But, since that missing boat left at six—"

"I may have three more passengers for you, but they won't be boarding at six."

There was a long pause. "They'll be boarding after we leave Memphis?"

"Yep."

Another pause. "You can tell me about it later. I gotta go. Captain Dale is yelling about something and I have half a dozen little fires to put out before we go."

"Thanks. I'll fill you in once we're on board. We're on our way."

Joe and David left the house about two minutes later.

They drove to Riverside Drive, then turned onto the cobblestones. There were already two dozen cars on the bumpy, sharply slanted parking area and people streaming through the canopied walkway onto the dock. They drove slow and easy, even though Jim had told David a car had never slipped into the river off the cobblestones. He had no desire to be the first to accomplish that little trick.

They followed a couple dressed in formal evening wear onto the dock then veered left to the *Showboat* where Jim was talking to a couple of crew members. As soon as he had each one clear on responsibilities for the cruise, he took David and Joe back to his office behind the gift shop.

"Okay, Jim, I'll need complete privacy on the third deck tonight, for about half an hour, as soon as you can manage it after we leave."

"What else?"

"I'm going to try to get three people off another boat that's cruising tonight. If I manage it, I'll need a place to take them. They'll require medical treatment."

Jim's eyes narrowed and his forehead creased with disbelief. "I'm not following."

"You don't have to understand it. Will there be a place for me to treat them, assuming I get them on board?"

"Bar on the first deck, stern. I can run everybody up front."

"Thanks, Jim. I owe you one."

"The next time you go on vacation, take me with you. Anywhere. Don't bring me back for at least a month. Someplace with palm trees and sunshine and girls who think wearing clothes is against their religion."

David laughed. "You got it."

When they got back outside, Bob was there. They boarded the *Memphis Queen III*.

Chapter Eighteen

"Where on earth could he be?" Lisette said aloud, echoing the phrase screaming through her mind. David would never have been gone so long if something hadn't gone wrong.

She went through the house again, checking every door and window, making sure they hadn't been disturbed. The house remained as quiet as a tomb. She tried to shake that thought.

She was halfway up the stairs before she fully realized what she was doing. But it didn't matter. She kept going, into her secret room, where she'd spent hundreds of hours of her childhood.

Opposite the attic, this room sat on top of the house like a crown, bestowing the finishing touch to the Italianate architecture. The trio of arched windows drew her like magic. She gazed toward the river and saw the top deck of the *Cajun Star*, awaiting passengers for its last cruise down the Mississippi. Black smoke curled lazily above the twin smokestacks. When the boilers were running at full capacity, smoke and fire would belch from the stacks in thick columns.

The watch Lisette had pinned to her left shoulder told her they had only an hour before they had to be on that boat, according to Andrew's ultimatum. Maybe David could find Jacob and Aunt Portia before then.

How many hours had she gazed out these windows as a child, dressed in Mother's old clothes, her feathered hats and boas on her head and around her neck? Lisette wondered.

She and Delia, her best friend in all the world, pretended they were fine ladies. Taking turns, they called on each other, served tea in chipped china cups, ate biscuits and cookies and sandwiches prepared by their cook—Aunt Portia—and gossiped about everyone they knew.

"Lydia has a new baby," Lisette would say, sipping tea with her little finger pointed daintily toward the ceiling.

"How marvelous," Delia would answer, brushing a crumb from her chin. "Was it a boy or a girl?"

"A girl. She has her mother's chin."

"How dreadful."

They would burst into peals of laughter over Lydia's chin, sometimes spewing cookies and tea across the table and onto the rug.

Mostly though, they stood at the windows, staring through the trees toward the river, speaking in hushed tones about private and scary things.

"The man I will someday marry," Delia would whisper, "will be tall and handsome, with flashing eyes and a quick wit. He will adore me above all he possesses and would throw it all away in a second if given a choice between his riches and me." At this, she would sigh. "I shall be the most beautiful lady in Memphis, except for you, of course, Lisette. You'll be the most beautiful too."

"Of course."

"I shall ride in an elegant carriage with matching horses with plumes on their harnesses. Everyone will sigh when we pass and say, 'There they are. Can you believe how beautiful she is? Such a perfect couple.' "

It would then be Lisette's turn.

"The man I will someday marry will be kind and gentle

and will love me more than life itself."

"Will he be tall?"

"Perhaps. Tall enough that I shall look up into his eyes when he holds me." More sighs. "But not so tall that I could not circle his neck with my arms and kiss him without stretching upward too far."

"Not too far . . ."

"Above all, he will love the world as I love it and take me to the farthest reaches of this continent, across the seas and around the world. Every wonder of the world will be ours to see and experience and share."

These dreams occupied them by the hour. They never tired of repeating them.

Before Lisette reached the age of twenty-two, Delia married Fenimore Byerly, an employee of the Tennessee Brewery, and bore him three children in three years. Fenimore was short, plump and balding. Delia swore he was the epitome of "the man she would someday marry."

Lisette heard noises below and rushed down the stairs, frantic to see David.

She stopped midway down the final flight. Andrew stood just inside the front door. The facing on the front door was splintered. Hot anger flooded through her.

"I've come to take you to the boat, Lisa. Get your things."

"I'm going nowhere without David," she said, as calmly and steadily as she could.

"Well, then you're going to be waiting a long time. He isn't coming."

Her heart pounded mercilessly in her chest. What had Andrew done to David?

He guessed what she was thinking. "Oh, he's alive and

well, although embarrassed and rather wet, would be my guess."

What on earth could he be talking about?

"He took another swim in the Peabody fountain and disappeared, just as he did the first time I met him. Isn't it clever the way the fountain has that effect on him?" He shook his head mockingly.

He came toward her. She backed up the stairs, searching for a way to escape him. He matched every step, his eyes gleaming wickedly, his forced smile chilling her as no north wind ever could. There was no way to leave the house, short of plunging out a window, on any floor except the first. She was trapped. But she would never surrender.

Lisette whirled and ran up the steps, around and up the next flight, desperate to reach the secret room, but his hands closed on her shoulders before she reached the third floor and he dragged her down. She tried to scratch or bite him, but he held her from behind, his arm so tight across her breasts she almost screamed with the pain. She kicked backward, hoping to dislodge his hold, but he twisted her around and struck her face so hard she almost blacked out.

"Stop it! I'll beat you to death where you stand! Do you hear me?" He struck her again.

Weeping, her head throbbing until she thought it might explode, she stopped fighting. She was no good to Jacob or Aunt Portia beaten to a bloody pulp.

Andrew dragged her roughly down the stairs to the foyer, through the front door, which he left standing open. A carriage waited. He shoved her inside, climbed in, then grabbed her wrists before she could orient herself enough to attempt escape. He yelled to the driver who slapped the horses sharply. They leapt away, jarring the carriage, throwing her back against the seat. Andrew raised his hand as though to hit her again.

"No! Please, I'll be still. I promise."

He lowered his hand. His eyes no longer held that same cold gleam she'd seen before. There remained only a frightening madness, pain she'd never imagined, and cruelty born of neglect and apathy.

Dear God, let David be all right, she prayed. She sensed he was no longer in this century. Through the past week she had come to recognize his presence like a signature, a feeling deep inside which lay warm and comfortable in her soul as nothing ever had.

The dock was alive with the fierce activity of loading trunks and baggage, cargo and supplies for the week-long trip to New Orleans. Arriving passengers chattered and laughed, eager to begin a journey she knew would end in tragedy.

The nonstop time required to reach New Orleans was probably no more than three or four days, but that duration doubled with the habit of stopping repeatedly to take on more cargo. But these stops were irrelevant on this particular trip. After midnight, the *Cajun Star* would cruise a different river. And all these people would be gone forever.

"We're here. Smile, Lisa. Let everyone see how happy you are to be going home to New Orleans." Andrew held onto her arm while she stepped down from the carriage. She had no baggage, nothing to qualify her as a passenger of the *Star* for the next week. Perhaps that fact would afford her an opportunity to alert someone to her plight. If she tried to attract attention by screaming or yelling, Andrew would knock her senseless and somehow explain away her distress. She had to speak directly to the one person on this boat known and trusted. The thought gave her a burst of optimism and hope.

David was nowhere to be seen. He must not have been able to return. It was up to Lisette to protect herself and her family and somehow get them off this boat before midnight.

She examined every face, hoping to see the captain supervising the loading of cargo, but he wasn't there. They approached the boarding plank.

Andrew whispered harshly, "One sound from you and I'll knock you unconscious and throw you in the river. You'll drown before anyone knows what's happened."

She nodded tersely.

He handed a ticket to the purser standing beside the plank. "Mrs. Westmoreland, bound for New Orleans. Her trunks are already on board."

The purser frowned, his forehead creasing. "I have no record of any trunks with that name."

Andrew laughed awkwardly. "Try the name Morgan. I may have used her maiden name by mistake when I brought them."

The Purser checked his cargo manifest, then nodded, the creases in his forehead easing. "Morgan. Two large trunks." He tipped his hat to Lisette. "Have a nice trip, Mrs. Westmoreland."

She nodded. Two large trunks.

"Not one word to the captain. There isn't a lot of air in those trunks. You wouldn't want dear Papa to run out of air, now, would you? Or Aunt Portia? What a pity that would be."

Lisette squeezed her eyes tightly shut. "Bastard," she breathed just loud enough for him to hear.

"I thought you might approve. Now, up the plank with you. I intend to see that you are comfortably settled before I leave you to your cruise."

"Where are those trunks?"

"I had them stored." He reached into his pocket. "The location is in this envelope. I'll give it to you when I leave the boat. Not one instant before. If you make a scene, I promise Papa and Aunt Portia will suffer for the mistake."

She said nothing. Rage threatened to blot out every bit of sensible thought needed to defeat this monster. At the very least, he should die with them.

Chapter Nineteen

People flooded onto the *Memphis Queen III*. David wondered if they were going to be able to find any place on this boat where they could be alone. All the preliminaries for casting off, the greetings and instructions, the opening of the bar for those who wanted to get a head start on the party, drove David crazy. Why couldn't they dispense with all of this and get on with the cruise! They made their way up to the third deck. It was crawling with people.

"Hey, Bro, you're letting it get to you."

David's first reaction was to lash out at Joe, but he was right. It *was* getting to David. Time was running out. Only a few hours remained until midnight. If the boilers were destined to explode, and the result as grisly as he'd read in a book about the *Sultana* tragedy, they had to be off the boat and a decent distance away to avoid being injured or killed by the explosion. The possibilities scurried in his brain, like mice fleeing a sinking ship. Joe patted his back. David hadn't answered because he didn't trust himself to say something polite.

"It's going to be all right, David."

That did it. "How the hell do you know that?"

Joe gave him apologetic look. "I don't. I just know we have to believe it, that's all. Looking for the worst means that's what we'll end up with. We have to be positive."

"Otherwise, I won't be calm enough to make this work." David took a long, slow, deep breath. "Not knowing is killing me. Not knowing about the boat and what's going to happen, not knowing about Lisette and what that bastard could be doing to her." He rubbed his eyes. How in the hell could anyone be calm?

"They're casting off now, so we'll be underway soon. Did Jim say this deck would be available? I can't see how, with this many people on board."

They were all over the boat, laughing, talking, drinking. The band was playing in the ballroom on the second deck where David had seen Lisette the first time.

A thought stuck in his mind. Why hadn't he seen it before? Up until now, he'd assumed the only place where they could actually move from one century to another and stay there for any length of time was the Peabody fountain. But they'd met on the third decks of the *Memphis Queen III*—and the *Cajun Star*. Lisette didn't go back to her own time until they entered the ballroom—on the second deck. The third deck had to be another portal—a link allowing them to walk back and forth between centuries.

"Joe, I may be onto something." David tried to fasten it firmly in his mind before saying it aloud. Could it be so simple?

"What?" Joe glanced around the deck at the milling crowd. "Did you see her? What's going on?"

"This boat—this deck—is the key." David had to get this deck cleared. "Let's find Jim. We can't have people appearing and disappearing in front of everyone, can we?"

"You think—hey, wait up!"

David threaded his way through the crowd, down the steps and inside the ballroom packed with people. No wonder they were spilling out onto the upper deck. He eased his way around the edge of the room with an odd sensation of déjà vu, went through the front doors and found Jim at the bow, yelling at someone up above.

"Jim, any chance the third deck will clear out pretty soon?"

"Shouldn't take long. As soon as we get under way, the wind will be too cold for most folks. They'll head inside."

"That room is already full."

"You weren't the only one who called late and asked to join the party. We're really overloaded for that room but nothing dangerous. This boat can carry a lot more people than we have on board, but that room may get a little close before the evening is over. If that sorority hadn't already booked the *Showboat,* we would've moved over to it."

David breathed silent thanks to the sorority. They had to be on *this* boat tonight.

Jim squinted into the breeze. "We have a south wind, so it'll go with us on the way back. Once we reach our farthest point south and head north again, the wind won't be a factor. People will come out for a breather and to escape the crush."

"Then we have until that southern-most point. How long before we get there?"

"It's two hours down and four back. Gotta go."

"Thanks." David went back to the third deck. Once the boat was up to full speed, the wind blew as briskly as Jim had predicted, slicing across the deck, chilling everyone in the open. Before long, only a couple of stragglers remained.

Bob joined David on deck, pulling his coat tighter. "Any chance we could get behind something or do this inside? I'm not sure any of us can concentrate if we're freezing to death."

"Hypnosis may not be necessary, Bob. I have an idea this will be easier than we thought."

"Sounds great to me. The idea of putting you under again goes against my better judgment."

"Both of you can go below. I have to be alone."

"No problem." Joe tugged at Bob's sleeve. "Let's give him a chance to do this by himself. If he can't, you can zap him back like you did before." Without protest, Bob followed Joe down the port staircase.

David stood at the bow, the cold south wind blowing straight into his face. In a few seconds, his skin felt numb. He closed his eyes, remembering when he'd stood with Lisette on the bow of the *Cajun Star*. The railings had not been brilliant, freshly painted white, as they were on the *Queen III*, and they weren't iron filigree, but wood. The deck had also been wood instead of metal. There was no wood on the *Queen III* at all, but nineteenth century riverboats had been heavy with wood. Floating firetraps.

David focused on that difference, imagining a wooden deck beneath his feet and wooden railings.

The pulsing of the diesel engine, turning the paddle-wheel at the stern, changed suddenly. He smelled the smoke of burning coal.

Chapter Twenty

Standing by the rail of the *Cajun Star*, Andrew never took his eyes off Lisette, daring her to make a move. For a moment or so, she glared back, but then looked away, disgusted with what she saw in his eyes and in the smirk she'd seen repeatedly since he produced the marriage license.

She couldn't help wondering what had happened to the person who had come to the house, asking forgiveness, rendering aid to her father when he was stricken. She still had difficulty reconciling the two as one man. If only Andrew could let that kinder self surface and dominate, he might become a decent human being. Could she reach that other personality?

He was staring at something on the dock. She rose slowly, hoping to escape notice, but he instantly pinned her with his gaze. She sank back into the chair. Before long they would pull the plank. Andrew would no doubt disembark at last call for going ashore, leaving them on board. She urged time to move faster, knowing she would not be able to get to Jacob and Aunt Portia until they were away from the dock. It was agony to think of them packed in trunks like cargo, while Andrew forced her to sit idle. They might be dying.

The captain came on deck, just past the boarding plank. Her breath came harder and faster. There were too many people between them for a shout to reach him. She would have to wait until he came closer.

Andrew saw him too. He inched closer to her chair,

blocking her view of the captain.

"Don't even think about it," he muttered, and gripped her shoulder.

She shook her head once and clamped her lips tightly shut, demonstrating she understood the warning. Andrew withdrew his hand.

"All ashore that's goin' ashore!" the purser called, one hand cupped around his mouth.

"That's me. Why don't you go inside now, Lisa."

"The envelope. You promised."

He reached into his coat pocket and drew it out slowly. "This envelope? I almost forgot. How good of you to remind me." He gripped her elbow tightly, pushing her toward an entrance just aft of her chair. He opened the door. She held out her hand. He gave the envelope to her, shoved her through the door and slammed it closed. By the time she regained her balance he was gone.

Lisette tore open the envelope and jerked out a single sheet of paper. Her hands shook so badly she could hardly read the few words scrawled there.

If you really thought I would tell you where those trunks are, you're not as bright as I thought. Have fun looking for them.

She crumpled the paper into a tight wad. Tears of anger and hatred spilled from her eyes. She threw the paper against the floor, then hurried outside. They were well away from the dock, away from Andrew. The realization gave her a surge of strength and new hope. She had to find the captain.

She told the first deck hand she passed she had to see the captain about a matter of life and death. With a doubtful expression, he took her toward the bow where the captain stood, waving to someone on the bank.

"Captain! You have to help me!"

"Mrs. Westmoreland! I had no idea you were on this boat. What's wrong?"

"My father and my aunt. They're somewhere on board."

"And you've become separated. Don't worry, I'll help you find them."

"You don't understand. They've been locked into trunks. We have to find them before—"

"Trunks! Who would do such a thing?"

"My stepson."

Eyes narrowed and mouth tightened, his chest swelled with a deep, angry breath.

He yelled to several men, explained quickly, then sent them running through the boat.

"You wait here, Ma'am. It won't take long. They know every inch of this boat." He offered her a chair, but she was too overwrought to sit. What if they were too late? There was no way to know when Andrew had put them into the trunks, if that's actually where they were. He might have lied about that too. Please, God, let them be all right, she prayed, squeezing her eyes tightly shut.

Seconds crept by like hours. She paced the deck, desperate for a glimpse of someone coming to say they were all right.

The captain was pacing too, but in a much tighter circle. Lisette could tell he wanted to join the search, but felt his duty was with her.

"Sir!" A man on the deck just above us leaned over the rail.

"Report!"

"We found them." He hesitated. "You'd better come up here, Sir."

Chapter Twenty-One

David turned around slowly. His heart pounded and his breath came in gasps. The deck was rimmed with wooden rails that had not been painted in a long time. The insignia on the pilothouse bore the name of the boat. *Cajun Star.*

The boat hadn't cast off. He didn't see Lisette anywhere. Had she already boarded? The captain—David guessed his position from the matching insignia on his cap—issued quiet orders to deck hands running around like ants.

David eased around the rail, watching for anyone he might recognize. If he'd told the truth, Andrew would be bringing Jacob and Portia on board just before six. David's watch indicated it was two minutes of.

Andrew emerged from a door about twenty feet away on the starboard side. Anger knotted David's gut when he saw Andrew's self-satisfied smirk—an expression David had come to expect from him.

With his head bowed slightly to prevent Andrew a direct view of his face, David made his way through the tangle of deck hands and passengers until he stood only a few feet away. Andrew headed for the plank, intending to leave the boat. That meant Lisette, Portia and Jacob were already on board.

When Andrew turned to head down the plank, David edged past a deck hand, rushed forward and grabbed Andrew's arm.

"Excuse me?" he blurted. "You!"

"Before you go ashore, Mr. Westmoreland . . ." David

pulled his arm behind him and jerked once to emphasize the willingness to break his arm if necessary. "I have a few questions for you."

"Let go of me! I have to—" He stopped his protest when David lifted his elbow an inch higher.

"Deserting the ship like the rat you are? I don't think so." Seeing no one looking their direction, David took the opportunity to land a solid punch in Andrew's gut and let go of his arm. Andrew gasped and doubled over, clutching his middle with both hands.

"Now, you bastard, we're going to have a talk." David dragged Andrew around and through the first door on the port side and dropped him into a straight-backed chair. His face had turned a ghastly shade of gray. David knew he shouldn't feel good about causing pain, but he did. Let the bastard taste a bit of what he'd dished out to Lisette and Portia. David had the urge to punch him again, in the face this time, but didn't. He wasn't worth the damage it might do to David's hand.

"Have to—get off—" Andrew wheezed and coughed. His face reddened with the strain of speaking.

"Off this boat? Not on your life. The fun is just beginning. Aren't you curious to know what's going to happen to this grand old lady?" David tried to sound flippant. The truth be known, he wanted to find Lisette and her family and run down that plank with them, away from the doomed riverboat. Since he could feel movement, he knew the opportunity had passed. They were under way.

A deck hand spotted Andrew, bent double, and came to investigate.

"He's all right," David told the hand. "Just a little stomach discomfort. I'm a doctor. I'm taking care of it."

"Very good, Sir." He left.

David spoke softly into Andrew's ear, which was still quite red, matching his face. "Do I need to treat your stomach again, Mr. Westmoreland, or do you think you've had enough medication for today?"

Andrew's face was livid with pure hatred. His eyes had watered to such an extent that David almost felt sorry for him.

David had to find Lisette, but couldn't leave Andrew alone. In a few minutes, he might be recovered enough to jump overboard and try to swim for shore.

The deck hand David had spoken to came through the far door with the captain and pointed.

"Sir, Clancy tells me you're a doctor."

"I am. What's the problem?"

"I don't know yet, Sir. If you'll come with me, we need your help."

"I can't leave this man unattended. He may try to jump ship."

The captain studied Andrew carefully. His eyes widened with recognition. "Westmoreland. Your stepmother has told me what you've done on my boat." He signaled for the nearest hand, who came straight away. "This man is not to move from this chair. If he tries to get up, knock him out. If necessary, kill him."

"Aye, Captain!"

"Follow me, Doctor."

Chapter Twenty-Two

Frantic to find Jacob and Aunt Portia, Lisette followed the captain to a stateroom at the far end of the fourth deck. Twin smokestacks belched great volumes of thick, acrid black smoke, now that the boat was moving downriver. The farther they went down the walkway, the harder it was to breathe in the dense smoke. The idea of Jacob and Aunt Portia being in one of these airless rooms, imprisoned in trunks, filled Lisette with dread and grief. How could Andrew do this to anyone? The deck hand refused to tell her anything, no matter how she prodded him for information.

"Are they alive? Surely you can tell me—" She saw two trunks standing in the way. They stepped around them. The lids were open, revealing rough boards lining the interiors. They were hardly large enough for a child to curl up inside. Lisette wanted to scream in rage and pain.

The man stopped at the next to last door, turned around, and waited for the captain to enter first. After a moment, the captain gestured Lisette inside.

There were two beds, practically touching in the center of the stuffy room. Aunt Portia lay on one, Jacob on the other. At first glance, Lisette thought they were dead.

"Aunt Portia! Papa! Dear God, please—" She knelt between the beds, clasped their hands and wept bitter tears of anger and helplessness.

The deck hand finally spoke. "We found them in those trunks, Captain. The ones outside. Clancy says there's a doctor on board."

"Where?"

Lisette didn't hear his reply. The captain left immediately. If only David could be that doctor. With his miracle medicines from the future, her father and Aunt Portia might have a chance to recover from this travesty. In only a few minutes, Lisette heard the captain's deep, booming voice, getting louder as he came closer.

"This way, Doctor. They were found in those trunks. Look lively there! Let the doctor through."

At first, Lisette thought she must be dreaming. "David." She fell into his arms. He held her a brief moment, his breath warm on her cheek, then eased past to the bedsides. For the first time, she allowed herself to hope everything might be all right.

He peered into their eyes, pressed his fingers to their pulses, then turned back to her.

"There isn't enough air in this room for a baby to breathe. Captain!"

He came into the room. Lisette stepped back outside onto the walkway.

"Is there somewhere they can be moved where there's ventilation? It's stifling in here."

The captain gave brisk instructions to his men to move Aunt Portia and Jacob to his own quarters.

"Thank you, Captain," Lisette whispered. In only minutes, they were on a lower deck where Jacob and Portia had been carried gently and laid side by side on the captain's wide bed. The porthole was open. A cool, moist breeze swept into the room. David resumed his examination while the rest waited outside in a sitting room. The captain coaxed Lisette to take a glass of sherry, but she asked for water instead. She had to keep her head clear. How long had they been under way?

"Captain, do you have the time?"

He frowned, puzzled by the question, pulled his watch from his pocket and peered at it. "Quarter past seven, Ma'am."

"Thank you." Less than five hours.

David emerged from the room. She prayed for him to smile, to indicate everything was all right. He didn't.

"Lisette, go to your father. I'm afraid—"

"No!" She ran into the room, knelt between the bed and reached for her father's hand. It felt cool, the fingers stiff and unresponsive. "Papa, can you hear me?"

He opened his eyes with difficulty. She touched his cheek. He turned toward her and smiled.

"Lisette. Home at last. I'm sorry. So sorry."

Tears poured from her eyes, streamed down her face. "Don't talk, Papa. Just rest. You're going to be well again. David is here. David will take care of you."

"Hush, child, and listen. I never got to tell you . . . how sorry . . . about Westmoreland . . ." His eyes fluttered closed for a moment.

"Papa!"

When he opened his eyes again, she could see a cloud had obscured his vision. The brightness in his eyes had dimmed.

"Forgive me, child. Forgive . . . me . . ."

"Of course I forgive you. I love you, Papa."

His eyelids drooped, his chest fell and did not rise again for a very long time.

"David, help him!"

"There's nothing I can do. His heart is too weak."

"You're saying he's going to die?" It was too much to bear. Too much.

David hesitated before speaking, his expression full of

frustration and anxiety. "Time will tell. If I had modern equipment and medicines, it would be a different story." He closed his eyes. "I've done everything I can do here."

She understood. In David's clinic, her father would have a chance to live. She could see it was tearing David apart not to be able to do more.

Aunt Portia called her name softly. Lisette nodded to David she was all right and knelt beside the bed. She was so weak, hardly able to hold her eyes open.

"Lisette. Thank God you came. Is Jacob all right? He was having trouble breathing."

She fell silent. Lisette's tears refused to dry and she had no power to be stronger. "He's here." She touched Jacob's shoulder. His breathing had become so shallow; it was difficult to detect.

"Oh, Jacob, Jacob."

Chapter Twenty-Three

David left Lisette and Portia and joined the captain, standing just outside the door. "I think it might be wise if Westmoreland were locked up, with a guard posted. Jacob Morgan will probably not live through the night, and Westmoreland will be responsible for his death. Perhaps, if they'd been found earlier, or if I'd had adequate facilities, I could make sure he's alive in the morning." David's inability to help without drugs or machinery not yet invented made him want to smash something. Preferably Andrew Westmoreland. Maybe Joe was right. Being a doctor in this century would drive him crazy with worry and regret. David took a deep breath. "Miss Morgan is stable. She'll be fine with rest and care."

The captain nodded once, tersely. "I'll take care of Westmoreland. Clancy, stay close by. Assist the doctor in any way he or Mrs. Westmoreland requests."

The name grated on David. "She'll soon be Mrs. Stewart. We're to be married. Until then, please call her Miss Morgan. I don't think she'll object."

The creases in the captain's forehead eased. He managed a smile. "Well, now, that's good news, indeed. Doctor Stewart, is it?"

"David Stewart. I wish we could have met under happier circumstances."

"If there's anything at all I can do for Mr. Morgan or the ladies, just send word by Clancy. I wish we could take her back to Memphis, but there's a town closer that has a decent hospital that we'll reach by six in the morning. We'll drop all of you there. Excuse me, now. I have a prisoner to deal with." He strode off, his heels heavy on the wooden floor.

David went back into the room. "Lisette, I need to talk to Aunt Portia, now that she's awake."

Lisette's expression displayed sudden fear. He hurried to allay those fears.

"She's going to be all right. I just need to monitor her vital signs."

"Monitor. Of course." She hugged Portia and eased past David out of the room. He sat on the edge of the bed.

"How do you feel?" He took her pulse again. It pounded beneath his fingers, strong and healthy.

"Angry. And grieved. How could Andrew have done such a cruel thing to us? And get away with it!"

"I promise, he isn't going to get away with anything."

"But he left us on this boat to die."

"I detained him. He's one deck below us, locked up and guarded. He isn't going anywhere."

Portia squeezed her eyes tightly shut. "Thank the Lord." A tear ran down her cheek. "And thank you, David."

He kissed her forehead and found it cool beneath his lips. No fever he could detect. It would take more than a trunk and a bastard to defeat this lady.

"Rest now. Lisette will be nearby and so will I if you need anything. I suspect you'll be stiff and sore for a while, but there's nothing seriously wrong with you. You're a tough old bird."

Her eyes widened, then she smiled. "That I am." After a moment, her seriousness returned. "Jacob isn't going to survive this ordeal, is he?"

"I can't say for sure what will happen, but I don't think

so. The trauma was too much."

"No need to explain." She reached for her brother's hand. "Thank you for telling me."

Lisette started back inside, but David waved her away. "Aunt Portia needs to sleep. Your father is resting quietly."

Lisette followed him to a divan and nestled against him. He felt complete, holding her, feeling her breath against his throat.

Just then, a boy of about ten or eleven, with a wild shock of carrot-orange hair, came running through the sitting room swinging a skinning knife, yelling at the top of his lungs about pirates and scoundrels. A deck hand followed, close on his heels, puffing, falling behind. Clancy tried to grab the boy as he came by but missed getting a firm grip on him. He shook his head, disapproving of either the boy, the man chasing him, or both.

"Master Crump! You can't come in here. These are the captain's quarters," the deck hand pleaded.

The boy seemed not to hear, or if he did, to ignore what he'd heard. He disappeared through an aft door at the far end of the room. The deck hand stopped, shaking his head as Clancy had done. "Sorry, Sir, Ma'am. He's a feisty one, for sure."

"Excuse me, but did I hear you call him Crump?"

"Yes, Sir. Eddie Crump. He isn't a bad boy, just full of mischief and always playing pirate games. Into everything. He wasn't supposed to be aboard until next week, but his aunt—he's been visiting her—brought him to the dock and begged us to take him home early. The poor woman looked terrible. Said she had to have rest."

A commotion interrupted. Eddie bolted back through the door where he'd exited, saw them staring at him, changed his mind and dashed back out the door, slamming into a passenger who happened to be coming in at the time, bringing curses and shouts.

"Excuse me, Sir. I'd better see where he's gone now. The captain assigned me to the boy, I'm afraid. He's only going a short way downriver. We'll be letting him off at first light in the morning."

First light. Where would the *Cajun Star* be at first light?

"At least he isn't going all the way to New Orleans." The deck hand took a deep breath and let it out noisily. "Something to be grateful for." He hurried through the aft door, calling Eddie's name in a pleading tone.

"David, is that the boy—the man—you told me about?"

"I told you about Edward Hull Crump. Whether or not Eddie's the same Crump from Memphis history, there's no way to tell. The deck hand did say he wasn't supposed to ride the boat until next week." The possibility this boy could be "Boss" Crump weighed heavily on him. Memphis without "Boss" Crump. An entirely different Memphis.

"We'll have to save him, won't we?" she said quietly.

He nodded. They couldn't assume this Eddie Crump was *not* Edward Hull Crump. For better or worse, Eddie would have to leave the boat before midnight.

Chapter Twenty-Four

David was right. They had to save this rude boy.

"How soon before we'll be able to move Aunt Portia?"

"She needs to rest. A couple of hours at least." He looked at his watch. "It's going on eight o'clock. We still have four hours, but I don't want to cut it too close. I think we should leave the boat by eleven at the latest."

"Can we be sure the newspaper article was right about the time?"

He frowned. She guessed he'd not thought about it before now. "We have no choice but to believe it. Aunt Portia has to have rest or she'll never make it off the boat. She could have a stroke or a heart attack if she's stressed too much after the ordeal she's been through. By eleven I'll have found a way to get us all off the boat safely." He smiled. "Trust me."

"Of course I trust you." A wave of dizziness passed through her. She leaned against him.

"What's wrong?"

"Just a little dizzy, that's all."

"You need rest too. Do you have assigned quarters?"

"Not that I've been told. There hasn't been time to ask."

David left her on the divan and went to find the captain. Her thoughts instantly returned to her father, memories swarming through her troubled mind. She gave in to them gladly, needing to reconnect with a time when he was sound of mind and body, when he still recognized and cared about her.

Growing up, she had depended on her father devotedly. Annoying him most was her stubborn refusal to select a husband. The five years after she'd turned sixteen were especially difficult for him. He feared she would be a spinster—exactly what happened. She never could explain to him that being a wife and mother would be wonderful. But not for her. Not yet. She wanted more. All she could think of then was seeing more of the world. She remembered the night she confided in him.

"Papa, come out on the terrace. There's something I want to talk to you about." She took his hands in hers. The gesture always worked magic on him as nothing else could. She suspected it was a gesture her mother might have used, but he never confirmed her suspicions and she hadn't dared ask for fear it would lose its effectiveness.

"All right, I'll listen." They sat on wrought iron chairs near the marble wall enclosing the terrace. A mockingbird sang its final song of the day while fireflies glimmered among the roses.

"I want to go to San Francisco."

"San Francisco!" He frowned. "What nonsense is this? You know I can't leave Memphis right now." He paced across the terrace and back again. "I'm in the middle of business negotiations that cannot be neglected. This could mean—"

She tried to get him to sit down again, but he refused. "Please, Papa, won't you listen? I didn't mean *you* should go."

His eyes widened. "You cannot mean you would go alone! You'd actually consider such an outrageous thing? Unmarried women do not travel unescorted. You know that as well as I do. Aunt Portia is not able to—" His expression changed. He looked squarely at her. "Is this your way to tell me you—" He stopped suddenly, waiting for her to respond.

She rushed to quash this notion with no possible misinterpretation. "I meant no such thing. I have no intention of announcing my engagement to anyone in the near future." She almost added she might never choose to marry at all but decided to avoid angering him further. "I do not wish to be married, Papa. I've told you my feelings about marriage time and again."

"And I've told you that you are going to be past the age for marriage if you don't stop this insistence on seeing the world and make your choice. There are several fine young men here in Memphis who would swim the length of the Mississippi if you showed them any interest at all. If you don't choose soon—"

"Then what? Will you drag me off to a convent? Or marry me off to the first man who offers to take your spinster daughter off your hands? Really, Papa, sometimes you are so old-fashioned, I'm surprised you don't have river moss on that bald head of yours."

His face flushed bright red and his eyes blazed with anger. She had gone too far.

"I was not going to tell you until tomorrow, but you give me no choice."

Her heart beat faster. "Tell me what?" She stood, feeling the need to be on more of an equal level with him.

"I have observed the young men who come to this house to call on you."

He had come to a decision. She could see it in his face. His eyes drilled into her, eliciting fear and anxiety—emotions never in her life associated with her father.

"In order to see to it you are provided for in the manner to which you have become accustomed, I intend to arrange a marriage for you—"

"No! Don't say any more. You can't—"

"With the suitor of *my* choice."

She felt as though the floor had dropped from beneath her. She reached for the marble wall to steady herself. "There's no reason why you must make the decision for me. You've always said I could decide for myself. You can't—"

"I can and I shall! I will hear no more about it. I have pleaded with you to marry the man of your choice, but you have refused. I will not stand by and watch my only daughter wither on the vine, left to go to seed. I want a grandson before I die, to carry on the work I've begun and to take my place in Morgan Enterprises. If I wait for you to make up your mind, I will forfeit any chance I have for immortality. You need a husband and I intend to see to it you have one at the earliest opportunity. I shall inform you when I've made my decision." He clamped his lips together and bolted toward the house. The door bounced several times before settling into its familiar niche in the doorframe.

Tears streamed from her eyes, only to be dried in the night breeze blowing across the terrace. That's all she was to him, his chance at immortality.

The saffron plague struck him before he had a chance to carry through on his threat. After months of recuperation, he insisted on getting out of the house for a while. He went to the Peabody, got completely inebriated, played cards with James Westmoreland, who had been in Memphis on business, bet his spinster daughter's hand in marriage—and lost. The next thing she knew, she was on her way to New Orleans on the *Cajun Star*.

Now, here she was on the *Cajun Star* again, waiting for midnight and an unknown fate. Her father was near death, Aunt Portia gravely ill, and David struggling to save them all—along with an obnoxious redheaded boy who might not want to be put off the boat in the middle of the night.

David came through the far doors, slowed, then gathered her into his arms again. "Are you all right? Is there anything I can do to help?"

"I was just remembering . . . What did the captain say?"

"He assigned you to the compartment directly across the way from his. Do you have any baggage?"

"Andrew didn't give me time. He said I wouldn't need it."

"Bastard. He thought he'd put the three of you on this boat, then go back to Memphis as though nothing had happened. Straight to your house, no doubt."

"He ruined the lock on the front door when he broke in and dragged me away. There would be no one to stop him from taking possession."

"You mean your house is unlocked and unoccupied?"

"There's no need to worry. No one will bother anything. Besides, Andrew took Sedonia when he took Aunt Portia and Papa from the house. With no need to hold her any longer, she's probably back home by now, worrying herself to death over us."

"I hope you're right. In the meantime, you need rest. Why not sleep a while? The captain is sending someone to watch Jacob and Aunt Portia. I'll be back in an hour or so."

"Check on Andrew too. I can't bear to think he might be allowed to roam this boat."

"Don't give it another thought. I promise you, he's going nowhere."

In her compartment, with a small bed and a tiny water closet, she lay down immediately and marveled at how tired she was. Waves of sleep began to overtake her. David sat on the side of the bed and kissed her gently. She felt a surge of desire, pulled him closer and took her time kissing him. He pulled her into his arms, stroking her back, then her breasts. After a moment, he stopped.

"Not now, my love," he whispered. "When I come back. Dream about me while you sleep."

"I'll close my eyes, and you'll be there."

He covered her with a quilt from the bottom of the bed, then stepped to the door. "We're almost home now."

Chapter Twenty-Five

David pulled the door closed gently. She'd already fallen asleep. He wished he could let her rest until morning, but time was slipping away.

The captain was on the second deck talking to a deck hand. David had no idea how to approach him with the idea of leaving the boat, or whether there would be an appropriate vessel for such a task, but he had to try.

"Captain, may I have a word with you?"

He finished his conversation then led David to an office adjoining the ballroom. With sudden recognition, David knew this had to be the ballroom from which Lisette had come the night they met. It gave him the oddest feeling to walk across the room and picture her leaving, walking up the staircase to the third deck, standing at the bow, her black veil slipping from her hair in the wind. He marveled at the memory of their meeting and how it had changed his life.

"Doctor?" He sat down behind a heavy mahogany desk. He gestured toward a chair opposite. "Are the ladies resting? And Mr. Morgan?"

"Yes, thank you, Captain. I have an unusual request. What I'm going to tell you will no doubt sound odd. I promise you, though, I'm dead serious."

His eyes narrowed, producing a deep crease between his eyebrows.

"I intend to leave this boat tonight."

His eyebrows shot up in surprise. "Tonight?"

"Yes, before midnight. And I must take Miss Morgan and her aunt with me. And her father, if he survives." He decided not to mention Eddie. It might sound like kidnapping, a complication he didn't need.

"May I ask why?"

"An urgent matter involving a patient. I cannot afford the time it would take to go all the way to New Orleans and back. I have to perform an operation first thing in the morning, in Memphis."

"Then why did you board this boat?"

"When I learned Andrew Westmoreland had kidnapped Jacob and Portia Morgan, and Lisette, I had to stop him. I'd hoped I wouldn't have to stay on board past departure."

"I see." He sat back in his chair, producing squeaks and groans from the shift of weight. "I can let you off first thing in the morning but not before. We have a planned stop at six."

"You don't understand, Captain. I have to be in Memphis in the morning." It was time to assume a frantic physician posture. "We have to leave the boat before midnight. Miss Morgan needs to rest for a couple of hours before she'll be able to travel, otherwise, I'd want to leave now."

He shook his head. "I'm responsible for the safety of the people on this vessel, Doctor Stewart. In my opinion, it would be unsafe for you to leave the boat before morning."

"I'll assume all responsibility, sign a statement, absolving you of any liability should something happen to us, state that you allowed us to leave against your better judgment—anything—but we have to get off this boat!" So agitated by this time, David was afraid he might blurt the truth if he wasn't careful, eliminating any chances they might have.

He stood. "I'm sorry, Doctor. I can't allow it. We'll be

docking at six in the morning to drop off Master Crump. At that time I'll allow you to leave."

Further discussion was pointless. His features were as set as his mind. David nodded, then left the office. They'd have to do this without his help.

He stared at his watch. Less than three hours until midnight.

Chapter Twenty-Six

Lisette awoke to the touch of David's hand on her cheek.

"I hate to wake you," he said softly, "but it's getting late."

"What time is it?"

"We have an hour."

Panic shimmered through her. "Only an hour?" She tried to sit up but a wave of dizziness made her abandon the effort. "Have you spoken to the captain?"

"He won't help us."

"What are we going to do?"

"I've located a small boat that's used for sounding when the river is low, the way it is now. We're going to leave in it just before midnight. If we try to go sooner, we could be discovered and brought back on board. We can't risk it."

"Isn't there any way we could warn the captain?"

"Not without changing history, we can't. There's no telling what the result might be if we prevented the *Cajun Star* from disappearing. We can't risk it, just as we can't risk letting Eddie Crump disappear with the *Star*. He may not be the Eddie Crump in Memphis history, but then again, 'Boss' Crump had red hair, just like Eddie. Could be coincidence, but I'm not willing to risk it."

"At least we can save one person." Lisette was suddenly overwhelmed with the realization they might not succeed, that they might have only two more hours to live.

"Love me, David, please."

Without a word, he locked the door, took off his clothes,

while she managed to get out of hers, and slid into bed with her. They lay there a moment, enjoying the sensation of bare skin against bare skin, then began what could be their last exploration of each other's bodies. David's caresses made her tremble with desire. She traced the contours of his arms, shoulders, back, before drawing his lips to hers.

Gradually, their passion increased until they could delay no longer. No matter how tightly she held him, she longed to be closer. When he slipped inside her, the pace of their lovemaking quickened. She clung to him, desperate to keep him this close forever.

Afterward, they lay in each other's arms for too short a time before he rose, took his clothes and went to the water closet. She felt like half a person, a shell with the soul missing.

After he came out, she went to the water closet, bathed her face in cool water and wept for all that had happened, all they still had to face. When he came up behind her, she turned and pressed against him, felt his arms come around her.

They had less than an hour.

Chapter Twenty-Seven

David left Lisette dressing and made his way forward to the sounding boat, to get it ready to put over the side before fetching Eddie Crump. What could David say to get Eddie to come with them? The last thing he could tell him was the truth. Or was it? A boy of his age and exuberance might warm instantly to the idea that the boilers were rigged to explode. Of course they weren't rigged to David's knowledge, but anything was possible. A strange man claiming to know Eddie would be the mayor of Memphis by 1907 might be exactly the push David needed to get Eddie to "play the game." It was worth a try. If he refused to come willingly, David would just have to drag him along, kicking and screaming—or knock him out. Not his favorite choice.

The captain stood near the sounding boat. He caught David's eye, frowned.

"Just checking in before retiring, Captain. You're sure you won't let us off the boat before morning?"

"Sorry, Doctor. First light. Not before."

"You're the captain." David gave him what he hoped would look like a reconciled smile and went toward the stern. He found a shadowed corner and waited, hoping the captain would leave the deck soon. Since Portia and Jacob were using his quarters, David wondered where the captain would sleep tonight.

The captain wandered around the deck, staring at the river, paying attention to nothing specific David could detect. He decided he must be settling his mind before sleep.

It was the longest five minutes of David's life.

When the captain finally left the deck, David rushed to the bow and untied the ropes securing the boat. He picked up one end, testing weight. Barely eight feet long, it wasn't too heavy to lift over the side. He had to get Lisette, Portia, Jacob—and Eddie. David prayed the boat would be big enough for all of them.

Lisette wasn't in her quarters. David found her across the way with Portia and Jacob. Again, he wished he could let them rest until morning, but they were out of time.

When David entered the room, he knew something was wrong. After a quick exam, he verified Jacob had died in his sleep. Not expected. And unavoidable, *damn it,* under these primitive circumstances.

Lisette's eyes glimmered with tears. "It happened an hour ago. Aunt Portia didn't want to disturb us." She squeezed her eyes tightly shut, her shoulders shaking.

Portia waved away David's question about why she hadn't called them. "There wasn't a thing you could've done, David. One minute he was breathing, the next he wasn't. It's exactly the kind of death I would've wished for Jacob. Peaceful and calm."

"I'm sorry," he whispered, unable to say more.

"David, how can we leave him?" Lisette gripped David's hand until his fingers stung with the pressure.

"We have to. It's time. Bring Aunt Portia quickly, all the way to the bow."

"But, David—"

"Hurry! I have to find Eddie."

Lisette, resigned, helped Portia to stand. She seemed shaky at first, then stronger. David had to trust both of them to find the strength for what had to be done.

In his search for the sounding boat, he had seen Eddie

Crump entering a stateroom on the port side of the third deck. Staying in the shadows, David went directly there, avoiding several deck hands on the way, losing precious time waiting for them to pass through on their way to other parts of the boat. Sweat trickled into his eyes. He squelched the impulse to look at his watch again.

In the gloom of night, every door looked the same. When he'd narrowed the choices to two, he tested each door—unlocked, oddly enough—and peered into the room. In the first, a man snored loudly.

In the second, he heard faint breathing coming from the bed, and once his eyes were adjusted to the dark, saw tousled hair sticking out above the covers. Eddie was traveling alone on this trip. Unusual for a boy this age, yet David knew from his reading that Edward Hull Crump was no ordinary boy, just as he was destined to be no ordinary man. David sat on the edge of the bed and touched Eddie's arm lightly.

"Eddie, wake up. Eddie!"

He came from deep sleep, a difference in his breathing marking each level as he rose to consciousness.

"What's wrong?"

"You're Edward Crump, isn't that right?"

"Yes." He rubbed his eyes with his fists.

"Edward Hull Crump?"

"What's this all about? Who are you? Are we there?"

"You have to come with me. I'm a doctor. I'll explain as we go."

"Go? Where are we going?"

"We don't have much time."

Whether it was his half-asleep state or just his upbringing, Eddie rose, pulled on his clothes and followed David out of the room and toward the bow. On the way,

David whispered urgently, trying to simulate an action adventure movie in tone.

"We're leaving the boat."

"Leaving? Why?"

"The boilers." He would string out the information to keep him moving. A kid like this would never run from the end of a story this fantastic.

"What about the boilers?" His eyes were wide open now. Sleep had left him completely.

"They're rigged to explode. Hijackers."

"Hijackers? What's that?"

Damn. A twentieth century word. "People trying to steal the boat. I just found out. There's no time. We have to get off."

His voice rose from a mimicked whisper to normal volume. "Shouldn't we tell the captain?"

"I've told him, but he won't listen. He's trying to keep us all on the boat. He may be one of the hijackers. We have to escape. Hurry!"

He balked. "Why are you saving me?"

Good question. "Because you're Edward Crump."

"So? I don't know you. Why aren't you saving everyone?" His eyes grew even rounder. "You're trying to kidnap me!" He opened his mouth to scream.

David slugged him. Not too hard. Just enough, right under the chin, to knock him out. Then he caught him when he sagged. David swung him over his shoulder, then headed for the sounding boat. Lisette and Portia were standing beside the boat. A third person stood beside Lisette, holding her arm behind her back.

Andrew Westmoreland.

Chapter Twenty-Eight

When Andrew stepped from the shadows and grabbed Lisette, blood trickled from one corner of his mouth. His clothes were filthy, as though he'd been wallowing on the floor. He twisted her arm painfully into her spine. Aunt Portia was too weak to be of any help whatsoever.

"David is coming. If you harm us—"

"Shut up. I'm counting on the good doctor to be here any minute. I want all of you to watch as I sail away."

She was about to plead with Andrew to have mercy when David appeared, carrying the red-haired boy like a sack of flour.

"David!" Andrew gave her arm a cruel twist.

"Well, Doctor Stewart, I see you've stooped to kidnapping too. Perhaps you and I are not that much different."

Lisette could see anger boiling in David. The boy moved, groaned.

David didn't say anything to Andrew at first. He propped the boy against the nearest wall and approached them. "Lisette, are you and Portia all right?"

"Yes."

His eyes were hard and fixed on Andrew. "If you so much as redden her skin, I'll—"

"Now, Doctor, I wouldn't make any threats if I were you." Andrew shoved her hard against the rail. "Unless, of course, you want to see how well she can swim."

Lisette could swim quite well, thanks to Aunt Portia, but David had no way of knowing. And neither did Andrew.

"I can't swim, Andrew, and neither can Aunt Portia. We'll die if you throw us into the river. I can't believe you'd be so cruel." He'd already proven how cruel he could be. Would he believe this lie? He paused to consider, then loosened his grip just enough for her to twist out of his grasp. David didn't waste an instant. He rushed toward Andrew, knocked him flat on the deck, pinned him down, and pounded his face until blood spattered everywhere.

"You're killing him!" She pulled at David's shoulders, hoping he would realize what he was doing. "He isn't worth it!"

Relief surged through her when David stopped his assault.

Breathing hard, David said, "You're right. He isn't worth skinning my knuckles." He looked at her, then to Aunt Portia. A backward glance produced a long sigh.

Eddie was gone.

"We can't look for him, David. We'll have to hope he isn't the same Edward Crump."

"The same as what?" A head of tousled red hair popped up from the sounding boat. "Who do you think I am?"

David turned Andrew facedown on the deck and secured his hands behind him with a belt while Lisette went to speak to Eddie.

"If you're the Eddie Crump we think you are, you're going to be a very important person in Memphis. That's why Doctor Stewart and I want to save you from dying on this boat. Won't you come with us? I don't think you want to die."

He digested this information, then climbed out of the boat. "Let's get out of here!"

David left Andrew bound and unconscious and came over to the boat. "Help me get it over the side and into the river?"

"Sure!" Eddie looked over the edge, to the second deck and pointed. "Why don't we get those guys to help?"

A dozen deck hands heard Eddie and immediately headed for the stairs. They'd be here in seconds. David gripped Eddie's shoulders. "Now, Eddie! They're the ones who've rigged the boilers to blow!"

Lisette had no idea why David told Eddie that ridiculous story, but it made an impression on him. He grabbed one end of the sounding boat and lifted it as far as he could. David lifted the other end. Lisette ran to help Eddie. The boat teetered on the rail before plunging into the river. The *Cajun Star* moved past it so fast she feared they would lose it before they could climb down and inside, but a rope tied to the front caught and held. David must have planned this too.

"You first, Eddie."

"Aye, aye, sir!" He scrambled over the rail and dropped into the boat, appearing terribly small, bobbing in the wake.

Shouts and voices converged on them. They put Aunt Portia over the rail next. She was almost spent. Eddie grabbed her legs and caught her as she fell into the boat.

"Now you, Lisette."

Climbing over the rail, she shouted, "I love you, David!" and dropped into the blackness below. Her knees crumpled when she landed in the boat. Eddie wrapped his arms around her and kept her from pitching into the river.

There was barely enough room for the three of them.

"David!"

He had just climbed over the rail when the deck hands surrounded him. Lisette screamed his name, but he'd been dragged away. She couldn't see him anywhere. One of the hands reached down to grab the rope.

"A knife! We have to cut the rope!"

"I have one!" From his boot, Eddie pulled the skinning knife they'd seen him brandish earlier. He sawed away at the rope. It broke free just as one of the hands was climbing down from the rail.

The sounding boat shot backward, bouncing in the wake of the *Cajun Star*.

Frantically, Lisette searched every face, trying to locate David, but they were already too far away. He had to escape the boat!

The *Star*'s whistle blasted through the night.

"The boilers!" Eddie shouted. "That man said they were rigged to blow!"

Lisette's throat clamped shut, her lungs refusing to draw breath. David! Her mind screamed his name again and again, until she found her voice.

"David!"

Chapter Twenty-Nine

David was almost over the rail when they caught him. The captain was among them, shouting, "Hold fast that man!" At least four hands seized David and dragged him from the rail.

"We have to get off this boat!" David shouted to the captain. "It's going to disappear and everyone on board with it. We have to go now. Midnight! Do you hear me? Midnight!"

The captain gave David a look of horror and disgust. He'd classified David a mad man.

"Secure that sounding boat! Get those people back on board."

"No! It's midnight! We're all going to die if we don't leave this boat!"

"Shut him up," the captain ordered.

A hand clamped over David's mouth, and an arm came around his throat and tightened until speech was impossible. How could he make him understand?

An eerie stillness settled over the *Cajun Star*. A tremor passed through the bow, as though the riverboat had shuddered.

A horrendous, thundering explosion tore through the boat!

The captain was thrown to the deck, then David and the men holding him were struck by the force of the blast and smashed against the railing. Steam hissed when the decks in the center of the boat fell in upon themselves, crushing everything below. The pilothouse collapsed into the bottom of the boat. Live coals from the ruptured boilers were flung upward in a macabre imitation of a fireworks display. The massive smoke stacks swayed, then plummeted into the river. Red-tongued flames and acrid black smoke engulfed the boat like thick fog. People screamed in fear and pain.

Squinting through the haze, David spotted bodies on the deck and in the river. Had Lisette been far enough away to escape this nightmare? There was no way to tell. Bodies hurled high into the air by the blast were falling into the black waters of the Mississippi with heavy splashes and agonized screams of terror.

Blood ran into David's eyes. A piece of shrapnel had imbedded itself in his scalp, but the wound was nothing compared to those he saw around him. He pulled the iron shard from his skin, tore off a piece of his shirt and wrapped it around his head to soak up blood and keep it out of his eyes. Summoning everything in his training to delay his shock and horror, he went to help the injured. He was a doctor. People were dying all around him.

Chapter Thirty

Lisette thought her head would burst. She could only stare at the *Cajun Star*, sailing farther and farther down the river.

She screamed in terror when the percussion of a thousand bolts of lightning knocked her down. The *Cajun Star* exploded, engulfed in a fireball, red and orange and white. Lisette was thrown on top of Aunt Portia. The riverboat splintered into a million shards, pelting them, piercing bare skin, raining about them until they were covered with debris. She thought surely they must be dead and descending into hell.

By the time Lisette was able to sit upright again, the last thundering report had died. The *Cajun Star*, what was left of her, burned, the crackling of the flames punctuating the pitiful screams and moans of the dying.

"David." She closed her eyes, grief crushing the life out of her.

Chapter Thirty-One

David realized within minutes there was no use in trying to doctor these people. Their wounds were too extensive, their numbers overwhelming.

The captain was shouting, "Abandon ship!" People flung themselves into the river, some of them able to swim for shore, others disappearing beneath the water, littered with the debris of a dying riverboat. David saw a large clump of white material floating on the surface of the water and realized, with sheer horror, it was a baby! A woman, shrieking the baby's name, managed to swim to it and save it from sinking into the river. The baby's voluminous clothing had saved it from drowning. Incredible. The mother pulled the baby back on board. Its chances of survival might have been better in the river.

Wind stripped the smoke from the boat, gusting in such strength David could hardly stand. Lightning webbed across the sky, producing thunder so loud people around him screamed, thinking the boat had exploded again. David expected torrents of rain, but there were none. The heavens ripped themselves apart, yet there were no tears for the dying.

Andrew Westmoreland hurled himself at David, screaming, "You did this! We're all going to die because of you!"

David braced himself against the railing, arms raised in defense. When Andrew slammed into David, he pushed him around, into the railing. Andrew tumbled into the churning river; his face grotesquely illumined by the red glow of the riverboat. He sank beneath the dark waters and did not rise again.

The captain jerked David around, his face livid with what he'd seen. "How did you know?" he yelled into David's face.

David knew what he had to do.

Chapter Thirty-Two

Lisette had never seen such lightning nor heard such deaf-ening thunder. Yet there was no rain, no torrents that should have accompanied such a cataclysm. The *Cajun Star* was sinking. Lisette searched the waters in vain, hoping to see David clinging to one of the scraps of wood, that af-forded many survivors a way to stay afloat until they could get to the riverbank. But his face was not among them. Lisette wished there could be a way for her to help these people.

A hollow space opened inside her when she realized David—a doctor—would never leave injured, dying people, to save himself. "David, how can I live without you?"

The wind began so suddenly; it took her breath. They clutched the sides of the sounding boat, fearing it would capsize and they'd be thrown into the river.

The wind stopped. Just stopped. The skies shone with stars. How could this be?

Lisette wiped the soot from her eyes with her skirt and peered into the still, dark night.

There was no evidence of any boat on the river.

The *Cajun Star* had disappeared.

No one spoke for a long moment while they tried to comprehend what they'd just seen. Eddie was first to react.

"Are you all right, Ma'am?"

Lisette nodded. He asked Aunt Portia. She, too, had es-caped serious injury.

They managed to get to the east bank and out of the

sounding boat. They couldn't have done it without Eddie. As a man would have done, he took responsibility for the two women entrusted to his care and brought them to safety.

Once on dry land, he left them to rest while he went for help. No one had heard an explosion and no one, even people fairly close to where the blast occurred, had seen fire or smoke. When Eddie took them back to the river, the sounding boat was gone. Eddie begged Lisette to tell them it was true, but she couldn't speak. She no longer cared for herself, anyone, or anything. Part of her soul had been ripped away, leaving an unbearable emptiness behind.

Aunt Portia answered everyone's questions. When they realized she was describing the explosion of the *Cajun Star*, everyone seemed to talk at once.

The doctor who was summoned to treat their wounds gave Lisette laudanum to help her rest. She welcomed sleep when it came, but awoke screaming, the *Cajun Star* exploding again in her dreams.

The next day, when they finally got home to Memphis, Sedonia met them at the front door, with Seth.

Home.

After a while, Sedonia brought tea and sandwiches, but Lisette couldn't eat. She heard Aunt Portia tell Sedonia that David had died on the riverboat, and it would take time for Lisette to heal.

Time.

That night, Lisette's dreams were filled with David's anguished face, calling, begging her to come to him. She awoke again and again, sobbing, wishing the dreams would go away.

The next morning, Aunt Portia roused her. "Lisette, you have to get dressed. Hurry!"

Lisette's mind was clouded with grief. "Please leave me alone."

"I won't! We have to get to the Peabody."

Lisette managed to open her eyes. "The Peabody?"

"To the fountain. He's there! Don't you see?"

"But, Aunt Portia, didn't you see the flames, feel the explosion?"

"Of course I did. I can't explain what happened to that boat afterward, but it exploded, it surely did."

"Then why—"

"I can't explain why. I just know we have to get to the Peabody."

Lisette dragged herself from bed, wishing Aunt Portia would leave her alone, let her grieve.

"Perk up, now. You don't want David to see you like this."

The delusion brought a fresh spill of tears. Portia's mind must have been affected by the blast, and she had not been able to accept the fact David had died on the boat and she was living in a dream world. "Aunt Portia—"

"You've been so intent on grieving, you haven't been listening. I dreamed about David last night. He told me the two of us should meet him at the Peabody today, as soon as possible. He tried to tell you, but you haven't been listening. The laudanum has turned your mind into mush."

"I, too, dreamed about David, begging me to come back to him."

"He's alive, don't you see?"

If only it were true. Lisette sat on the side of the bed, letting the dizziness pass before Portia helped her dress. Did she dare let herself believe it could be possible?

Seth brought the carriage around front and helped them inside. Lisette scarcely saw or heard anything as they drove down Adams Avenue toward town. David's face, his voice, pleading, consumed her totally. No matter where she went in the world, no matter what she might ever do, nothing could be complete without David.

At the Peabody, Aunt Portia urged Lisette down from the carriage.

"Aunt Portia, can this possibly be true?"

"Never mind the truth. I have no idea about what's true anymore. Let's get inside. Hurry, now."

Entering the lobby was like losing David all over again. She remembered him standing by the fountain, leading her upstairs to the Memorabilia Room, the scandalous clothes on women of the twenty-first century, his tender kisses. If believing David was alive was part of a fantasy world, then living in that world would be preferable to her never-ending nightmare.

Aunt Portia took her hand and dragged her toward the fountain. "You have to be at the fountain, or you can't go through, isn't that right?"

"Yes, the fountain." Lisette's heart pounded until she felt faint. A tingle began in her hands and feet, circled on the crown of her head, then slid down her spine. The same tingle she'd experienced once before when she and Aunt Portia had come to meet David. She stepped back toward Aunt Portia. The tingling stopped. "What if it's true? How can I leave you?"

"How can you stay? I have Sedonia and Seth, and Morgan Enterprises to run. They're coming today to ask me more about the explosion. I'll tell them you and Jacob and David were on the boat. History will stay the same." She clutched Lisette's hands tightly, tears dampening her lined cheeks. "Your happiness has always been my happiness. Go to him, child. Be happy."

Lisette held her, cried with her, kissed her cheek, then turned back to the fountain.

When she reached it, she took one look at the water, placid and unmoving, and squeezed her eyes tightly shut. Another tingle shimmered through her, crown to toes. The melodious tones of a piano intruded softly, then louder. Ducks quacked. Lisette opened her eyes, saw the mallards swimming, watched a woman walk past, wearing pants so short, Lisette could see practically every inch of her legs.

There. In the shadows.

Holding his head with both hands, elbows propped on knees, David reclined on a sofa, asleep. A uniformed man approached him, shook his shoulder. "Doctor Stewart, you really must go home, Sir."

Lisette pressed her hand against the man's shoulder. "I'll take him home."

In one motion, David was in her arms. He wept like a child, his shoulders shaking, his body trembling. "I thought I'd lost you."

"How did you get off the boat?" she whispered between frantic kisses.

"The captain and I appeared on the third deck of the *Memphis Queen III* with our clothes on fire, in front of a dozen people. Scared the hell out of them. And the captain."

Relief and joy flooded through Lisette. She laughed when she'd thought she would never laugh again. "You brought him with you?"

"He's still in shock. I had a lot of explaining to do. Captain Dale and Jim had a million questions for him." His expression became solemn. "What happened to the *Cajun Star?*"

"After the explosion, it disappeared. Even the smoke and

debris were gone. The stars came out. No one believed us at first. It was as though it never happened."

"Just like the article said."

" 'Only Ol' Man River knows.' " He said the rest along with her. " 'But he don't say nuthin' at all.' "

He smiled. "Your house is here."

"I can't wait to show you my secret room. It's where I first dreamed about you."

"And there's no need to worry about Aunt Portia. She lived to the ripe old age of ninety-six after bringing Morgan Enterprises into the twentieth century with a bang. And, you won't believe what happened to Eddie Crump. There's a lot more, all of it good. I'll tell you everything."

"We have a lifetime. But first, I want to sample some ice cream. Lots of ice cream."

David grinned like a small boy. "We'll taste every flavor. Then, we're going to buy you a bikini."

"What on earth is that?"

"You'll see."

They left the lobby of the Peabody Hotel. The twenty-first century wrapped its arms around them and welcomed them home.

About the Author

Linda George has been a professional writer for more than 25 years. Her career as a novelist began in 1998 with *Gabriel's Heart*, under the name Madeline George for Harlequin Historicals. Linda has also published two novels with Deep South Press and more than fifty nonfiction books with Children's Press, Franklin-Watts, KidHaven Press, Blackbirch Press, and Capstone Press for YA and young readers.

Linda has been a speaker at writers' conferences and an instructor for inspiring writers throughout her career as a professional writer. After writing nonfiction for the past nine years, she's turning her attention back to fiction and to telling the stories she's always wanted to tell.

Linda lives in West Texas with her husband, Charles, who is also an author. Their website, Linda's Heart, part of Spotlight on Writers, features newsletters, writing tips, personal columns, and information about their upcoming books and conferences where Linda will be speaking.

www.spotlightonwriters.com